Praise for 'The Porc

Winner of the Luigi Bonomi Prize fo

Jacob Ross, Fellow of the Royal Instit
'A wonderfully observed story about Irene who, in the twilight of her life, finds herself surrounded not only by her children and grandchildren but also by their personal crises and uncertainties... The tensions between Irene's failing body and her healthy recalcitrant mind which insists on maintaining her independence and her dignity, is one of the highlights... A remarkably accomplished, wholly absorbing portrayal of family, the love and tensions that bind them, and ultimately, an old woman's gracious retreat from life. The Porcupine's Dilemma is not only about ageing and dying, but also about life: the gift of offspring and perpetuity through those who come after.

Katie Isbester, Founder of Claret Press
Falls into a well-recognised genre of a comedy of manners set in a genteel English cottage, with a theme of gross injustice and lack of autonomy expressed with considerable good humour. Similar to Jane Austen - writing is witty and charming and all the barbs are gently swathed – only here, the injustice is... a bright old lady denied control over her own life. It's a fabulous updating and pertinent given our aging populace.

Cherry Mosteshar, The Oxford Editors
Great story line that should appeal to the 'sandwich generation', those taking care of both children and parents while having their own mid-life crisis. Gentle and moving, with dialogue that is totally natural and believable. Wonderful writing.

Praise for 'The Amazon Girdle'

Dennis Hamley, author of *Spirit of Place*
Beautifully written... To keep hold of such a subtle plot ... is a high novelistic skill.

Barbara Lorna Hudson, author of *Timed Out*
Complex fascinating characters and a plot to match. If you like Ruth Rendell writing as Barbara Vine you will like this.

Published by Genver Books 2016
Abingdon, Oxon, OX14 2QJ

enquiries@genverbooks.com

ISBN 978-0-9935375-2-3 paperback
ISBN 978-0-9935375-3-0 e-book

Cover design: Ana Grigoriu ana@books-design.com

For Akita

About the author

Elizabeth Mapstone is a former psychotherapist and consultant to the Family Court, now writing fiction. As well as contributing to academic books and journals, she was Founding Editor of The Psychologist, and published two non-fiction books with Random House. Since her retirement, she has also published several short stories and a mystery novel, available in paperback and as ebook.

Also by Elizabeth Mapstone

Fiction

The Amazon's Girdle, Genver Books - a mystery novel set in Paris, London and Cornwall in 1959 and 1977. Available on Kindle, as epub and in bookshops: ISBN 9780993537509

Non-fiction

War of Words: Women and men arguing, Chatto & Windus - on the psychology of arguing. (Translated into German, Dutch, French and Mandarin Chinese).

Stop Dreaming, Start Living, Vermilion. A self-help book that really works, ISBN 0091894611. (Translated into German, French and Dutch)

The Porcupine's Dilemma

by

Elizabeth Mapstone

*The closer you get to someone you love,
the more painfully you can hurt each other*

GENVER
BOOKS

1

Irene

I saw Death in the garden today. She grinned at me, tombstone teeth gleaming in the shadows beyond the apple trees. She wanted me to know: Time may not have caught up with her yet, but it amuses her to stalk her victims, to remind them she always wins in the end.

I'm not afraid, I told her. But not now. Not when David and his family are on their way. When Death makes her final visit, I must be alone. And let it be swift, no lingering, no opportunity for anyone to interfere. Other people always want to do something to make themselves feel better - summon a doctor, an ambulance, send the afflicted off to hospital. I don't want that to happen to me.

"I realize," I say aloud, "it is a truth universally acknowledged that an old woman near the end of her journey must be in need of a guardian."

Susan snorts with laughter at the other end of the telephone.

"Oh, ha, very ha, Mother. You do know you're being bloody unfair, I trust?"

"Oh?"

"I only suggested a live-in companion because you don't get enough help in the house. It was just an idea."

I remember her tears, and her pleading, 'Come and live with me, let me look after you.' And I did think about it, briefly. Susan would be an easy companion, and there could be pleasure in it. But no. I manage perfectly well. The last thing I want is to inflict this failing old carcass on someone I love.

"I wasn't getting at you, Susie darling. You've always been good to me, never make me feel a burden."

"I should hope not. So what's this dig about guardians?"

I coax a laugh from a constricted throat. "I was being silly. Just thinking about the coming week. With David and family."

"Ah. I see. And I bet poor old Danielle is quaking in her Jimmy Choos at the prospect of coping with you. Be kind to her, Monster Woman. She means well."

"That, my darling, is precisely what bothers me. If there were a God, my one prayer would be to be preserved from people with good intentions."

"Don't worry, Mother. She won't dare tell you what to do - not after last time. Your sharp tongue will protect you."

So even Susan sees me as an old harpy, with a tongue like a Biblical flail. "I don't want to defend myself, you know. I'd really like this visit to be pleasant."

"Go on, it'll be lovely, you know it will. Dave and I both adore Hart House, and even Danielle praises your cooking. So don't worry. You know you'll enjoy the children anyway."

"Of course I will, darling. And thank you. Courage restored."

I replace the receiver and resolve to be tolerant and forbearing. I shall behave perfectly, so long as she does.

My hands are twisting in my lap: once graceful, now lumpy, with swollen joints and twisted fingers; spattered with brown splodges, ridged with blue veins. Not my hands, my mother's. My grandmother's. Hands that still serve, though: clumsily, sometimes painfully, but I can still cook and care for myself. And my guests.

All is prepared: fresh sheets on the beds, towels piled in the guest bathroom, a casserole simmering in the AGA. Freshly-cut lilies perfume the sitting room.

Through the open window, I hear the hum of an engine approaching through the beech trees. People rarely come this way - it must be them. Yes, there's the swish and crackle of gravel as the car turns into the drive, the distinctive clang as it crosses the drain. I push against the upholstered arms, drag my body out of the chair, grab the stick that for once has not fallen to the floor. My heart is beating too fast. I close my eyes, take a few deep breaths. Then I tap my way out onto the terrace.

A hatchback is parked beside the garage, bags are being taken out of the back, and a small girl struggles to drag a case across the slates, one wheel spinning in the air.

I wave, begin my tortoise-like progress. I can no longer help with their luggage, but I can greet them with a hug. The smile that spreads my lips and gleams in my eyes will, I hope, mask my fears. Though I am delighted to have my family gather round me again, I dread the coming invasion.

**

"Like your suitcase, Tanya." The five-year-old frowns as she yanks the pink trolley at a tipsy angle. "Shall we get both wheels on the ground?"

"It's mine, Grammar. Daddy gived it me."

"Lucky girl."

"I know." She grins, tossing the golden curls that mislead the unwary into thinking her an angel, and drags the trolley case towards the house. "I'm gonna bags the best bed."

"No need, my darling. Yours is the one with roses on the pillow case."

The little girl stops, swivels those blue eyes, glares at me, guns at the ready. "Is it the one what's got the window?"

I shake my head at her, and laugh. "You know it is, Miss Bossy Boots. The one you always sleep in here."

The blue eyes crinkle, safety catch back on. "That's all right then." She pokes her tongue at her brother, who has just drawn level with us, and starts chanting: "Simon can't have it, Simon can't have it."

The eight-year-old is laden with soft zipper bags almost as big as he is. "Hello, Granma."

"Hello, Simon darling. You all right with all those things?"

"O'course."

I blow him a kiss and he marches on, as determined as any marine recruit.

"You're a pain," he tells his sister. They both struggle through the swinging screen door with their luggage. "I don't want your stupid bed."

I hear her giggle, "I know," before the screen door bangs shut.

Danielle approaches, graceful as a ballerina: pale hair smooth and shined into one of those sharp-edged, lop-sided styles the fashionable wear on television at this turn in the century; embroidered tee shirt,

3

designer jeans, cobwebby cardigan; poppy red lipstick unsmudged, matching nails clutching several bulging supermarket bags. How does she manage to look photo-fresh after a long journey, when some of us fail to maintain a cared-for appearance beyond the bedroom?

"Irene. How are you?"

She plants a lipsticky kiss on my cheek, while I kiss the air near hers, and breathe in the heady fumes of Lancôme's Trésor. Good heavens, that used to be my perfume.

"I'm fine, Danielle, thank you. How was your journey?"

"Rapid. Dave, as usual, drove like that proverbial bat out of hell." She smiles, forgetting my aversion to careless clichés. "He's been dying to get down here to see you, make sure you're still in the land of the living. I'll just take this lot inside. Some wine and a few things I thought you could do with."

"Thank you, Danielle. That's very thoughtful. Do let me see what's there first, won't you? Before you put it away. Otherwise, it might get overlooked."

"Don't you worry about that." She struts away, swinging the bags.

A large brown bear puts arms round me, hugs me until my breath almost fails.

"Hello, Ma dear. You look wonderful."

David. My baby. How he longed to be big, and now he is: six foot high and six foot wide, cuboid as his sister rather unkindly says. Ink black hair just touched with grey at the sides, wide mouth, laughter lines at the corners of brown eyes. That prosthetic is marvellously real. And the scars barely show at all.

"David darling, so lovely to see you. Are you well?"

"Bearing up, Ma, bearing up." He hoists the largest suitcase I have ever seen onto his shoulder, picks up another shopping bag, and we proceed towards the house.

"Why are you not pulling that case, David? It has wheels."

"Just easier this way, the slates are so uneven. Glad to see you're using a stick, it'd be horribly easy to trip on this terrace."

"You're not going to start too, are you?" I look at him carefully, and

4

am startled to see his father's face: the same dark hair, the same nose, the same blue chin in the afternoon. So many years, I'd almost forgotten Martin. Then he winks, and I see he is a plumper, gentler version.

"Just glad you're taking a bit of care, Ma. That's all."

We both smile at that.

"Garden's looking glorious. You really have done wonders here."

We have now reached the upper pond with its blue iris, striped acorus and small red water lily James Brydon, and David lifts the suitcase down from his shoulder, so that we can contemplate the view. The house is built on the side of a hill, overlooking a wooded valley, so the garden drops below us, shrub-covered banks down to a much larger lower pond. Air-borne drops from the fountain sparkle in the sun, froth a pattern on the surface of the water, slashed by vermilion flashes as goldfish swim by. All around, in a protective circle, are the greens and greys, browns and reds of trees and flowering shrubs: beech, red maple, sweet chestnut, Japanese acer, photinia, and magnolia; fuchsias crimson, white and magenta, hydrangeas blue and lilac.

"Remember how we found this house?"

"Yeah, though I can't have been much older than Simon is now. You really scared me, you know. When you led us all past that gate saying PRIVATE?"

"That broken gate. It was all overgrown and abandoned." Everywhere invading brambles had thrown their hooks over struggling fruit trees and blanketed large areas of what was, we learned later, an acre of garden.

"True. Susie said it was like Sleeping Beauty, and we should have had swords."

"And you said, 'Gosh, do you think they're all asleep?' And Susie teased you that the princess was waiting for you to kiss her."

He laughs. "I almost believed it. Especially when we saw the house. I think I really thought it was a castle – you know, with that huge studded door, and all made of stone. And so quiet. No sound at all. Weird. As though Susie was right - everyone was asleep and covered in cobwebs."

"Yes. It was an amazing find."

"I've just realized," he says in tones of astonishment, "it's over thirty years ago. No wonder you don't want to move - nearly half your life has been in this house."

I smile at him. Takes some people a long time to acknowledge important truths.

"I'll leave when you carry me out in my eco-friendly coffin."

***

As expected, Danielle has commandeered the kitchen, stowed away the goodies she brought, poured out juice for the children, and clearly plans to make the tea. Fine. That sorts out the difficulty of carrying a tea-tray into the living room. I had planned to use the trolley.

Presumably, she is now upstairs, dealing with the children, so I'll visit the loo. Anxiety seems to have put pressure on my bladder, and my muscles are ill-equipped to cope. Annoying not to have installed a downstairs lavatory. I make my way up the stairs, slow as liquid helium. Voices in the children's bedroom, someone in the guest bathroom, but mine is clear.

When I've managed to negotiate awkward modern clothing and washed my creaking hands, I sit on the lid of the lavatory and scrabble in the medicine cupboard for the Tramadol. Two more allowed before bedtime. Glass of water from the sink. I wait for the capsules to work before I can venture back downstairs.

They've only just arrived, and already I'm feeling tired, and every joint is complaining. This body of mine must have been made of shoddy materials. Dear God, if you exist, please help me cope with this blasted woman I know I should learn to love, but can't. And please don't let this wretched carcass let me down.

Tap, tap on the bathroom door.

Blistering hell. Can't even remain unmolested in my own bathroom.

"Granma..." Simon. "Granma!" Tap, tap. "Mummy says, tea is ready."

"Yes, my darling. Coming."

I manoeuvre past the bidet, holding on to the wall, making damn sure I don't fall again. Breaking a rib against the edge of the claw-foot iron bath is not something to repeat.

I unbolt the door, and give the boy a smile. He's nearly as tall as I am, I must have shrunk more than I supposed.

"Have I been a long time?"

"Dunno."

"Oh dear, I've forgotten my stick again. Can you fetch it, darling?"

"Course." He scampers into the bathroom, collects it from the floor. "Why do you need a stick, Granma?"

"I'm a bit wobbly these days, that's all."

"Mummy says you're bound to fall and break something because you're old, and you shouldn't live in a house where there are stairs. And steps in the garden."

"Does she, Simon?"

"Yes. But why does she say that, Granma?"

"Why don't you ask her yourself?"

"I did, but she told me to mind my own business." The boy puts out his youthful stubby fingers to touch my grossly misshapen ones on the banister. I close my eyes, savour his innocence as love floods my throat. "Granma."

'What is it, my darling?'

"Just, well, I don't want you to go anywhere else," he confides in a low voice. "I want you to stay here, in this house. I like it."

An unexpected ally. "So do I, Simon. So do I."

2

Irene

I'm scrubbing new potatoes at the sink, pondering mint. Eau de cologne? Apple? Perhaps spearmint for the children?

"Let me do that." Lancôme's *Trésor* assaults the clean smells of earth and root. Designer Woman oozes into the kitchen.

"I'm perfectly fine, thank you, Danielle."

"Why not take advantage of my being here? You should be taking things easy." She hovers at my shoulder.

"I am still capable of making a meal for my guests, thank you."

"Yes, of course you are, Irene. All I'm saying is, why keep a dog and bark too? When I'm here, let me do the cooking."

The woman has that bit right. A pestilential yapping pekinese.

Irene, really – you did resolve to treat her decently. Even inside your head.

I sigh and so does she, and we catch each other's eye briefly. Laughter bubbles in my throat, but I swallow it. How nice it would be if she and I could laugh together, but I've never known her have a sense of humour.

"Perhaps you'd like to prepare some green vegetables for the steamer - whatever the children would prefer. In the fridge."

"I don't mean to upset you, Irene." Danielle extracts French beans and broccoli from the cooler, piles them onto the central worktop. "It's just, well, you're not in the best of health and we worry about you."

"Please don't."

"In this house, all alone. What if you're taken ill again, or have a fall?"

"I'm not a fool, Danielle. I've taken precautions." Why is it Designer Woman who claims to worry? Susie and David don't badger me like this. I cover the scrubbed potatoes with cold water, realize the saucepan is now too heavy to carry across to the AGA, heave it onto the draining board. "When you've done the veg, perhaps you could put the potatoes on? I'll go cut some fresh herbs."

The woman smiles, as though given a gift, and an apron floats off the hook, wraps itself around her torso. Marigolds glide over long pale hands. So that's how she keeps her painted claws.

Irene! Give her some credit - she is being far better natured than you deserve. Shamed by the admonitions of my inner mentor, I add: "You might like to check on the casserole in about fifteen minutes. It's in the bottom oven."

"Of course I will."

I take the small colander and a pair of kitchen scissors in one hand and my stick in the other, note how Danielle compresses her lips as she watches me tap my way through to the living room.

"Grammar, Grammar!" Tanya scrambles to her feet, waving a battered child's book. "Guess what. I can read it all. Let me show you."

"You clever thing. That's a hard book."

"I know."

"Help me cut some mint, and then you can read it to me."

"Okay."

Sunshine still fills the conservatory. Beside the plate glass windows, roses thrive on well-dug-in horse manure: scarlet, heady-scented, sculptured whorls of *Wendy Cusson;* sweetly perfumed, multi-petalled flat magenta flowers of *Gertrude Jekyll* and lilac *David Rennie Mackintosh;* spicy scented, yellow sculpted heads of *French Lace;* and the blousy, pink-tinged, pale yellow petals of *Peace.*

David leans on the big table placed there for the view, elbow on crossword, chin on hand, dreaming.

"You look earnest. Contemplating the importance of being?"

He looks up, startled, laughs. "Oh, very witty, Ma. Though I wasn't so much thinking of playing Jack Worthing as wondering how I could do a Bunbury."

"To escape what?"

"First week of school, of course, Mother dear. As soon as we go back, it's timetabling and streaming the brats and yet another year of my prison sentence."

I laugh, kiss him on the cheek. "You really are an actor *manqué*, my darling. *Quel drame!*"

"Can I help?" he calls, as Tanya and I go out through the screen door.

"You could set the table, darling. And if you hate teaching, quit. Do something else." Through the window, he throws up his hands, sobs theatrically.

Tanya skips ahead down the gently sloping path that zigzags across the steep gradient, allowing me to reach most parts of the garden. People who instruct me to "take things easy" mean well, but have got it wrong. Arthritis has colonised every joint in this recalcitrant body, and my half-dead heart has made hip or knee replacement impossible, but I refuse to lie around in a heap waiting for Death to call. My garden keeps the music playing.

"Grammar. Are you really old?" the little girl asks, as I cut some sprigs of Bowles mint.

"Pretty old."

"Are you gonna die?"

"One day."

"Mummy says you're gonna die if you stay in this house. I don't want you to die, Grammar."

"I have to die one day, sweetheart. But it's nothing to worry about. Really. And when I do, I want you to remember all the nice things we did together."

"What did we do?"

Laughter waltzes round my heart, and I hug my granddaughter. "Oh, Tanya darling, I do love you."

***

"I'd like to feed the children right now, and get them to bed," Danielle says as Tanya finishes reading to me. "If you don't mind, Irene. I don't want their bedtimes disrupted."

"It *is* holidays, Dani," protests David. "Give them a break. They've only just arrived, and the sun's shining. They'll never get to sleep."

"Fine. You take over then."

"Have it your way. You always do. G and T, Ma?"

10

I watch them glare at each other, then Danielle turns, goes upstairs.

"That would be lovely, David." What has got into them? I thought they had the perfect marriage. Well, not perfect: perfection and marriage are incompatible. But I did think theirs was as good a marriage as any could be.

"Lemon or lime, Ma?" David calls from the kitchen.

"Lime, please." All couples have minor tiffs from time to time. Probably nothing serious.

I push myself off the settee, and tick-tock my way into the kitchen. A saucepan is bubbling on the hotplate, with a small number of potatoes, and a steamer on top with green vegetables for the children. I slide it over to the simmer plate.

"David darling, could you please put that big pan of potatoes on the hotplate for me? I'll get them started, and they can finish off in the bottom oven. It won't matter how long we leave them then."

He looks at me and grins. "My Dani *is* a trifle on the domineering side, but she means well, Ma. "

That phrase again. Heaven preserve us. "I know, darling. But I do have things organised for your first meal here. I'm not completely useless."

"Course you're not useless, Mother dear. You're a feisty old woman."

"Less of the 'old', *if* you don't mind."

The children are fed and marshalled, protesting, to bed. When they come to kiss me goodnight, I quote R.L. Stevenson to them:

"In winter I get up at night,
And dress by yellow candle-light.
In summer, quite the other way -
I have to go to bed by day."

"You see?" proclaims Simon. "It's even written down it's stupid to go to bed so early. I bet nobody else has to, not when it's holidays. Granma wouldn't make us. Would you, Granma?"

"If your Mummy wants you to go to bed at the proper time, then that's when you go." Tanya snuggles up against me, watching her mother out of the corner of her eye.

"'S not fair."

"Just think if you were living in the Land of the Midnight Sun," says David, playing the schoolteacher. "In the north of Norway and Sweden, the sun never sets during the summer. Everyone has to go to bed by daylight, or they'd never sleep at all."

"Right. And in the winter, the sun never appears either," Danielle adds, in a voice sharp enough to split logs. "Not a good place to live, in case you were wondering. Now upstairs, both of you. You can read, but you are not to get out of bed. For anything."

"Why does the sun go away at different times?" Simon asks as he obediently climbs the stairs. "I don't understand."

"I'll explain in the morning."

Danielle's return is marked by a noticeable drop in temperature, as though a cloud were obscuring the sun that persists in its efforts to tantalise Simon.

She looks unhappy. Something has happened between these two, and they don't want me to know. Caution colours their every exchange. I unexpectedly think of porcupines making love: the closer they get, the more likely they'll get hurt.

It makes me suddenly very sad.

3

Irene

An insistent drumbeat intrudes on my mind, and the sun is bright on my eyelids. The duvet is too hot. I push it away, carefully turn my head, hoping not to activate flaming stilettos in my neck. Just after ten. I'd no idea it was so late.

Just have to get my muscles to wake up: hope they won't take their usual hour to release the overnight blockage. I stretch my right leg towards the foot of the bed, feel calf and thigh muscles twitch and jag, resisting, then slowly relax. The second leg is easier, but my right hip wrenches, like bones of the earth enduring the drills of miners deep below the surface. I close my eyes until it passes.

The rap rap rap of the drum is now accompanied by a voice calling, "Irene? Irene?" I pull back the duvet, reach for the control to raise the bed. Fallen to the floor. Again.

"Yes? Come in."

"Sorry to intrude, Irene." Danielle, with a welcome cup of tea, its steam wafting like an astilbe flower.

"Thank you, Danielle. How thoughtful." But I can't sit up. Hells bells. My muscles are refusing to cooperate. "Could you give me the wand, please? On the floor."

"Of course." She hands it to me with an anxious smile that says she doesn't want to upset me. I smile back, hoping I convey the friendliness I'd like to develop between us.

"I seem to have overslept - sorry about that." The button on the wand raises my head and shoulders. I reach for the cup, praying not to wobble and spill the tea, and savour the warmth in my throat. "This is just the thing to wake me up."

"I wouldn't have bothered you, but your gardener is here. He says you asked him to come up today, even though it's Sunday, and he needs your instructions."

Indispensable Ivor, carrying out our agreement. Someone in the house? He checks that I am still around, still free to act as I choose; I send a message that he can know is from me, and he leaves well alone; if he's worried, he's to enlist the aid of my neighbours, Alex and Joan, or phone Susan. A jewel. He comes up every day, just to make sure I haven't fallen or had a heart attack.

"Would you please tell him I don't need him today after all? But I would like to see him tomorrow." Danielle nods. "Thanks."

"Anything I can get you?"

"Thank you, Danielle. I'm fine. I'll get up in a minute."

"Grammar, Grammar!" Tanya bursts into the room, and her mother scoops her up.

"Out. Come on, leave your grandmother alone."

"But I wanna tell her something."

"Later."

The door closes behind them, and I realize I'm never sure whether Danielle tries to keep Tanya away in a misguided attempt to protect an old woman, or because she is possessive.

Forget it, Irene. Take advantage of the lovely hot tea to swallow your morning medication.

Snapping the different tablets from the foil dispensers is a recurring tactile pendulum: the packaging that resists and pains fingers; the foil that tears too far, like opening a Kit Kat; the tough foil that curls back like the top of a sardine tin; and the long smooth capsule that slides through a membrane that splits gently, gives pleasure every time. Susan on her last visit decided to count the daily pills and tablets and capsules, and reached thirteen. I deflected my daughter's anxiety with the old joke 'Now you know why I rattle,' and we both laughed, indulging each other. Susan's total didn't include the pain-killers. Only Patrick, my doctor, knows about them.

***

By the time I get downstairs, it's gone eleven, and David is about to take the children for a walk across the fields and back through the valley. Must be fifteen years since I've been able to make that round trip. I used to climb over the stone hedge beyond our garden, drop onto the grass below, and there, stretching in a semicircle to the sea, were the stone-wall-stitched patches of fields, embroidered with creamy sheep and burnt sienna cattle, swathes of laurel green grass sequinned with the gold of buttercups and hawkbit. As I passed, skylarks still rose carolling into the empty sky, not yet dissuaded from nesting in the grass by premature haying, or pesticides.

"You might see signs of badgers over in the field beyond the barn," I tell them. "I saw several holes that appeared freshly dug last time I was near there."

"So you can get to Three Gates, can you, Ma? That's pretty good."

I laugh. A round trip of a quarter of a mile, and a very minor slope. "Not completely past it, you see?" David smiles approvingly at me, so I refrain from adding that the slope is beginning to feel like a hill, and I have to be feeling at my best to tackle it.

"Can we see the badgers?" demands Simon. "Please, Dad."

"We can see their holes. But I don't expect they'll come out when people are around. They're mainly nocturnal anyway."

"What's that mean?" Tanya frowns.

"They come out at night, stupid."

"That'll do, Simon. I don't think farmers like badgers much, so we may find their holes have been blocked."

"Crikee! Why would they do that?" Simon looks so shocked, I put out my hand to stroke his shoulder, and his mother protests:

"Now you're upsetting him, Dave. Can't you ever let well alone?"

"Always know best, don't you, Dani." David's eye is the steel of a garden spade. "I wonder the Pope hasn't asked you for advice."

Danielle compresses scarlet lips, then turns to me. "Let me get you some breakfast, Irene. Coffee or tea?"

"Coffee, please, with hot milk. That'd be lovely."

Her smile is like the sun emerging from behind a cloud. My son is behaving like a barbarian, and when he bends to kiss my cheek, I frown at him.

"I know it's not my business, but is it necessary to keep needling Danielle?"

"Not your affair, Mother. Sorry we put on a performance. Nothing to worry about."

The set of his jaw reminds me again, forcibly, of his father: Martin in his Rock of Gibraltar phase, when words made no impact, determined to remain unmoved by the most irresistible force.

"Right, kids, I'm off. Who's coming?"

"Me, Daddy, me." Tanya takes his hand. "Simon's a slow coach."

"Bye, Granma." The boy scampers after his father and sister, laces dangling.

"Simon," I call. "Laces." He stops, hesitates as the others go through the gate. "Don't worry, you'll catch up easily. You're fast." He grins, bends to tie the laces properly. "Have a lovely walk."

Danielle brings me a tray of coffee, with a bowl of fruit salad and yoghurt. My favourite breakfast. Her thoughtfulness makes me uncomfortably aware that I was somewhat ungracious yesterday when she offered to help. How sad that after living seventy years, I still allow awkwardness to spoil what should be a happy visit.

"You're being very considerate, Danielle."

She stops, halfway through the screen door, turns and smiles. Her hair is immaculate, her skin flawless, though I see incipient lines around her mouth, and she has painted lips and nails the scarlet of Wendy Cusson roses.

"Come and join me."

She hesitates. "You sure?"

I raise an eyebrow, point to a chair beside me, and she lets the door bang, sits down.

"This fruit salad is very good. Must have taken quite a time."

"I enjoy preparing food. You know, as a break from people's damaged bodies."

"I can understand that. How is your job?"

She flushes, and looks out over the garden. The sun is high, and beyond the shelter of the awning, roses and lilies radiate scarlet, pink, magenta, lemon and gold.

"I'm doing quite well, thanks. They've even offered me promotion. Except that it means being on duty several evenings a month, and travel."

"Is that bad?"

"It does conflict with what Dave wants to do. So we have a problem."

"Oh, dear."

"We'll sort it."

"Was that why didn't you go with the others?"

"No, no. I just felt like being alone for a while."

"I know the feeling." I hope my son hasn't forgotten all I taught him about treating a woman as an equal. "You mustn't let a husband ruin your career, you know."

She laughs, like a tambourine with a cracked membrane.

"Yeah. Women's Lib, and all that. Except it doesn't work, does it? Not in practice. I often wonder how many of those women's libbers actually had husbands and children."

I laugh too, remembering the stridency of the militant feminists I met as a mature student at Exeter, and the realities of juggling the needs of two children, absorbing work and a husband I loved. "You're right. In my day, it was called 'having it all'. I thought perhaps you and David had found the magic formula."

She puffs out a sigh. "Some hopes. But never mind that, Irene. Just let me feel I'm some use while we are here." I look at her with as little expression on my face as I can manage. Dangerous territory. "I... I know. You live alone, you can manage. But ... while I'm here, let me take care of you."

"Why should you want to do that? You're my guest, not the other way round."

"That's partly why, really. It isn't right that you have to cope with four more people in the house. Why not let me help you?"

"I'm delighted to let you help me, my dear. But I would rather you didn't take over my kitchen completely. If you don't mind my saying so."

She flinches, as though wounded by my words. "I'm sorry, Irene. I didn't mean to give that impression."

I spoon up the last juicy remnants of yoghurt. "This breakfast has been delicious, and much appreciated." She smiles, a little uncertainly. "What I mean is, I'm very happy to be spoilt by you in this way, when you ask. But you did sort of take command, don't you think? From the moment you arrived. Even putting away the things you brought, when I asked you not to?"

"Oh, dear. I'm really, really sorry if I've offended you."

I reach over and pat her hands that are clutched together. "It's all right, I'm not offended, my dear. I just felt I should say something. I am still an independent woman, and it needs to be remembered."

"Yes, you're right. I can see how that must have been very annoying." She trembles a small smile, and I savour a delicious sense of relief. Even triumph. I made an effort to communicate with my opinionated daughter-in-law, and actually succeeded.

"You see," she goes on, "your body simply can't do the things you want it to, and at the end of the day, I feel I should help. Especially since we've brought the children."

"But I love having them here."

"Of course you do, Irene. But we have to face facts. They're young and thoughtless and climb all over you, and you're frailer than ever - and – well, I don't want our visit to make things worse for you."

"Goodness. The children make it all worthwhile. Don't try to protect me from them - that'd really make me unhappy."

"You imagine I haven't seen you wince with pain when Tani leans on your thighs?" She shakes her head as though she doesn't know what to do. "I just wish I felt you had the best treatment down here. You'd be much better off in the Oxford area. So many brilliant specialists at the Radcliffe. Sorry. I didn't mean to bring that up again. Forget I said it."

"No. Best not go down that path again." We gaze at each other, and I can see she is finding this conversation as uncomfortable as I am. "Look, Danielle. I know you're a physiotherapist, and understand all about bodies, and I know my own body is decrepit, and deteriorating, and won't stay alive for ever. But. It still functions. And so does my brain. I'm still perfectly capable of looking after myself."

She shakes her head, and I begin to lose the sympathy I had so recently developed.

"Sorry, Irene. I wasn't going to bring it up, but since you want to talk about it. I don't think you're safe here on your own. The whole place is an accident waiting to happen."

"And how do you make that out, may I ask?"

"You've had two heart attacks, you're riddled with arthritis, and you hobble around like a tortoise with a stick. What would happen if you fell down the stairs? Or in this garden? You'd be bound to break something. And if you fell in either pond, it just doesn't bear thinking of."

"All old people run this risk. It'll happen to you one day."

"I can assure you, I won't be living in a dangerous place like this." I wave my hand in a 'Have it your way' gesture. "And you could have another heart attack at any moment."

"What is your solution?"

"You could come and live with us. The Oxford area is lovely. You'd like it."

"I don't think so."

"Or you could take a flat in a sheltered housing estate. There's an excellent one near us. This house should bring in enough money to make it affordable."

"You've certainly thought it all out."

"We needed to. You're so far away down here, we can't possibly keep an eye on you. And Dave gets so worried about you, I just had to think of a solution."

"I seem to remember we've been through this before, Danielle. And I said no."

She sighs, puts her head in her manicured hands. How trying for her. What a tiresome mother-in-law she has.

"You'll have to give in sooner or later. Why not now? While you still have your faculties and can decide for yourself?"

"I take it that means you'd move me against my will. Once you could legitimately claim I was senile, of course."

"Please, Irene, we all need to face facts. The bottom line is, if you have another heart attack, Dave would have to decide what's best for you."

"I see. Even though I've made it quite clear, to you and to David, to Susan and Frank, and to my doctor, and to my solicitor, that I wish to die in this house. Not in hospital. Not in a nursing home. Not in any sheltered accommodation. I wish to die here. And if I take a while over it, then I shall borrow against the value of this house to pay for private nursing. I hope you are really clear about this."

She sighs. "I do know that's what you want. But it's so unrealistic. You could be incapacitated for years, and end up having to move into some ghastly nursing home when you're too frail to fight."

I laugh. A bit short, but a laugh all the same. "Are you sure you're thinking of me? Or are you worried about the money?"

"What a terrible thing to say!"

"I'm not a fool, Danielle, however decrepit I am. I know David hates teaching, while you talk of turning down promotion, which usually means an increase in salary. You'd just better hope I do die soon."

She stands up. "You really can be very hurtful, you know."

"Good. Just tell yourself that any hurt I have inflicted is just recompense for your insulting insistence that I can't be trusted to make my own decisions. I shall remain here, in the house I love, surrounded by the garden I created, until I die. Whenever and however that is. I shall not be moving anywhere."

She stares at me, and I stare back, firm, unmoving. She turns away, goes inside.

I drag the recliner cushion over to the vine-clad pergola, lie back in the dappled shade. If Danielle wants to take over the cooking, she can do just that while they're here; no point in expending energy on that front. My main aim must be to ensure that if - or perhaps when – I have another heart attack, Danielle and David cannot overrule my explicit wishes. From now on, I must somehow prevent anyone ever taking me to hospital on any pretext. A fall would be seriously inconvenient, and would certainly involve medical intervention. So I'd better not fall. I don't want to end up like my mother, breaking a hip, needing an operation, and dying in the damned hospital before she could return home.

Everything has been written down, but I must make sure copies are sent to all concerned: David, Susan, the doctors' surgery. Patrick has agreed that I'm free to choose whether or not to accept hospital treatment, but suppose he's not on duty? Thank the Lord, Susan understood. She resisted, but she did agree: her mother should be free to choose how her life ends.

Tomorrow, I shall phone my solicitor, Charles.

How is it that I can have spent so many years as a mediator, helping others discover ways of resolving conflict, and yet at the end of my life, I find myself in a battle for survival? Talk, say all the experts. Negotiate. Exchange points of view. But as every mediator knows, talking never works when one side refuses all concessions, and is determined to win. I feel like a small country threatened by overwhelming forces. My desire for independence carries no weight at the negotiating table, and my longing for peace at the end of my life is casually discounted.

War has been declared. I shall fight – literally - to the death.

4

David

David needed to run and run, until the tension in his blood dissipated, borne away by the wind gusting in from the sea. At the gate, he hoisted Tanya onto his shoulders, and jogged along the lane beneath overhanging beeches, puffing with the unaccustomed exercise, his daughter jolted by his uneven gait and giggling. The sharp pain in his scalp as she held onto his hair felt appropriate. I'm a bastard, he thought. But oh, for a wife who is not always so bloody sure she is so bloody right.

"Daddy! Daddee! Wait for me!"

The boy was dawdling, as usual, his head in a bush, or down a rabbit hole, or up a tree. Odd that. Susie and I were never that keen on wild life.

"Come on, Simon, keep up."

With Tanya chanting "You can't catch us" in her most annoying voice, David increased his pace, but it was a relief to reach the corner and lift her down. The blood had started to flow more freely round his muscles, and the boy he used to be scrambled over the wall into the field below. Barbed wire? That was new. Mother said old man Curtis had died, and his son-in-law was running the farm. He wondered if Susie ever told her the old lecher gave her a lift up the lane in his Land Rover, and tried to fumble into her knickers. She couldn't have been more than twelve. Certainly gave them both a new perspective on country life.

"You two climb over while I hold the wire out of the way. Just slide under. That's it."

They were in another place. Open. Free. Nothing but a wide expanse of green disappearing below the slope of the hill, a circle of blue-grey ocean to the horizon, and above, clouds like scudding soap suds in a sky blue as Dani's eyes. Out here he used to believe that the world could open, there was space for him, he need not be trapped. But then he'd return, and bloody reality would claim him. Just as well there was no internet then. There were times he'd felt like killing himself. Who knows what might have happened if he'd found a chat room for adolescent suicides? Poor Mother. She had no idea, never seemed to notice he was unhappy. He watched his children dancing in the wind, and thought, I'm forty next month. It's now or never.

Striding through the long grass, he savoured the salt sea tang mixed with nostalgic smells of earth, dung and vegetation. Half-hidden, the children bounced through the tall growth, and Alex and Joan's black cat from next door stalked them like a panther in the Serengeti.

"If you want to see badger holes, we have to go to the field at the top."

"Come on, Tani."

5

Simon

Simon ran on ahead into the next field, but came to a sudden halt. Where he had expected to find badger holes there now was a wide excavation and piles of earth in great mounds. The badger setts had been dug out.

"What...? what happened, Dad?"

"It's what farmers do, Simon. Sorry, should've given this a miss."

Simon couldn't move. Grandma didn't know what the farmer had done, and he didn't want to tell her. It was horrible. You could see a horrible great hole like a cave where the horrible farmer had dug and dug, and piles of earth all scrabbled over. He imagined the poor badgers trying to fight back, and horrible men hitting them with their shovels. He wanted to cry. But he didn't.

Dad didn't seem to care. He just said, "Farmers are like that, Simon. They kill any creature they think is a pest."

So Simon knew the farmer was stupid as well as horrible. It was stupid to think a badger was a pest. Badgers were beautiful. One of the best things ever, ever, ever, in his whole life was watching badgers.

When he was six. He never told his parents, cos they'd laugh at him. They never believed him when he told them amazing things. And he could remember every bit. Tani fell off her tricycle and blood spurted all over her face and she was crying, so an ambulance with blue lights took her and Mum to the hospital to make her better. Dad drove him down to Cornwall to stay with Grandma. All by himself, for a whole week. It was really fun.

One night, Grandma woke him up, and it was nearly midnight. They went outside. The moon was really round and full and bright, and the garden was nearly like the day-time, except the colours were more grey and silvery. Grandma said they must be very quiet. He heard rustling in the bushes, and a twig snap, and birds twitter briefly in their nests. The moonlight seemed to make them wakeful, he'd never known that before.

A barn owl with large round eyes floated silently towards him, and he caught his breath. Then it turned, flew high into a tree. Its flight must have moved the air, but he heard nothing. Except bats. Suddenly there were lots of bats swooping and squeaking in the air around them.

Grandma walked a bit faster then. She wasn't so wobbly. So they went through the gate, and along the lane. They were going to look at the moon on the sea. But instead, they stopped at a gap in the hedge, where they could see into the field above her house. And there, dancing in the moonlight, was a family of badgers. It was really truly, truly true. Two big badgers, the parents, and a lot of little ones, he counted four, and they were all dancing. Really dancing, under the moon.

Nobody would believe him, so he didn't talk about it. But he and Grandma knew. It was true, because they'd seen it together. So he and she must be special.

"Come on, Simon," Dad said, and his voice was a bit gentle. "Tani's nearly over the stile already."

But she'd stopped on the top, of course. Simon knew she would. The next field was full of bullocks, and she might have been mobbed without Dad to ward them off. "Bullocks are clumsy and inquisitive," he told them every year. As though they were too stupid to remember. "Never go walking through their field without a grown-up with a stick, and shout at them as loudly as you can if they come near."

Simon had thought once that he'd like to be a farmer. But farmers only kept animals to make them into meat. He wouldn't like that. There had to be some other way he could live in the country, like Grandma, and be with animals.

At the bottom of the field, Dad got a bit aerated, like Mum would say. The stile was all over-grown with brambles and tall stinging nettles, and you couldn't use the gate, because it was padlocked.

"*Cry havoc and let slip the dogs of war.*" Dad shouted as he swung his stick at the nettles and brambles, but they fought back and scratched and stung his bare legs and arms. "*Doomsday is near,*" he cried, bashing at the waving brambles. "*Die all, die merrily.*" He trampled them all down at last, and laughed, waving his stick in the air triumphantly. He had slain

25

the enemy. Then he bowed to both children with a flourish, and handed them over the stile like a knight out of Tales of King Arthur.

That's my Dad, Simon thought with pride. He beats his breast like a gorilla when something makes him mad, and pretends he's the hero in a story who has to kill the baddie. And then he laughs. Makes me and Tani laugh too.

6

David

Fields and woods helped him feel he was on holiday: paved roads and houses were too much like being back home. So David hurried along the lower lane, past cottages ancient and comparatively modern, towards the wooded valley that led back to Hart House. As they passed the big old house at the end, he was reminded of years of piano lessons in Norman Fleetwood's music room: the shiny rosewood case, the yellowed ivory keys slightly chipped at the edges through years of use, and Norman towering over him, a gentle-voiced but intimidating giant. He never dared be late, or forget to practise, though he had no special talent. Amazing what Norman could do with such unpromising material.

And Belinda. He must have been, what? twelve, maybe, when she first appeared. Just a plump little girl of three or four, with no particular charms. But he remembered her barging into his lessons, and Norman crossly trying to banish her, without success. Perhaps it was that - her defiance of the Gentle Giant, who so over-awed him. He would never dare. Had never even considered failing his teacher in any way. And there was this little dumpling, saying "Won't!" and stamping her foot. A brat. But her amazing refusal to obey her towering uncle, even when he became angry, did drape his memory of her in a thin muslin of glamour, which her subsequent metamorphosis into decorative blonde woman only enhanced.

Extraordinary that, her turning up for his drama course. Not that he would ever have recognized her if she had not made herself known. Apparently, she had realized their old connection when she enrolled. She wanted to learn to act, she said. And it was a pleasure to be able to help.

Except that the wretched woman had no talent. He shook his head ruefully, recalling the painful experience of carrying her through four public performances of *The Importance*. She had seemed such a natural for Gwendolyn, but her own instinctive, flamboyant charm deserted her entirely on stage, and he could coax nothing remotely vivacious from her. An embarrassing business.

"Tanya! If you want to paddle in the water, for heaven's sake take off your shoes. What are you thinking of?" She turned her blue eyes on him, ready to fire with both guns, and he melted. As he always did. "Come on, then. Give them to me, I'll carry them."

She half handed her shoes and socks to him, half threw them, giggling, then turned and trotted into the water.

"And roll up your trousers! Good heavens, *think*, girl!"

Simon had left his shoes and socks on a rock, and had already moved quite a way downstream. Didn't children ever think ahead?

"Simon, tie the laces of your shoes together and hang them round your neck."

The boy sighed audibly, and grudgingly returned to retrieve his belongings. Weary. Put-upon. His acting is better than Belinda's, David thought, and laughed out loud.

Slowly they made their way upstream, both children negotiating the rocky bed of the shallow river. David waited for the inevitable: one at least would get a soaking. He insisted they come back to the path to skirt the deep pool under an ancient tree where he used to catch tiddlers. They were near what he and Susie called the Slippery Stones. Not safe to go further, for the water fell precipitately over the rocks, and where they were free of water, they were shiny with algae.

Tanya, defiant as always, put one foot too far, slipped and fell. She shrieked and Simon tried to reach her. David dropped what he was carrying and lifted her out of the water. She was shaking and squeaking with fright, but she was also giggling. Like her father, every dramatic event thrilled.

David made sure she was not hurt, then hugged her tight. Her clothes were sodden. "Just as well we're nearly back at Grandma's."

They began the long climb up to his mother's house and he thought, Such a shame she can't enjoy this beautiful valley any more. It's one of the reasons we came here. How far up from the river is the house? Three or four hundred feet. Which we have to climb. Breathless, he watched his two young children running on ahead, apparently quite unaffected by the steepness of the steps. He was like them once. Not the happiest of notions.

Simon came leaping back down, called in a loud stage whisper, "Dad, Dad! Look! There's two deer up there, and they're watching us."

David peered through the trees that sprawled across the hillside, but saw no sign of any living creature.

"See?" whispered Simon, impatient. "Oh-ooh, they're going. Ohwer. They were so pretty."

"You must have sharp eyes, Simon. I couldn't see them."

"Oh, well. See ya." The boy turned and scrambled effortlessly back up the steps, reminding his father once again of the realities of ageing.

Back to my mother, he thought. Poor old dear, she must be so frustrated. Dani doesn't understand you need to be near the things you love. My mother loves her house and her garden, and this valley she can no longer visit. I don't want to drag her upcountry if she wants to stay.

Just as I don't want anyone to drag me away from what I think is important.

One day, I'll be as decrepit as my mother, which is a seriously depressing thought. Like a condemned man, ageing focuses the mind. I must fulfil this one dream before it is too late.

7

Irene

"**G**ranma. Hey, Granma! We're back." Simon bounds up the steep steps, followed closely by his sister.

I lean into the cushions. In any other circumstances, I'd drag myself to my feet, hobble inside, put on the kettle. But Danielle will undoubtedly decide when refreshments are due. My anger is no longer bubbling with the destructive potential of an underground geyser. I have drawn away from the heat. The fact is, negative emotions are exhausting, and I'm tired of fighting my daughter-in-law. Quite literally, overwhelmed with fatigue. Somehow, I must recall that early training in relaxation and auto-hypnosis we mediators were given, designed to protect us against aggressive, abrasive personalities. Breathe in, slowly... slowly. Hold, gently let it out. Danielle, I swear your well-intentioned interference will be the death of me.

"Grammar, guess what." Tanya leans across my thighs, and arthritis bayonets knee and hip. I gently shift the child, put an arm around small shoulders, feel curls dribbling onto my fingers.

"You're all wet." She giggles, and tries to climb on my lap. I hug the child, then push her away as her weight awakens miners drilling into my hip. "You made me soggy too, you monster."

"Daddy! Daddy!" The girl bounces like a nursery song, coils round her father's legs as he puffs to the top of the steps. "I made Grammar all wet too."

"What a horror you are." David's face is red and perspiring, plump thighs bulge beneath Bermuda shorts. "Whew! I'd forgotten what a long haul it is up from the stream."

"Tanya, Simon. Inside. Get cleaned up." Danielle's voice slashes into my head. The woman must have some good qualities, her children are lovely. I close my eyes against designer jeans, appliquéd tee-shirt, sculpted hairdo. "Leave your grandmother alone. She's tired."

30

"Nice walk, David?" I ask in a wide-awake voice, and smile my most beguiling smile.

"Great, thanks, Ma. We had a lovely walk, didn't we? Eh, kids?" Danielle is already ushering the children through the screen door, and he shrugs his shoulders, drags over a chair so that he can sit in the sun as I lie in the shade. "Ah, well." He closes his eyes and appears to bask in the hot sunshine.

My maternal instincts get the better of me. "David, darling. You do have sunscreen, don't you?" Ever since my short bout with skin cancer on my face, I have warned everyone in my family to be vigilant, but doubt if they ever hear.

He opens those dark bedroom eyes inherited from his father, crinkles them at me in a knowing grin. "Would any of us dare not to?" He then declaims in his 'Old Actor Laddie' manner, clutching his brow: "Oh, no! Not Mother Harper Country! Beware the rays of the sun, my son! Slather on the 30 plus. Never mind the dark storm clouds, is that a gleam of light I see before me, the handle? No, no, getting carried away there. Remember Mother Harper's Rants, my son, and keep slathering. Block the sun. My son."

I laugh. "Glad you remember. So how was the valley looking?"

"Glorious, Ma, glorious. A lot of fallen trees, though, brought down by ivy which is taking over. Doesn't seem to be anyone looking after it now, which is a pity."

"I expect the neglect is because of a few incomers who made such a fuss when Jesse – you remember Jesse? Other side of the valley? He owned all that land, fields and the woods below, used to have a regular logging lane hidden in the woods above the stream. We used to visit him occasionally."

"Yeah, I remember. So what was the fuss?"

"A few romantics who'd never lived in the country before started a campaign to stop Jesse cutting or moving anything in the valley. Ecologically damaging, they claimed."

"Quite the opposite, I'd say. You'd think anyone with a garden would realize you'll just get ivy and brambles in the end."

"Exactly. Anyway, Jesse didn't like fighting battles in the newspapers, and sold up. Moved somewhere on the moors, I believe."

"The woods are still beautiful, but the ivy is definitely strangling trees and suffocating seedlings. Sad."

"Perhaps I don't miss much not walking there any more."

"I could drive you to the other end, where it's level. Why don't I do that this afternoon?"

I smile at him. How lucky I am to have such a thoughtful son. "Sounds a lovely idea."

"Is that old music teacher still there? I wonder if he'd let me park in his driveway?"

"You mean Norman? Norman Fleetwood? I see him quite often, with my music group. I'm sure he'd be happy to see you again, and let you park in his drive."

"You still playing, Ma?"

"Yes. When I can. Five of us now." Michelle with her dancing violin, Cheryl and her beautiful cello, Norman nodding to us from the piano, and versatile Leonard who plays violin or viola or piano, whichever we need, while I glory on with my clarinet - what bliss at last to play without anyone complaining.

"I was afraid to ask. In case your poor old fingers couldn't manage."

"Sometimes they don't, but I haven't given up. That really would be the end."

"And the piano, is it in tune?"

"Of course."

"Great. We should have a musical evening tonight. Dani's a talented singer, you know."

"Really?"

I find my enthusiasm for the best kind of home-made entertainment has dwindled, lies around my feet like the wrinkled remains of a deflated balloon. Danielle listening to my fumbling on the clarinet? I don't think so. For I know that all my energies would be engaged in expressing proper grandmotherly pleasure in everyone's performance, and my fingers would fail to cooperate. Music is no longer something I can take casually.

"Let's wait and see how the fingers feel later on," I suggest. "But I'd love to hear you and your family."

I look towards the house, and see that Danielle has enlisted her children's help to set out lunch under the awning. Where does David stand now that war has been declared? Here he is, being charming and offering ways in which I can take part in their holiday activities, while I know that his wife is plotting to oust me from my home. Is he softening me up, perhaps? Hard to believe he knows nothing about her intentions, even if he hasn't yet learned we are officially in a state of war.

"Granma, lunch is ready," Simon calls, running across the terrace.

"Let me help you up, Ma." David hauls himself out of his chair, holds out a hand.

"Don't feel like lunch, David dear."

He looks at me with a half-smile, and then nods. "All right. I'll tell her." He strides over to the laden table beneath the awning, bends to give Tanya a quick kiss, then goes inside.

Simon stands beside my recliner and his brown eyes spark joyously. "Guess what, Granma. I saw two deer in the trees while we were down the valley. Daddy says I have sharp eyes."

"You must have, Simon. Not many people see them." He smiles to himself, and nods, as though he had been sure this was special. "Enjoy your lunch, darling. I'll see you later."

This damned, blighted body. Where's my bloody stick? Hastily, I scrabble beneath the recliner, scraping painful knuckles on the slate as I chase the elusive wooden aid to the decrepit. Why does it always fall out of reach? Finally. I drag it towards me, knowing it will be a miracle if I can reach the loo in time. Not the one in the annexe: I can tell I shall have to change my clothes. Oh, damn and blast and blistering hell, why must this bloody body always let me down?

I stop swearing, close my mouth firmly, clamber to my feet, click clack my tedious way across the terrace.

"Can I help in any way, Ma?"

I shake my head, gripping too tightly to all my muscles to speak, manoeuvre through the screen door, the conservatory, the wide hall. Up the steep stairs. Why did we never install a loo downstairs? Concentrate. Down the passage, through the door, trousers down, pants down, God, God, why did you give me such a bloody useless body? At last, a blessed release. And the flooding not so bad this time. Just as well they're all outside, gives me time to change and clear up. God, I hate this decrepitude. Don't see how even the greatest determination can maintain dignity when every organ in your body increasingly threatens to fail.

Dammit all to hell.

"Grammar! Grammar!"

Here I am, trousers round ankles, wrinkled thighs bare, unable to stem the flow, and the door is wide open. The top of a fair curly head appears briefly through the banisters. What the devil does that bloody woman think she is doing, sending her children to spy on me?

I lean over to push the door shut, but can only catch it with the end of a finger. It moves half an inch. I hear Tanya clomping up the last steps at the half landing, pull off my shoe, take hasty aim. It hits the side of the door, which closes another half inch, then clatters to the floor. Never was good at throwing things.

Emergency measures. Ignoring the continuing stream, I half stand and hobble over to the door, slam it shut, push the bolt. Feel the warm trickle down my legs as the flow finally ebbs. Now I know why most people choose to have a bathroom leading off their bedroom. It would certainly ensure more privacy.

"Grammar, what was that bang?"

"Nothing, Tanya. Nothing to worry about."

"Did you fall over, Grammar?"

"No, no, darling, nothing like that. Just threw my shoe at a mouse, that's all."

"A mouse? Did you get it? Can I see?"

"No, I missed. It's run away now. Did you want something?"

"Mummy said, are you okay?"

I sigh. "Tell Mummy I'm fine, and I'm having a bath. So please not to worry."

"Okay." She scampers off, shouting, "Mummy, guess what? Grammar threw her shoe at a mouse."

Congratulations, Irene. Succour to the enemy. Hart House is now not only fraught with accident hazards, but is also unhygienic, overrun with rodents and a threat to health.

What a happy family holiday we all do have together.

8

Danielle

"So now we know another of her problems."

David frowned. "We do?"

"Well, I do, anyway. Another difficulty that won't get better over time." Danielle sighed. "I feel quite sorry for her. But if she won't face unpalatable facts, I don't know what to do. You will have to talk to her."

"You do nag, Dani. Give it a rest. Let everyone enjoy themselves."

"Can't you see? Your mother's strength is failing, and she shouldn't be living in a place like this. It's a nightmare."

"Suffering Thespis! Leave it." David stood up. "I'm going to phone my old music teacher, see if he'll let us park in his drive."

Danielle raised her eyes to heaven. He never listened. And she had no idea why he wanted to park in anyone's drive. This whole Harper family operated as though other people could read their minds.

Or as though there were secret rules everyone else knew how to follow, like The Family in The Godfather. With Irene as Godmother.

Like that time in the hospital: all of us gathered around The Godmother's bed. You'd have thought the sharp smell of chlorine, the click of the monitors attached to her anatomy and the way she lay against the pillows, skin like tallow, tangled hair uncombed – you'd have thought all that added up in any intelligent mind to a clear case of Aged Person in Need of Care. But no. I dared to breathe the smallest hint of a suggestion that Dave and Susan might investigate care homes, and the bloody Harpy pulled herself upright and started berating me for an interfering busybody. Which naturally set her blood pressure rising and alarm bells ringing and nurses rushing in from all sides. For which I was blamed. I was simply being practical and caring and foresighted. Perhaps I could have waited till we left her. But how was I to know she'd react so unreasonably to my spelling out the obvious?

And now The Family appeared to take it for granted their frail old mother should be left to die prematurely in this dangerous place.

"Where's Daddy going?"

"Why're farmers so stupid, Mum?"

"I asked first. Mummy. What's Daddy doing?"

"For goodness sake, eat your sandwich, Tani, and be quiet."

"S'not fair."

Danielle glared at her defiant daughter, who grinned and chomped more of her ham and tomato on wholemeal.

"Why do farmers want to kill badgers? It's stupid. So why?" Simon was as tenacious as his bloody-minded grandmother.

"You really want to know?" He nodded with vigour. "They believe that badgers spread a serious disease that kills their cattle, so they want to get rid of the badgers before they lose their livestock. See?"

"Oh." He frowned. "I'm definitely not gonna be a farmer. They kill animals all the time."

"If you really want to think about it, it's a bit more complicated. Because all those bullocks you see in the fields, enjoying the fresh green grass in the sunshine - they wouldn't even exist if farmers didn't want them for beef. So they have a short life, but it's not unhappy. Without the farmer, they wouldn't have a life at all. See?"

Danielle watched her clever eight-year-old try to grapple with issues of life, death and responsibility that baffle older, more experienced minds, and patted his hand. "Don't worry about it, Simon dear. Life is full of puzzles like that. I don't think we can solve it today, do you?"

"I still don't think it's right," he muttered, and examined his sandwich, which happened to be cheese and cucumber. "I'm gonna be a vegetarian, so there."

David returned so Danielle decided to ignore the vegetarian issue. Simon would probably forget again, and she smiled at the memory of his earlier brief flirtation with that tiresome regime: succulent golden-brown sausages seduced him. One more dream that couldn't withstand too much reality.

"We've been invited out to tea, everyone," David announced, "with my former music teacher. So I want everyone on their best behaviour."

Danielle stared at her husband: where did this come from? He didn't tell her anything these days. Making arrangements without even consulting her was beginning to piss her off.

"Music?" said Tanya, perking up. "Has he gotta piano?"

Irene appeared, smelling of flowers and changed into a swirly summer skirt down to her ankles. An improvement on her usual baggy old lady trousers, Danielle thought, and wondered why she always chose to cover her legs. Varicose veins? Swollen ankles? She watched her mother-in-law's unsteady progress out to the patio, fears nagging inside her head. How did she manage when Dave was not around to stop the screen door knocking her over?

"You look summery, Mother dear." David pulled out a chair. "Just the thing for going visiting."

"Oh?"

He flashed her a dentifrice-ad smile, and fluffed up the cushions. "Come and join us. We're making plans."

She hesitated. Danielle, aware the woman was embarrassed by their earlier bad-tempered exchange, avoided looking at her directly, concentrated on piling dishes onto a tray. Irene sank back against the cushions.

The sun was still high and the brilliance of the sky beyond the awning reminded Danielle of the Mediterranean. Before the children. Before concern for The Godmother. The fishing boat off Corfu; Dave's tanned muscles glistening and the dark hairs on his chest tempting her fingers; the smell of salt and the boatman's coarse bread soaked in olive oil and garlic; the rough red wine; the heat on her skin, and how they swam together in the deep clear water, glad of each other, and how everyone smiled.

9

Irene

"**D**id you really see a mouse, Granma?" Simon asks.

"No, not really. I was joking." The boy looks disappointed, and opens the book he's been hiding under the table.

Tanya wails, "Ooooh. That's not fair."

I shake my head at her, and mouthe, Sorry!

"You're naughty, Grammar. Growned-ups mustn't tell lies, must they, Mummy?"

"Do stop being silly, Tani. Your grandmother told you it was a joke. And nobody wants to see a mouse."

"I do." Simon raises his head briefly, and his mother frowns at him.

"What's this about visiting, then?" I ask.

"Aha." David has a definitely smug air, and I remember his father when he thought he'd "pulled a fast one", as he put it. Why does Martin keep turning up in my head? Do I have to relive all my mistakes?

"I telephoned Norman to ask if I could park in his driveway, and he said, of course, and would we all like to join him for tea this afternoon?"

"Really? Good heavens. How brave of him."

"We're not as bad as that, Mother. Surely."

I laugh. "I only meant that I was surprised at his invitation. Ever since Joseph died, he's been a bit of a recluse. You remember Joseph?"

"Of course I remember him. Lovely chap. In every sense of the word. A real luvvie. And what a scandal! Not only queer, but black. Or perhaps the other way round."

"You remember the scandal, but I remember how everyone came to love him. By the time he died of that terrible cancer, almost everyone was really upset. Poor Norman. If it hadn't been for his music ...." Three years ago now, and I still ache for him. For them both. Beautiful dusky Joseph, whose burnished copper skin faded to a yellowish mud, whose velvety midnight eyes glazed with pain. And tall, muscular Norman, built like a rugger player, who shrank over the months it took, until he resembled an old-fashioned wooden clothes peg, his round head atop a long thin body, belted into trousers that sagged, as he sagged, unable to comprehend the fate of his lover.

"Yes, sorry. I was forgetting poor Joseph's horrible end."

"So what's the plan?"

"He invited us for about four. So I suggest we drive down about 3.30, and go for a walk in the valley. What do you think? Can you manage about half an hour?"

I smile at him. He is being so thoughtful, I feel quite proud of my son. Even if he did allow Joseph to slip from his mind. "I should think so, darling. No more. But a gentle walk would be a real treat."

He stands up to help Danielle with the tray, and I lean back, put my feet on the ledge under the table. How beautiful the garden is from here, glowing in the sunshine. Blush pink *Devonshire Lass* roses clambering through the magnolia leaves, apricot-streaked astromeria and blue delphiniums vying with golden and scarlet lilies on one side, while behind me, a variety of hydrangeas clothes the bank in white, pink, blue blossoms. I am a lucky woman.

Simon sits opposite, engrossed in *Harry Potter and the Goblet of Fire*. A seductive series. I too have read all four volumes so far. Books and music - without them, life would be barren. Thank you, Lord, though I know you don't exist, I am grateful I was born into a cultured society, and to parents who valued the arts.

My father was like an army tank, smashing down obstacles, oblivious of people's feelings, impervious to argument. Perhaps that's why I married a pig-headed man myself the first time around. But he did value books, of many kinds: history, novels, science. I didn't need to go to the library very often, for I chose to work my way through my parents' bookshelves: Dickens, Trollope (so many novels, they took me more than a year), Thackeray, Walter Scott, George Eliot, Jane Austen, Mrs Gaskell, the Brontes, Tolstoy, Dostoevsky; and from my mother's shelves, the Romantics, Jeffery Farnol, H.E. Bates, Elizabeth Goudge. I was a voracious reader, and learned eventually some discrimination.

"Grammar. Can I play the piano? Please?"

"I don't know, my darling. Can you play? Do you know how?"

"I bin gived lessons," Tanya says with unmistakeable pride. "Daddy told me how to read the notes. And I can play some songs. So there."

"Lovely. First you must wash your hands, and then we'll open the piano and try it out."

"OK." She marches purposefully inside, and I look at my watch. Quarter to three. Plenty of time for a short musical interlude.

My mother's gift to me was music. She taught me the piano, persuaded me to pass all the exams. Martin too was musical, had perfect pitch. But no sign of real gifts in my children, though David was certainly competent, passing all the formal piano grades. A musical granddaughter would be a benison.

My true love has always been the soprano clarinet. When I first heard it, on the Third Programme, I couldn't believe a musical instrument could create such a glorious sound. I heard it through my belly and the music rose to my lungs and I could scarcely breathe. I had to play. One of the girls in the school orchestra let me try hers, and I knew this was for me. Unfortunately, my father refused to let me practise when he was around, even after I had persuaded my favourite uncle to fork out for a second-hand, second-rate soprano clarinet. Still, I did learn to play. And now I have a beauty, nestled in its velvet bed, and most days my fingers allow me to coax a melody from its slender windpipe.

"Grammar. Come on."

"Coming, Miss Impatience." I tap my tedious way through to the music room, where I open the Bluthner boudoir grand. "Your hands are clean?"

Tanya shows them to me, her attention snagged by the shining ivory and ebony keys, and she climbs onto the piano stool, which is set for tall Norman, and so is far too low. Even swivelled to its fullest extent, she needs extra height, and her attempts to climb onto the big cushion I suggest make us both giggle. Determination wins in the end, and I sit beside her on one of the upright chairs.

"I don't know whether I have any easy music, Tanya. Can you

41

remember anything that you can play?"

"Easy peasy." And she starts to play the nursery song, "Boys and girls come out to play" using both hands. A simple tune, but accurate and in time. "I don't need the music really, cos I sing it in my head."

"Do you really? Let me sing one to you, and see if you can play that."

Her eyes gleam with excitement. "OK."

"Sing a song of sixpence, Pocket full of rye." It's the first one I think of, but is perhaps an unkind test, as it has a series of intervals that only a child with a good ear could promptly transfer to the piano. She does it. First with the right hand, accurately playing the notes I sing, and then with her left, transposing all the notes down an octave.

"That was very good, Tanya."

"Sing another, Grammar."

I'm still trying to think of another nursery rhyme when I hear a lovely mezzo-soprano singing, "Nymphs and shepherds, come away, come away..." and Danielle walks in. Tanya is trying to follow the notes, but this song is tricky. Danielle repeats her singing of the verse three times, and to my astonishment, Tanya succeeds in playing this comparatively complex tune, and laughs with delight.

"That was good, Mummy. I like that song."

Danielle's pale face looks as though lit from within as she smiles, white teeth flashing against scarlet lips. "You're a clever, clever Tani," she says and hugs her daughter. "That was a really difficult song to pick up so quickly."

"Time to get moving, if we're going for that walk." David is standing in the doorway.

Danielle sighs. "Fine. Come on Tani, come and get tidied up for this tea-party."

"Oower, I wanna play the piano."

"Later." Danielle takes her daughter's reluctant hand, and they go upstairs.

"That child is really gifted, David."

"Yes. We think so."

"Does she have a good teacher?"

"Well, me, at the moment." He turns away, and I can see he is embarrassed.

"David, darling. She really should be taught by a professional."

"Yes, I know. But..." He starts to walk away. "Let's talk about it some other time."

"David. If money is the problem, I will pay for proper lessons."

"Mother dear, please. You've done enough for us. Don't forget, you might need every penny you've got before this world has finished with you."

I stand quite still, so that I can put all my strength into my voice.

"This is not for you. This is for Tanya. My granddaughter. She needs proper music lessons and I will pay for them. Please don't argue. Just make the arrangements and let me know."

"Mother, you're a darling. And as bossy as my wife. Between the two of you, I have no chance. Let's talk about it later."

Turning down an offer that would benefit his daughter? That's quite unlike my David. Music lessons for a beginner are scarcely a major expense, so why would he not want me to give Tanya this gift? What on earth is going on in this family?

Perhaps they have money worries they haven't told me about. Oh, dear, I do hope Danielle hasn't been running up credit card debts the way you hear about on television. What did Susie say? "Quaking in her Jimmy Choos." All those stylish clothes the woman struts around in, all that make-up, all the shopping she arrived with ... She does seem to spend money like a wedding guest throwing confetti. So yes, that could be it. Poor David.

10

Irene

Beneath ancient beech and sycamore draped in ivy, the cool green valley is like an old beloved friend. Sunshine tumbles through leafy branches, tangos over the path, skitters on the water; a hidden waterfall fills the air with *bass continuo*, and high in the trees, song birds chitter brief arpeggios. I breathe in the music-laden air. Even if I never walk here again, I couldn't leave this valley for a Midlands town.

The children run ahead, with Danielle trying to keep them from getting wet and muddy. I hear her laughing. And laughing again. So she *can*. Why is she so dreary, so hard on the children? Is it me?

David walks beside me, matching his pace to mine though the sun moves across the sky more swiftly.

"Such a lovely day. Did you not want to take the children to the beach?"

"But it's too difficult for you, Ma dear."

"I don't need to come with you, darling. It's just a pleasure to see you all."

"Such a short visit this time. I want you to enjoy it too."

I smile at him, noting the anxiety behind his long black lashes. I suppose, like all children of elderly parents, he worries about not doing enough, fears how it will end. He smiles back. Overweight he may be, but big dark eyes, white teeth and full red lips make him a sexily attractive man. Like his father.

"This is a treat for me, David. Thank you."

I sit on a fallen tree and release him to join his lively family as they play along the water's edge, among the pink campion and wood anemones. The river is shallow after a long drought, and sings as it hastens over stones, gurgles through tree roots and spurts occasional crystals into the air. The slight mud smell of the water mingles with the sweetness of honeysuckle, and beneath it, the sharp musk of a fox leaves a bitter taste in the throat. Even that I have missed.

**

Norman stands, tall and stooped like a heron, as we walk up his drive. Or rather, Danielle and David walk, the children skip and dance, and I, well, I shall be glad to sit in a chair once I manage to climb this damned slope.

"Irene, my dear." He bends to kiss my cheek.

"Do you remember David?"

"Of course. David. Welcome. It's been a long time."

As David introduces his family and we all go inside, I think, yes indeed, it has been a very long time. What made my son renew his acquaintance with his music teacher this visit?

Norman's house has been in his family for several generations, and little has been changed in his lifetime. The rooms are high ceilinged but small in dimension, he has few modern conveniences and a great deal of beautiful old furniture. But he does have a noisy, chain-flush, mahogany-seated lavatory downstairs, which I visit as a precautionary measure. We women of the music group no longer blush to confess our urgent needs, for we know that our elderly male friends envy us the ease with which we pee.

Everyone is seated around the dining table when I return, for Norman has provided a traditional Cornish cream tea, with what I am sure are home-made scones and home-made cherry almond cake. Yes, and even the raspberry jam comes from his own prolific stand of raspberry canes, now cared for by Ivor. I can see that Simon is not sure about this fare, but his sister has red jam on her cheeks and a gleam in her eyes as she crams scone into her mouth.

"What a feast, Norman," I say, as he hands me a welcome cup of tea in his mother's best Spode china.

"It's a pleasure to bake for other people. Not so much fun just for one's self."

"Oh, I do know what you mean, Norman," Danielle says. "I too like to cook, but one does need an audience. Scarcely feels worth the effort otherwise."

45

"My dear. My sentiments entirely." Norman nods at her with approval. "I do hope your little family is appreciative of your efforts."

"Ah, that depends." She laughs, like the ringing of a copper bell. "You can see that one of my children loves your scones. I think, Tanya, you had better wait before you take another, in case someone else wants more too."

"This is really, really yummy."

"I do like cake," volunteers Simon, and I laugh, while his mother frowns, shakes her head at him.

"Splendid, boy. Let me cut you a piece."

"Thanks, Mr er.."

"Fleetwood, Simon." His father glares at him, then turns to our host. "Do you remember, Norman, I met your niece, Belinda, when I came for lessons? She was only about Tanya's age then?"

Norman frowns. "Belinda? Yes, you might well have met her. She used to come here with her mother every summer. Pretty little thing, but not what I'd call musical."

"I remember," says David, "because, by a happy coincidence, we met in Oxford. She said to give you her love if I should see you."

"Well, well. How odd that you should mention her today. I haven't seen her since Joseph's funeral, and she telephoned last night to ask if she could stay."

"Really?" David frowns.

"Such a surprise. I expect her this evening. Someone else to cook for, my dear." Norman turns to Danielle with a smile, which she returns half-heartedly, for she is sitting very still, watching her husband. All her earlier animation has vanished. "Belinda tells me she's now in films, you know."

"Yes, so I understand," David says, and I can see he is monitoring his wife's reaction. Which is to remain motionless. Oh dear.

"Good heavens, Norman, you're going to be very busy," I say. "Perhaps we should be going."

"Certainly not, Irene, my dear. You must all finish your tea, and then we must have a little music before you leave me."

"Ooh, yees." Tanya's mouth is so full, the enthusiastic words are barely audible. Her mother moves at last, leans over and whispers: "Mouth. Keep it closed." The child chews as fast as she can, clearly bursting to talk.

"Norman," I say. "I discovered today that Danielle has a lovely singing voice. Perhaps the two of you might play a few songs for us when we have finished?"

"It would be a pleasure, Irene."

I turn to Danielle, whose expression is a complex melange of astonishment, shock and pleasure. "I hope you don't mind my mentioning it. Music can be such a joy."

Her smile could light up a darkened room. "Irene. I just don't know what to say." I see tears in her eyes.

"Don't say anything. Just delight us with a few songs, my dear."

"Can I go in the garden? Please, Mr Fleetwood?" Simon asks.

"Alas, not all my family is musical, Norman," David says. "Simon here prefers nature."

"Does he? Well, now, Simon. You are perfectly at liberty to explore my garden. But you might perhaps like to examine my *Encyclopaedia of Natural History* instead?"

"Gosh." The boy stares at the tall, thin old man, as though he's been offered a glimpse of treasure.

"Come with me, into my den. I'll show you the books and you can decide."

"I remember those volumes," David tells me as they leave the room. "Great heavy things with dark red covers. Leather, I think. And amazingly intricate drawings of bugs and animals from all over the world. Simon will be in his element."

I want to ask how he met Belinda, and how he could have recognized the child he had known in the decorative, blonde thirty-year-old I saw at Joseph's funeral. But we all make our way to the music room, where our little group plays.

Danielle appears to hold Tanya back as Norman lifts the lid, flexes his fingers ready to play. "Just behave," she whispers in the girl's ear. "We are visitors."

Tanya looks sulky. "I know." She shakes her shoulders until her

47

mother lets go, then creeps over to the piano, to stand beside Norman.

He smiles, looks down at her. "What would you like to hear?"

"Nim – er nimps 'n shepherds. What my Mummy did sing."

"Ah. 'Nymphs and shepherds'? All right. I'll play the notes and you and your Mummy sing." He glances round to make sure of Danielle's acquiescence, then launches into a complex arrangement. The room is filled with a mezzo-soprano, rich and smooth as hand-made Belgian chocolates, and the voice of a child, true as my clarinet.

The next half hour is a feast of song. Norman produces a well-used copy of *The Parlour Song Book*, edited by our late friend Michael Turner, and we all join in. My own voice has become thin and absorbent as blotting paper, but at least I sing the right notes, and David has a pleasing, hot-buttered-toast-and-honey tenor. The songs are of the Edwardian era, and redolent of nostalgia: 'Jeannie with the Light-Brown Hair' and the haunting 'I'll Take You Home Again, Kathleen' that my mother used to sing; sentimental gems like the 'The Grandfather's Clock', 'Woodman, Spare that Tree' and 'My Old Kentucky Home'; and Danielle enchants us all with 'O for the Wings of a Dove'. All the tensions of the past days forgotten, we try singing 'Sweet and Low' as a part song. Tanya astonishes me, once she has learned the melody, by strongly holding her own line, and the afternoon ends in triumphant harmony.

We find Simon deep in an ancient armchair, immersed in an enormous volume, reluctant to leave.

"Super book, Mr Fleetwood. Thank you for letting me read it."

"Very glad you liked it, young man. What a charming family, Irene. Please do bring them again."

"A lovely visit, Norman dear."

Amid a chorus of thank-yous and expressions of mutual admiration, we climb in the car, wave good bye to our host.

"I wanted to play the piano too," complains Tanya as we drive away.

"You've learned lots of new songs today," says her mother. "Let's see if we can remember them when we get back."

"That was a very enjoyable visit," I say. "Thank you, David. I felt very proud of my family."

"They were reasonably well behaved. Thank heaven."

"You should see those books, Dad. They're cool."

"Which volume did you choose?"

"Dunno. I just opened one and it was super. About animals in the Amazon rain forest. I'm gonna be a explorer when I grow up."

"I thought you were going to be a vet."

"Yeah. That too."

As David approaches our driveway, and I feel the car bump over the drain, then crunch through the gravel, I realize I am extraordinarily tired. But the visit to my old friend, which might have been difficult after this morning's Declaration of War, was almost undiluted pleasure. Even my relationship with Danielle has benefited. I am happy.

11

Simon

"**Y**ou've got half an hour to play in the garden, and then it's bath-time. Go on. Shoo."

Simon grabbed his sister's arm as she opened her mouth to protest, muttered, "Come on, Tani. Mum's gonna explode. Can't you hear it in her voice?"

"What did we do?"

"Nothing. Come on, I don't think it's us she's mad at."

"I wanna play the piano."

"Come *on*!"

"Ohwer."

"Let's go feed the fish." Simon ran down the path towards the lower pond, and Tanya skipped after.

"Fish are boring," she told him.

Simon didn't care what she said. He measured out the fish food from the sack in the greenhouse, carried the plastic container carefully over to the pond, started scattering the pellets over the surface. Fish of all sizes rapidly converged on the area, black, pale yellow, vermilion, snapping at the food as though a motor has been set going.

"Why is Mummy mad?"

"Dunno. I 'spect Dad's done something. He usually has."

"What does he do?"

"You know. You heard them, Tani."

"Oh."

Simon didn't want to think about his parents. What he wanted to know was, why were the fish all different colours? He remembered when Granma got the fish, 'cos he helped her put them in the pond. He was five, like Tani is now, but he liked the pond and all the creatures you could see in the water. There were newts and tadpoles and funny little black beetles swimming around, and water skaters paddling like racing boats across the surface, and snails with pointy shells, like witches' hats, that seemed to move through the water by waving their squishy bodies. Weird. Granma got a plastic bag with eight bright orange goldfish, and together they dipped it into the pond and he held it carefully until the water in the bag was the same temperature as the pond water. Then Granma said he could slowly open the bag, while she held his legs to stop him falling in, and let the fish swim away. It was brilliant. You could see them a lot because they were such a bright colour. And they swam all over the place, all together in a bunch to keep each other company, and explored the whole pond. He watched them for a long time. Sometimes they hid under the lily leaves. But what he liked best of all was when he fed them, and they all zoomed up like tiny orange torpedoes.

So how could eight bright orange goldfish make dozens of baby fish that were black and yellow and white, even spotty and striped? Very puzzling. No good asking Dad, not if he'd been getting an earful. Mum going on at him just made him mad.

12

David

David, too, heard the irate tones in Danielle's voice, and rather hoped that his mother's presence might tone down the promised diatribe. But alas, the older woman fell asleep on the sofa. Danielle indicated with her head, Come into the kitchen, and he complied. Get it over. He was getting used to ructions at home.

"Bastard. Another of your sneaky performances. How *could* you drag us all into your sordid affair?"

"What *are* you talking about?"

"Come on. Don't pretend with me. It's sheer chance, is it, that we visit the uncle of the very same Barbie you've been shagging?"

"You're talking nonsense. I haven't been shagging the woman. I may have flirted a bit, to encourage her to put a bit more oomph into her stage performance. You know how it is. Doesn't mean a thing."

"Yeah, right."

"Norman is a friend of my mother's *and* my old music teacher. As you saw."

"Uh-huh. And just in case we all have a good time, and forget about the Great Lover for five minutes, you have to bring that stupid bitch into the conversation."

"Would've looked odd if I hadn't."

"You think I'm a fool, don't you? As though it isn't obvious that you wanted to check on whether dear Barbie is going to join you. You're a sodding bastard. I could murder you, bringing her down here."

"Don't be ridiculous, Dani. I wouldn't *do* that."

"You wouldn't *do* that? My eye."

"I tell you, I've no idea why she's coming."

"Really? Well, I have. She's following you. Obviously."

David snorted. "Well, if she is, she's wasting her time. You *know* that." He summoned his most seductive tones. "Come on, come here. Give us

52

a cuddle. You know there's nothing in it." A hand on each of her arms, he slowly turned her round to face him.

"How is it you always think you can get round me, you bastard?"

"You love me, really. That's what it is."

"Don't flatter yourself."

He drew her closer. "Oh, Dani, why are we fighting? Let's not spoil what we have."

She appeared to be melting, but then she pushed him away. "I need some space here. You go fetch the children, get them in the bath. Just leave me alone for a while. I'll make dinner."

"The music was enjoyable, anyway," he tried as a parting shot. "At least my mother seemed to have a good time."

She pursed her lips. "That's lucky." As she unhooked the apron, wrapped it around her, then opened the fridge door and peered inside, he almost believed he did not exist for her at that moment. She, too, could act better than Belinda.

I give up, he thought. This afternoon was a great success, and now look at my blasted wife. An hour of singing to an appreciative audience - she should be happy. I'm sure I would be. But no. To hear her talk, you'd think it was a catastrophe.

She knows actors coax and cajole – it goes with the territory. But she can have no reason to believe I'm actually having an affair, not even with my recent very decorative leading lady.

His mother was sleeping in a corner of the sofa, her head tilted to one side, her mouth open. Relaxed like that, she looked older than he thought. Skin corrugated, eyes sunken, lips thinned and drooping, drops of saliva gathering at the lower corner: you could see the skull beneath, just waiting to be released. He hadn't realized.

I hope she has longer to live than her appearance right now suggests, he thought, and tucked a cushion into her shoulder, to hold her head up better. Poor old dear. He felt her chilled hand, and despite the summer weather, decided to tuck a blanket around her. Susie said she was fading. He didn't like the dull, empty feeling that thought gave him. But she was a game old bird, probably go on for years despite her heart attacks. Dani

53

said so, and she was probably right. She usually was.

In the garden, the children had disappeared.

Would Simon disobey the strict rule that they stay within the garden boundaries? He'd damned well better not. In fact, he'd better not argue with me, whatever he's done. What's got into him lately? It's argue, argue, argue at the drop of a hat, and who wants to listen to an ignorant boy pontificate? A brief flash of memory: Jeff, his stepfather, looming over him, like the giant at the top of the beanstalk, one hand raised to strike, '*Shut your mouth, boy, no one cares what you think.*' No, no. I'm not going back there. And I'm *not* a bully like him.

Standing at the top of the terrace, David roared in the voice that could stun an audience up in the gods: "Simon! Tanya! Time to come in! Right now!"

And he remembered the rhododendron cave. Thirty years ago. Still there, just below the badger run, a massive shrub of tangled branches, glossy dark green leaves and, in the spring, fragrant red blossoms that made a carpet inside as they fell. His secret hideaway. He kept his secret treasures there, in a large octagonal tin that had held Quality Street toffees. He hadn't thought of that for years.

His two children emerged from the shrubbery below, and started to climb the steps. Could they have found his old hiding place? Very unlikely.

"What've you been doing?" he asked as they came near.

"Nothing."

"Tanya?"

"What?"

"You been doing nothing too?"

The little girl looked at her brother, then shook her head. "Dunno."

David laughed. How idiotic he was being. "Of course, you've been doing nothing. That's why you're covered in dry leaves." They looked down at their dusty clothes, surprised, and he laughed again, his inner tension ebbing like the sea. "Never mind. I came to tell you, Mummy says it's bath-time. So come on. We don't want her to get cross, do we?"

"Did she shout at you, Dad?"

"You let well alone, boy." But he cuffed his son on the shoulder, and winked. Simon grinned back.

He hustled them inside. "Now, straight upstairs and have that bath."

"I wanna play the *piano*."

Tanya's wail startled even herself with its tones of betrayal, and she started to giggle. Her father scooped her up in his arms, laughing, and carried her up the stairs. "Come on, Monster Child. Enough theatricals from you for one day."

13

Simon

Simon veered into the kitchen, where his mother was sitting at the central counter, chin on hand, staring into space. He stood in front of her, waiting. Slowly, she returned from wherever she had disappeared, saw him and smiled.

"Simon."

"Mum, do you know why Granma's orange goldfishes have made babies in different colours?"

"Ah, a genetics question, eh? That's my lovely scientific son. Details, please."

"The baby fish are orange and yellow and white sometimes, and some are just black. Do you know why?"

"I can explain how genetics work. And I suppose that must be why those fish vary a lot."

"OK." He climbed onto a stool beside her, and gazed at his mother eagerly.

She laughed, and then frowned. "You've put me on the spot. The reason goldfish are gold or yellow or whatever is because of their genes, of course, and they have two versions of each gene in every cell."

"Why?"

"Because that's how bi-sexual reproduction evolved. You know babies are made by combining an egg from the mother and sperm from the father. Right?" Simon nodded. Everyone knew that. "So for that to happen, each egg has just one version of each gene from the mother and each sperm has one version from the father, and when they get together, the new baby has the usual two versions. Clear so far?"

"Mmm."

"If all your grandmother's original goldfish were orange, they all had at least one gene for orange in their cells. However, some of them must have had other genes that didn't show - they're called recessive. So if an egg was given a gene for yellow, say, and a sperm came along with its own gene for yellow, then you would have a yellow goldfish. That means that any fish with orange plus yellow genes would have to turn orange, and would pass on both orange and yellow genes to the next generation. But a fish with yellow and yellow would only pass on yellow genes. See?"

"Why are there black ones?"

"Baby goldfish are usually black to begin with, to help hide them from predators."

"Yeah. Some of the black ones are pretty big, you know."

"Perhaps the switch to turn off their black colour didn't work. Things go wrong sometimes - that's also part of nature. And some of the mistakes turn out to be a good thing, and help the animal survive. That's called genetic mutation."

"Thanks, Mum. You know loads of things, don't you?"

She laughed. "I did do biological sciences at university, you know."

This genes stuff is weird, Simon thought as he climbed the stairs to have his shower. I wonder if people are made like that too. I wish...

But then he didn't really know what he did wish, just that he could find things out when he wanted to, and he didn't know why his parents wouldn't buy a computer, because everyone said you could find out anything on the world-wide web. And *everyone* at school had computers at home. Except him. It wasn't fair.

Granma would understand. Maybe she could make Dad give him a computer. Trouble was, he kept moaning about money, which was stupid, because everyone knew that that was why you had two parents who went off to work every day. They went to work to make money. I'm gonna tell Granma. She'll know what to do.

14

Irene

"Night, night, Grammar." Warm hands scrabble in my neck, and warm limbs scented with Pears soap lean on my body, spiking breast and shoulder. I'm lying awkwardly against cushions on the settee, and back and neck scream silently as I try to move. Tanya giggles, perfectly sure her grandmother is happy for her to crawl on top. "Stop sleeping, Grammar. I need a kiss."

I open my eyes. The child is in her night things. "Is it bed-time?"

"Mummy says. Really I wanna watch a video."

Laughter quivers in my chest and I move enough to hug the girl. "Night, my darling." Tanya puts her lips to mine and we exchange a wet kiss. "Sleep well. See you in the morning."

Danielle takes her daughter upstairs, and I assess the situation. First thing is to get the body moving or I'll be trapped like this for hours. Falling asleep when not lying down properly is an error. Someone is in the kitchen, rattling ice cubes. With a bit of luck, David's preparing G and T. Might make these aches tolerable.

Second thing is to struggle up the stairs to the bathroom. And no way am I allowing myself to give in again, to haste or fatigue. I must never forget they are here. I can't stand up without help. Blistering hell. David enters at the crucial moment, stops me crying out as my back complains forcefully. I *have* to move. Even if I have to crawl upstairs.

"Slice of lemon or lime, Mother?"

"Lime, please. David darling, could you give me a hand up? I'm stuck."

"Why move?"

"I need to."

"Oh."

Operation Raise the Aged is difficult, prolonged and excruciating, and I'm unable to suppress every groan. But we succeed at last and I creep up the stairs, hanging onto the banisters at every step. At the top, Danielle gives me an awkward smile, but fortunately refrains from comment. I can hear Simon in the shower. At least I benefit from wearing a skirt this time. I take more pain-killers, even though I've supposedly had my ration. Without their help, I can't possibly venture back downstairs.

"You should have woken me," I tell them once installed in my reclining chair. Danielle looks at David, raises her eyebrows. So I'm being unreasonable?

"We did try. Really, Mother," David says soothingly. "You were just gone."

"We thought the best thing was to feed the kids and get them ready for bed."

"Sorry to be such a nuisance." No. Apologising makes you sound pathetic. Better simply to explain. "It's just that, these days, I always seem to need a nap after going out."

"Your mother's not a well woman, Dave. You do have to remember that."

I gaze at my daughter-in-law, and feel my lips tighten across my rather prominent teeth. Not more, surely? Not after such an enjoyable afternoon.

"Rubbish. She's a tough old biddy, aren't you, Mother?" He winks at me, and I raise my glass to him. He's taken out the Edinburgh cut-glass crystal I've always saved for best. Good. About time all my decent things are used, before it's too late for me, and everything ends up in a charity shop.

"Of course, I am, Monster Boy. Though as a teacher of English, you could choose your words more carefully. 'Tough', I acknowledge. 'Old' and 'biddy' are not terms that appear immediately appropriate. To me."

We both laugh, and I see Danielle raise her eyes to heaven. What *is* it with this woman? We all have a lovely afternoon, and already she seems to want to re-open hostilities. Admittedly, the exchanges between David and me are puerile, but surely most people find a little gentle joking helps overcome difficulties.

Simon appears in red shorts and green and red tee-shirt emblazoned with a footballer's head: the modern child's pyjamas, apparently. He is sent off to bed, protesting as before. I wink at him naughtily, for I sympathise with his desire to stay up. Children imagine adults do exciting and secret things while they are in bed. Would it were true.

Danielle serves a simple but delicious meal of new potatoes, smoked salmon and mixed tossed salad. I recognize herbs and flowers from my garden. It pleases me she is not hide-bound by convention. This hot summer's day would not have been enhanced, even in the relative cool of the evening, by a traditional Sunday roast.

But her skill in the kitchen is not matched by her charm at the dining table. When she pleads a headache and goes upstairs, I don't feel surprised.

"Is Danielle unhappy?"

"Perhaps."

"Shouldn't you go to her?"

"I don't think I could do any good at the moment." He stands up, starts to clear the table of the remaining mats, condiments, unused cutlery. I follow him into the kitchen, note that Danielle has put on the dishwasher, left everything as immaculately clean and tidy as her own soigné appearance.

"Shall we finish off the wine, Mother?"

"Good idea."

We return to the living room, and once comfortably installed in my recliner chair, I decide to play Miss Marple. But instead of approaching the tricky question of which side he's backing in the Newly-Declared War, my unruly mouth asks:

"What's all this about you meeting Belinda?"

He shakes his head, and laughs like a bassoon. "Ma, you're priceless! No beating about the bush with you. Here I've been, pussy-footing around, and you cut to the chase." His voice changes to a parody of a gossipy old woman. "Oh ho, she says to herself, Dave's been meeting little Belinda on the quiet, and poor Dani's feeling poorly. *What* is going on?"

"So, instead of mocking your old mother, tell her. What *is* going on?"

"My Great Surprise. I wasn't going to tell you until it was all signed and sealed, but maybe … just maybe I could let you in on the secret. I'll think about it."

He grins at me like a small boy given *carte blanche* in a sweet shop. Oh, dear Lord, I'm reverting to my own childhood – they don't even *have* sweet shops these days. My poor muddled brain. What *can* he be talking about?

"David. Stop being a tease. It makes me feel quite dizzy."

"Sorry, old thing." He stands up, bends to kiss my cheek, then wanders up stage. "You'll never guess. Not in a million years."

"David!"

He raises his hands in mock surrender. "All right, all right. So get this." Grand Macready pause, until I'm ready to hit him, and then he says, very quietly: "I've been offered a part in a film."

"*Really?*" A neat bit of drama. "Oh, my *darling!*"

"Quite a good part, in fact. Friend of the hero."

"That's *wonderful!*"

"Naturally, I had to shave a few years off my age, but apparently the screen test didn't let me down. So it's more or less settled, and filming starts in two weeks."

"How exciting." He's now grinning like an Olympic winner, and I can see that he could be a success if that bedroomy boyish charm translates to the screen. "So what's the film? Tell me more?"

"Oh, you know, another British romantic comedy. Can't tell you more, not until my contract is actually signed, but it looks good to me." He speaks lightly, but triumph is shining from every pore.

"Simply marvellous, David. You must tell me every detail, when you can. I'm dying to know all about it." He's almost dancing round the room, as though he's won a match on Wimbledon's Centre Court, and I wonder at his reticence till now. Took a lot of will-power. "And Belinda?"

"Yes, Belinda. It's quite a bit thanks to her that I got the screen test in the first place. She fancies herself as an actress, you know, and we met when she joined my drama course. Then she told me she worked for this film company, and they were looking for a male, mid-thirties, attractive and lively, but not too glam, well, I just knew I could do it. I could have kissed her." He grins again, looking up at the ceiling. "I *did* kiss her, actually. Anyway, it's all on a bit of a shoe string, and the director wanted unknowns for the main parts, maybe as a publicity gimmick. Or to save money. So I went for audition, and there we are."

"Darling, that's *amazing*. But what about your teaching?"

He raises those dark brows. "You sound just like my wife."

"Oh?"

"Didn't you say, 'If you hate teaching, do something else'? That's what I'm doing."

"Poor Danielle. I can see she would be worried. How will you pay the bills?"

"Dear God, Mother, I'll sort it!" He shakes his head again, and takes a deep breath. "You do get paid a fee when you appear in a film, you know."

I raise both hands. "Sorry, sorry. Not my business. And it came out all wrong." I watch as he regains control, but a dank gloom seems to descend, as though my unguarded questions had triggered a depression, and a vulture has landed on his shoulder, digging talons into his flesh. "You always were a good actor, I know that. All those plays you were in during your teens – I was so proud of you. We thought you'd go to drama school, and I never understood why you turned down the place at RADA. Perhaps this is better late than never."

"Yeah. At least they didn't make anything of my glass eye. That's one good thing."

"Oh, dear. Has it made such a difference?"

He glares at me, and I nearly drop my wine glass. Can that be hatred oozing from that dark long-lashed eye? "What do you think? Of course, it made a lot of difference."

"Sorry, David. I don't really see why."

He looks away. "Typical. Women never face reality."

"I think reality is one thing I'm good at, David. And your glass eye is a fact of life that both of us have to live with. But that prosthetic is so realistic, I always supposed most people don't even notice."

"Of course they do."

"*And* the scars have almost completely faded. How would it even show on stage? It doesn't stop you acting, does it?"

"So you think I'm seeing a sabre-toothed tiger where you're seeing a mosquito."

"Is it as bad as that?"

"You should remember how I got this injury in the first place. That might tell you."

I am almost back in the nightmare farmhouse that haunted me for years, making me relive events over and over. "Whatever are you talking about?"

"You never told me what really happened. So I had to guess. And I guess you had something to hide."

I grimace in disbelief as adrenalin makes my heart thump. "I can't believe what I'm hearing. Why on earth would I not tell you how you lost your eye?"

"I don't know. You tell me."

My hands open wide, gesture in emphasis. "There *is* no reason."

"Perhaps you could try telling me what really happened, right now."

The phone rings, startling us both.

"Could you get that, please?" It would take me so long to extricate myself from this chair, the answer service would have kicked in. I look at my watch: almost ten. Who could be phoning at this hour? I hope it's not an emergency.

David's voice is low, and he moves into the music room, trailing the long telephone cable, and shuts the door. I see.

Suddenly, I'm overwhelmed with fatigue. I have to go to bed. As I pass the door, I hear his voice raised: "No. Certainly not. You are not to involve my mother, not ever." And then his voice drops. Oh dear. My son does seem to have got his life in a tangle. Could resentment about a terrible freak accident in his childhood be a reason?

A pain is growing in my chest again. I need my medication.

How could I not have told him what happened? True, one tries to protect a child from the worst of horrors, and I certainly wasn't going to damage his memories of his father. But I was never the kind of mother who shielded her children from realities they needed to deal with. He was only two years old when his poor little face was slashed by glass, and the surgeon removed his right eye, so we've all lived with those injuries for years.

Oh, these stairs are steep. I need my angina spray. Please grow up, David. I won't be here for ever.

15

David

"**D**avey, dahling. Surprise! It's Linda."

David was acutely aware that this call was inappropriate. "What the hell are you doing, phoning me here?"

"Daahling! Don't be like that. You'll make me wish I hadn't come all the way down here, just for you."

Her husky voice, redolent with sexual provocation, irritated him like the whine of a mosquito in a darkened room.

"This is not on, Belinda. I told you, I won't have you involving my family. What the devil are you doing?"

"Oh, dear, and there I was, thinking you'd like to see a certain document just as soon as possible." In the dramatic pause that she failed to achieve on stage, but could do so well in real life, he realized what she was saying. "Ah well. Too bad. I'll have to tell my boss you aren't interested after all."

"You've got it? Really?"

"Aha, that makes a difference. All you want me for is your beastly contract, is that it?"

"Of course, it makes a difference, you silly girl. It's *wonderful, wonderful and most wonderful wonderful.* I'll come and get it from you right now."

"Oh, no. You can't do that. Uncle Norman's already in bed."

"Well, meet me. Meet me outside. I'll be there in five minutes."

"Daahling. What a lovely idea. Just one teensy little problem, Davey, my sweet. I don't want you to get cross or anything, but I haven't actually got it at the moment." She giggled in the most infuriating way, as though she believed her charms irresistible, and he felt an intense desire to slap her apricot cheek, and see those spider-fringed eyes open wide in surprise.

"What the hell are you playing at?" Thank the gods that protect all thespians, Dani had gone to bed.

"I had to send all the copies of the contract to Anton to get his signature, because he is, you know, the Director. But I asked him to send them to me here, at Uncle Norman's. Isn't that clever of me? I can bring them up to you tomorrow. If you're nice to me."

"*Oh, gods, prithee mercy!*" So it's really happening.

"Just think what a delicious visit we'll all have together. I'm so looking forward to seeing the lovely Reeny again."

"No. No. You can't come up here. I'll come to you."

"But daahling, Reeny and I are old friends, like for ever. Of course, I must come and visit with her."

Absolutely not. That could be disastrous.

"Belinda, my sweet. Just listen to me. It's wonderful of you to think of bringing me the contract while I'm here. But you must not involve my mother. Not ever. She's really not well."

"Oh, Davey." He heard the child-like pout in her voice. "That's so disappointing."

"I know. But you be a big brave girl, and I'll come and see you tomorrow, after the post has come." He warmed to the plans which sprang into his mind, fully-developed, out of nowhere. "You and Norman can witness my signature right away, then you can take the whole thing back to the studio."

"Hmmm."

"You're a positive angel to think of bringing the contract down here, Belinda darling. Sorry I didn't appreciate your plan at first. It's brilliant."

"Davey dahling, I get the strongest impression you want to get rid of me."

"Good heavens, Belinda. Don't be silly. I just want my contract sorted, that's all."

"Good. Because I won't be going straight back to work, you know. Dear Uncle Norman would think I was quite rude."

"Fine. Whatever." The air in his balloon was seeping out. "We'll take it to the post office then. Just so long as I can sign it and send it off. And after, we can have a drink to celebrate."

"Goody. I'm all for celebrating, Davey dahling."

He laughed. "Me too. So I'll come over to Norman's tomorrow afternoon. Wait for me, I'll be there."

"Night, night, daahling. Kiss, kiss."

"Goodnight, Belinda. Kiss to you too."

He put the phone down, and rubbed his forehead. Dear Belinda had become a liability. Such a pity. She reminded him of those blonde bombshells in movies of the fifties he had devoured in his youth, and flirting with her seemed to be part of his role as ageing Lothario and actor impresario. What could she want from a half-blind wannabe actor and drama teacher, with family commitments? He sighed. He'd been an idiot. Now he realized she was dangerous: like a buried roadside bomb, you never knew into whose life she'd explode.

His mother had disappeared, presumably gone to bed. He poured himself a whisky, wandered round the living room that had changed remarkably little from when he lived here: the same black leather sofa and easy chairs, the same purple carpet, now somewhat shabby and stained, the same curtains, now fraying at the edges. He gazed at them, as though seeing for the first time their enormous stylised pansies in purple, plum, violet, maroon. At least this house was wood-panelled throughout, so spared the garish wallpaper of the seventies, but its ethos remained reflected in those curtains.

New pictures on the wall, probably acquired from local artists: a nice little study of a canal in Venice; some abstracts; and paintings of heads, different styles, no theme, just odd, rather haunting; several sculptures, including the headless, limbless torso of a woman, beautiful but disturbing, and a naked couple closely entwined on the table by the window. Extraordinary things for an elderly woman to have on display.

At least she'd got rid of that Aztec model of a naked woman giving birth. Perhaps someone with taste accidentally broke it.

Why did she persist in pretending his glass eye was nothing? It had ruined his life.

He took a long swallow of the aromatic spirit, felt the warmth fill his chest.

What really happened? Why had she never told him the truth?

Of course, now that it seemed that his ambitions might be achieved after all, even this late in his life, perhaps he should let it go. Dani thought he should. And he knew his mother was not as strong and resilient as she used to be.

He drained his glass, picked up the whisky bottle, put it down again, walked over to the mantelpiece.

He felt so bloody resentful, and didn't really see why he should carry this around forever. What was she hiding? He really needed to find out once and for all. He had asked Susan what she could remember, because she was there. At least, he thought she was. But all she'd got in her head was some muddle about men shooting at her, which sounded as though she'd got her own memories mixed up with a scene from a war film. So she was no help.

Weird thing, memory. He and Susie never seemed to recall things in the same way. He was quite certain that he could remember his father, even though he was only three when Daddy left. But Susie always told him he'd got it all wrong. Why should her memories be right and his not?

A real sense of his father the last time they were together came to him. He could feel Daddy lifting him up, and the coat that itched his bare legs, and the smell of cigarette smoke that came out of his mouth. Daddy said Mummy sent him away, and he started to cry. David remembered he saw tears fill up his father's brown eyes and dribble down his cheeks, and his face was scratchy too, like his coat. Susie said Mummy didn't know he was going away, which was silly, because David knew that Daddy was crying. He couldn't remember if he cried too, which was odd.

Perhaps his mother's memories were also unreliable. That really would bring down the curtain before the drama was over. She was the only person left who knew what happened. He needed her to tell him everything, so that he could understand why his acting career was stifled before it began.

If he didn't talk to her soon, it might be too late. He'd talk to her tomorrow.

16

Irene

Danielle wakes me once again with a welcome cup of tea. I struggle out of a deep slumber, and give her a sleepy smile. She's bossy, but she's also thoughtful and kind. I could almost forget we are at war.

"Your gardener's here. Does he need instructions?"

She places the tea on my bedside table, her smile tentative, almost as though she is afraid of me. Which I doubt. She hands me the wand.

"Thanks. And thank you for the tea." I raise the bed-head "Just tell him, please, I'll see him at eleven as usual. He'll know what to do."

She nods, "Of course," then strides from the room. "No, no. Wait 'till your Grandmother is up, Tani," I hear through the door. "I've told you before."

The child wails, "I wanna ask her something ..." and her voice fades into the distance.

The still steaming liquid is too hot to take my pills, and I allow myself to relax against the pillows, sipping gently while I consider the situation. I can see now that David and Danielle have important issues to sort out, and worry about me is the last thing they need. But allowing myself to be dragooned into some care home, however nicely labelled, is not acceptable. I'd much rather they forget me, and get on with their lives. I still need to telephone Charles, get him to draw up whatever legal documents are possible to stop them moving me against my will.

If only I could have slept a few more hours. Yesterday has left me depleted, like a *floribunda* in late autumn still trying to produce a rose.

By the time my reluctant body makes it downstairs, it is past eleven and Ivor is already seated under the awning, eating his usual chocolate bar. Danielle has made him coffee. And when she brings me a tray of coffee and a bowl of sliced mango with yoghurt, I say warmly:

"Danielle, you're really spoiling me."

"My pleasure, Irene." She goes inside without smiling in return.

I tell Ivor that as family is here, he need not check up on me for the rest of the week. It's difficult to hide from those with whom you've worked closely for twenty years: I suspect he knows I mistrust the David Clan approach to Care of the Elderly.

Where is David, I wonder? And the children? Sun's high, I do hope he's taken them to the beach. Rock pools and sandcastles and swimming in the sea are why my grandchildren like to visit.

Time to put Call Divert on the telephone, and take my new mobile down to the terrace by the lower pond. Susan introduced me to the joys of modern technology in this year of the New Millenium, so I no longer need miss phone calls while in the garden.

Ivor is weeding inside the soft fruit cage below the lagoon terrace, but his sharp ears pick up the tock tock of my stick on stone, and he emerges, wide grin, stubble cheeks, to watch me move carefully round the paved edge of the pond.

"Aw'right if I cut back that rock rose? Her'll have you in the water soon."

I gaze at the mound of tissue-paper pink flowers atop dark green leaves, cascading down the bank and across the path. Determined to reach the water.

"Not yet. I'll go round the other side."

He shakes his head. "Just take care o' they fucksias, then. They'm near as bad."

I laugh. "I'm fine. Lots of room. Could you just open the parasol for me, please, Ivor? I shall sit down here for a while."

"I'll pick some o' they raspberries, afore they'm gone over. And there's logans, if you want 'em."

"Good idea. Thanks."

Comfortably installed on a recliner beneath a wide white parasol, I luxuriate in the knowledge of someone else doing the weeding. The sun shines through the fountain, throwing jewels in the air, diamonds, emeralds, sapphires. Goldfish drift lazily by, disappear beneath round green leaves. Bees visit the saffron stamens inside lily cups. Peacock-blue damsel flies dance together in coital bliss. Ivor closes the fruit cage, gathers up his tools, and moves away, out of sight, to the far side of the garden where deer have been gnawing at the bark on young trees.

I speed-dial Charles's office number.

"You've already made a Living Will, my dear."

"I am aware of that, Charles. My concern is that it's of no practical use sitting in your vault or in my desk drawer. I need to make sure it can't be over-ridden or nullified."

I hear him sigh, as though he's always suspected Irene Harper's memory is going. "You realize, I know, that a Living Will has no legal force. It is an expression of your last wishes, but can be overridden by your next of kin."

"Yes, I remember. And I *have* spoken to my children, and they understand I don't want my life prolonged unnecessarily. But I need you to add to it, Charles. I must not, under any circumstances, be taken to hospital."

There is silence, and I infer that this is not a normal request. Why not? Are most people afraid of taking a stand? Or are they simply afraid of dying? Probably hope that hospitals will provide the magic to keep death at bay.

"Would you like me to come and see you, Irene?"

"Yes, Charles. That would be a good idea. But only if you bring the documents I need, for me to sign."

"Very well." He sighs. "Tell me what you require."

"I wish to exercise my right to refuse all medical treatment I have not already agreed with my doctor, and that includes emergency treatment in hospital. I am prepared to accept treatment in my own home, and to pay for it myself, but I do not wish under any circumstances to be taken to hospital."

"I see. And is there any special reason for this?"

"Only that my daughter-in-law has made it clear she is prepared to override my wishes."

"Hmmm. A daughter-in-law has no legal authority. However, if she were in your home in the capacity of carer, her views might carry some weight."

"Heaven forbid."

"Can you not rely on your son and daughter to ensure your wishes are carried out?"

"Probably. But I want to be sure. Charles, I need you to send copies of the revised Living Will - certified copies - to my children and my doctor. And to anyone else who might be able to interfere."

"This is highly unusual." He sounds worried. What is there for him to be worried about? I'm the one who has reason to be worried.

"Charles, I'm instructing you. Are you going to let me down?"

He laughs suddenly, an odd unexpected sound, like a goose honking, and I realize I have never heard him laugh before. "I shall miss you, Irene, when your bloody-mindedness takes you off before your time."

"Sweet of you to say so, Charles. Come and see me tomorrow."

"Have to be Friday, my dear. About three."

Four more days. I must make sure the Emergency Services plastic canister in the fridge holds a new paper, wrapped prominently around the others: THIS PATIENT DOES NOT WISH TO HAVE HOSPITAL TREATMENT written in large red capitals. They say they always look there, if there's a green cross on the front door. And I'll tell David.

Can I rely on my own son? Unfortunately, I really don't know. It depends on how much he's influenced by his bloody wife, and really I have no idea. I don't understand men. Never have.

***

The fountain trills arpeggios and in counterpoint, a frog bugles among the irises and blue tits play piccolo in the apple tree. Brightness shines through the canvas of the parasol, creating a mandarin orange glow behind my eyelids. I have been asleep.

Simon, in shorts and tee-shirt, is kneeling on the slate, fair head bent near the water. He leans even further out, and fleetingly I think, Thank god, he can swim. Then he sprawls down till he teeters on the edge, stretches out both hands to catch a newt. A large jam-jar of earlier catches stands beside him.

Tanya I can't see, but can hear her singing, one of those tiresomely catchy advertising jingles I try to avoid. Lovely voice. How delicious to have a real musician in the family.

Voices filter through the background *continuo* of waterfall and fountain and birdsong, and I realize that David and Danielle think I'm still asleep. Strange how sound carries, straight downhill. They must be sitting on the terrace just above, unaware that I can hear every word.

"You need to take a hand, Dave. I've done my best, but she just won't listen to me."

"Why should she? You're not her daughter."

"That's a really unkind thing to say. Surely she knows I care about her. And it worries me to see how frail she's become. Even getting out of bed first thing seems to be a problem - the wand control keeps falling on the floor, and she asks me to pick it up. I just don't see how we can leave her like this, here on her own."

"Look, Danielle, my mother is a law unto herself. Always has been. Best to let well alone."

"And who's going to get landed with looking after her when she falls in this ghastly garden and breaks her hip? Or has yet another heart attack? It won't be you, because men never do. And it won't be your precious sister who's far too selfish to care about anything except her damned restaurant. It'll be me."

"No one's asking you to."

"Dave, listen to yourself. You're putting your head in the sand, like the proverbial ostrich. No one's asking yet, because no one but me ever seems to think ahead. But you can be damned sure that when the inevitable happens, it'll be, Oh dear, poor Irene, someone needs to look after her, good old Danielle is a trained physiotherapist, she'll know what to do."

"So what's wrong with that?"

I can hear the way Danielle takes in a long breath, and my sympathies are suddenly with the other woman. What a selfish beast my son turns out to be. He shames me.

"There's lots wrong. I have a full time job, for a start, and I'd like to see us pay all the bills without my salary. Not to mention two young children."

73

"We'd manage." David sounds remarkably casual.

"Pardon?"

"We'd manage. I've already worked it out,"

"You've worked it out. What have you worked out?"

There's silence and I hear chairs shifting, then David says, "I've been thinking about finances a lot recently. You know I want to quit teaching, become an actor. Just listen. If I do, I can do supply teaching when there's no work, and when there is, I'll grab it immediately, no hanging around. But acting pays too, so either way, our income is the same. More or less."

"Yeah. Right. Though as far as I can see, that makes my job even more essential."

"Well, maybe. Just at the beginning. Before I get established."

"Which is one more reason why you need to persuade your mother to move somewhere safer than this god-awful place."

"Flaming hell, woman! This is a beautiful place. The garden is famous, used to be shown to the public. You can't ask my mother to abandon it now."

Quite right. Good for you, son.

"This garden's a nightmare. Slate terrace, slate steps, stone paths, on the side of a hill so precipitous you could get vertigo. And your arthritic mother totters around with a thin wooden stick that slides and slips on slate, I've seen it. She's not even safe in the house. The stairs are steep, the place is full of polished floors and loose rugs. I'd sort it if it were my mother, but I'm not allowed to."

"You'd sort it."

"Please, Dave, before disaster strikes. Please persuade her to move into sheltered accommodation. Near us, then we could keep an eye on her."

"She doesn't want to."

"I know that. But she needs to, before it's too late and she has to go into a nursing home. She'd hate that more."

"Not if you and the kids came down here. If my mother needs you."

"That is precisely what I am trying to avoid. God. Sometimes I think you never listen."

Another silence clogs the spaces between them. I hear Tanya giggling among the trees somewhere nearby, and Simon growling, "A big hairy monster is gonna get you, and dunk you in the pond."

"So you *are* relying on me to do the nursing, when it comes down to it." Danielle's voice is quiet, cool.

"Course not. That's just one option."

"One option is that I quit my job at the Radcliffe - in which I am successful, I may add, and have been offered promotion. But I gather that doesn't count."

"You do exaggerate. I only mean that if my mother needs you, it's fine. From a financial point of view."

"Oh, good. And the mortgage?"

"Oh, I'd sort it. We have to be flexible. If I'm ever to break into acting."

"Flexible meaning Danielle does whatever her husband and mother-in-law need her to do. Slavery by consent."

"You can be a very annoying woman, Danielle. I hope you realize that."

A chair scrapes across the slate, and I hear the tambourine rattle of cups and saucers being piled together, then the sharp click of Danielle's heels.

"I'm not a fool, David." The swing door creaks open. "It's *your* mother we're talking about. Not mine. Just remember that." The screen door bangs. A wooden chair jangles on the slate, then leather-shod feet march loudly across the terrace in the direction of the garage. I hear the car start.

Well, well. Turbulence in Paradise. The Perfect Marriage falters once again.

But my attempt at cynicism fails. This is family.

What makes us think we can live with another person? Everyone dreams that love brings joy and happiness, overcomes all problems - that true lovers never quarrel but live in harmony for ever. And then, when you're not looking, the reality of the other person jabs you in the solar plexus, takes your breath away.

***

75

A sudden crash of cymbals and tympani startles me, and I realize I had dozed off again. Children's excited voices mingle with a man's deeper burr.

"Wow! That's a big branch, Ivor."

"It'll do the job. There now, we just need to thread this littl'un through. Budge up, maid."

Tanya giggles.

"Mind out the way, Tani, let me do this."

"That's the way, Simon. Pull. Pull hard. Good lad. And you poke that bit in there, maid. That's right."

"Seeeee? I c'n help as good as you."

Indispensable Ivor has enlisted 'help' as he repairs the boundary fence that the deer brought down. A man of unexpected qualities. I peer through the green shadowy woodland down to the right, see movement ill-defined behind dark-leaved rhododendrons, hear laughter though the words are now faint. A distant sapphire-blue hydrangea nods, as though a child has passed beneath. Being the offspring of warring parents can be a trial, as I know from both sides, but they sound happy.

Aware that this may not be the moment to return to the house, I settle back. Danielle is in the unenviable position of being caught between the Devil (her bloody-minded mother-in-law) and the Deep Blue Sea (her bloody-minded husband). Poor woman.

But I must not lose sight of her Declaration of Hostile Intent. Though diplomatic relations must be maintained for the sake of the children, the State of War between us must never be forgotten. A Cold War it is to be hoped, avoiding the use of weapons, nuclear or conventional. But war nonetheless.

17

David

David drove down the lane with an uneasy conscience. Admittedly, he had pushed Dani a bit, but he needed some excuse. The post must have arrived by now, even in this benighted part of the world, so he had to go out. It was her own fault. If she'd been more supportive, he wouldn't need to keep things from her. Not that he had, not really. She knew all about his screen test, and the promises they made. And when she saw the deal they'd be offering, then she'd stop worrying. He'd go back in triumph, the contract signed and sealed, and she'd be pleased. Dani was all right. She always bounced back.

"*O my prophetic soul.* I've got stage fright," he said aloud as he turned up Norman's drive. I'm about to make one of the most momentous commitments of my life. As important as my marriage. His stomach felt queasy, his neck and limbs were tense, and he was aware of every breath. Slowly and with care, he got out of the car and rang the bell.

"David. What an unexpected pleasure." Norman stared at him, smiling but perplexed.

"Norman. Sorry to disturb you. I was hoping to see Belinda." Idiotic female, why wasn't she on the lookout for him?

"Oh, dear. She's gone to visit an old school friend."

Judas priest!

"Was she expecting you?"

"I thought so." Apprehension hovered like a hawk, wings fluttering in rhythm with his racing heart. "She said she'd have some papers for me from her boss. Did any post come for her, do you know?"

Norman raised his eyebrows. "I really couldn't say, David."

"Of course." Breathing became difficult. "I'm waiting for a contract and it's really important, so I just wondered ... No. Right."

"I'm afraid I don't know when she'll be back."

In the pit of his stomach burned that familiar darkness.

"Thank you, Norman. I'm sorry to have disturbed you."

"Not at all. My best wishes to your delightful family."

David did his best to smile. "Thank you. We did enjoy our visit. Very much."

"Good bye." The door closed, and David reeled back to the car.

That was it. The final curtain. He should have known: there was no contract, and there never would be. To let her persuade him otherwise simply proved he was a fool. Why would they have sent his contract to Belinda anyway? Any normal business would have contacted him directly. And they hadn't. They had simply toyed with him, for he did not matter.

As flies to wanton boys are we to the gods;
They kill us for their sport.

Shakespeare understood it all, but even his words were not enough. For David had not been killed for sport: he was doomed to remain a plaything, though his wings had been torn off and he would never fly.

This final humiliation was incubating a fury that demanded physical expression. Where to go? Not the sea, too many holiday-makers. He needed a wide open space to rant and rail against his fate. Bodmin Moor. High up, where the wind never stops, and there is nothing but white granite boulders, coarse grass and the occasional sheep.

Trying to concentrate on anything but the non-existent contract, he drove inland towards the nearest town, crouched on the edge of the moor; past the squat buildings of the local comprehensive, where he had spent his adolescence resisting all forms of authority; thought back to the era when he cultivated a reputation as the school clown, and the one way he could obtain applause and admiration - amateur dramatics with the TrePolPen Players. Until he was outed as Frankenstein's monster.

Evading that thought too, he wondered what had become of old Mr Tyler, the one teacher who treated all pupils with courtesy. Without Tommy Tyler, he would never have got an A in English, never have gone to Exeter University, never have had the chance to appear at the Northcott Theatre. And never have thought of teaching as a worthwhile occupation. Extraordinary man, completely out of place in that godforsaken wilderness'. Oxford graduate, and a former actor himself, he'd stride along the corridors of their open prison, ancient chalk-dusted university gown flapping, exchanging greetings with the bolder pupils, instilling discipline by his mere presence. It wasn't fear, it was mutual respect.

"I hope I learned that from him at least," David said out loud, "or my years as a teacher have been a total waste of time."

Exactly. My entire life has been a total waste of time.

Almost instinctively, he had driven out onto the moors through back roads he'd never have found if he had stopped to think. Memory was weird, not always amenable to coercion. He wasn't quite sure where he was, though he recognized that hilly slope, the way the road skirted the bog, and came out at a fork high up, and he could hear the wind interrogate the car: what do you want up here? If he turned right, he could go higher, maybe climb that tor. Up a narrow road past granite boulders and coarse grass and sheep droppings. He parked on a flattish, comparatively rock-free area off the road, and got out.

The wind grabbed him, like a bull pit dog latching onto a victim, shaking and growling. Great. Let it chill him through, tear his ears, pummel his chest until he could scarcely breathe. Let it maul the pain in his chest. The wind recognized him.

He jogged towards its howling fangs, up a slope towards the boulder-strewn top of the tor, where the wind swelled and increased in violence, threatening to throw him over the edge. But his heart and lungs were molten rock, his belly churned with volcanic lava. No wind could cool the fires that raged inside him. He would never, ever be an actor. It was over.

The end. The end. The end.

Except that it could never end. He had a family, small children, a wife, an ailing mother - they wouldn't understand. So he could never ever end this *tale*

> *Told by an idiot, full of sound and fury,*
> *Signifying nothing.*

His rage would rumble on, an active Strombolian volcano, because he had to keep on ... and on ... and on.

Tomorrow, and tomorrow, and tomorrow ...
...to the last syllable of recorded time.

If he were not so angry, he could weep. But he was damned if he would cry. He could shed real tears on stage, or on film if the script required, but he was not going to blubber for real. Like a child. Not ever.

He gazed around in a circle at the grey green landscape, distant blue hills fading into clouds to the west. Few signs of habitation, save the dark line of the small town to the north, simply a bare country that mocked his belief that he would succeed. Lonely and bleak beneath a reluctant sun that seemed to disappear even as he watched.

Dost thou call me fool, boy?

Self-deluding, strutting ham that dreamed of playing King Lear. The Fool was right: Having no other titles, *that one thou was born with.*

In deliberate self-mockery, he stood on the highest rock, and declaimed in his best Actor Laddie style:

Blow, winds, and crack your cheeks! Rage! Blow!
You cataracts and hurricanes, spout
Till you have drench'd our steeples, drowned the cocks!
You sulphurous and thought-executing fires,
Vaunt-couriers to oak-cleaving thunderbolts,
Singe my white head! And thou, all-shaking thunder,
Strike flat the thick rotundity o' the world.

Yes, he thought. Good stuff. Dramatic, vivid and just how the wretched man must feel. No need to overdo, one could almost say that speech quietly, and still convey his deep and justified anger. Must remember that.

Then he laughed at himself again. Well, at least he still could appreciate the skill of a great dramatist. And the fact was, if he was never to have an opportunity to show the world that he was God's Latest Gift to the Cinema, he was still in demand as a lecturer for the university's Department of Continuing Education, he could still help other actors interpret their lines; and as director of amateur theatre groups not entirely

80

devoid of talent, he could still attempt some serious work. Am-dram. Not the same. But better than nothing.

He breathed deeply of the chill wind that blew from the east, where gathering dark clouds seemed to threaten a Lear-worthy storm, and rain began to mingle with the gusts that slashed his face. Getting soaked would crown today's coarse acting. He clambered back down over the rocks, strode firmly across the slope towards his car. Pull yourself together, man. Everyone has dreams that are not fulfilled. So they say.

A brief memory of Danielle brushing her hair at the dressing table, her reflection revealing the unshed tears she was trying to hide, and her lovely, seductive voice trembling as she said, "I always dreamed of being a singer. Not a good idea when you're born into a family that thinks a child banging on a toy xylophone is making music."

We should have chosen our fathers better, Dani. Yours determined you should follow him and become a dispensing chemist. Mine going AWOL. And my step-father a complete, total, utter bastard. East winds and fathers, destructive natural elements both.

He put the car into reverse. Back in Jeff's carpentry shop, twelve years old and trying not to listen to him rant, contemplating the chisel on the bench, and imagining how it would feel to stab the bastard in the neck. That'd stop him going on that I'm *fecking useless*, Mother would realize then that she'd married a bully. And as he reverted to the helpless rage of a schoolboy, the car hit a sharp rock, and the tyre exploded.

He leaned forward on the steering wheel, gripping with both hands, and swore. Loudly and unoriginally. Tears streaming down his cheeks.

Congratulations, David. You've just proved Jeff was right.

18

Irene

"Granma, Granma. Wake up."

I open my eyes and Simon is leaning over me, smelling of earth and leaves and summer-time, large white front teeth too big for his eight-year-old mouth.

"What is it, darling?"

He pulls back, and I see the sun has shifted: the parasol now is shaded by the pear tree.

"Mummy says, the gardener wants to go and should she give him money?"

I smile to myself. The woman's incorrigible. "You can tell your Mummy that Ivor gets paid regularly, and she doesn't need to worry about it."

Simon nods his fair head. "That's what he said."

"Good." I flex the muscles in my arms, and my tiresome back grumbles again. I need to move soon. Lying in the sun is a pleasure, but not always a good idea with arthritis.

"Guess what, Granma. I saw a baby fox."

"Really? Where?"

He points along the path below the greenhouse, towards the tall rhododendrons where the ground dips sharply. "He came over the wall, where the badgers go. You know, you showed me." Simon's face shines. "He just stood and stared at me. For ages."

"Gosh. You *are* a lucky boy."

"I know."

I shift my legs, and see that the swelling in my ankles has subsided, thank heaven. He perches on the cushion beside me.

"He was so pretty, and he wasn't scared a bit. Then Ivor came along with his saw, and he ran away. And I helped mend the fence. Ivor said the deer ate your hydrangeas so they mustn't come in the garden."

"You like animals, don't you, Simon?" He nods. What a stupid question: the boy is always either reading or watching wild-life. "Which animal would you like to be?"

"I wanna be a bird."

"Uh-huh."

"Birds're good. They can fly, and they make nests and they look after their babies. I like blackbirds, 'cos they eat berries. Don't wanna be a thrush, 'cos they eat snails." He screws up his face. "'S disgusting."

"Have you seen them?"

"That's a snail stone. See? Right there." He points to a large flat stone near the greenhouse, and I can see fragments of shell glinting in the late afternoon sunshine.

"You're an observant chap. Tell me, Simon, what animal do you see Tanya as?"

"She's a cat," he replies promptly. "Everyone thinks she purry and cuddly, but she's not really."

"A danger to birds, you mean?"

He looks at me, startled, and goes red. "Granma, you're naughty."

"I know, Simon, I know. So what about your mother?"

"Oh, she's a lioness."

"Uh-huh. And your father?"

"He's a gorilla."

"Good gracious. Why?"

"He's very hairy and can be angry."

David very hairy? I realize I see him in my mind as a boy, fourteen, fifteen maybe. Rarely as the man he has become. How unfair to him. But I'd have thought of him more as a gentle, unaggressive panda rather than a gorilla.

"Course, he's not really angry, you know, Granma," Simon adds, apparently worried when I crinkle my forehead. "He just likes play-acting."

I laugh. "So you noticed?"

"Granma. I need to ask you something."

"What is it, my darling?"

83

"Well ..." He hesitates.

"Go on, spit it out."

"Um, well, see, all the kids at school have got a computer, and I need one, but Dad says he won't get me one."

"Uh huh?"

"See, thing is, you can find out just *anything* on the computer. Everybody says. And then, see, I wouldn't have to *ask* when I want to know things. Grown-ups are always too busy."

"You have an encyclopaedia at home, don't you?"

"But it's *old*. And *everything* is on the internet, Granma. We use computers at school sometimes, and it's cool. You just Google what you want, and stuff comes up. Brilliant."

"We'll need to find out about computers then, and why your Daddy doesn't want to get you one."

"Yeah. I knew you'd help me, Granma." Then he sees his mother walking down the path between the lilac mophead and blue lacecap hydrangeas. "Oh, oh. Better not talk now."

"Oh? So this is a secret?" Danielle is now alongside the iris in the pond, a tray balanced in her hands. "Don't think that's a good idea, darling."

"She'll only say no."

"Made you a pot of tea, Irene." Danielle places the tray on the small table beside the recliner. I feel irritated to note she has used the Royal Stafford, which I would never bring in the garden. Still, her loss if it gets broken. Susan's getting the Wedgwood.

"That's kind of you, Danielle."

"Tanya's watching *Matilda*, Simon. If you want to join her?"

"Yeah!" He leaps up, narrowly missing the cup Danielle is filling with tea. "Bye, Granma." He runs up the steps, as though this won't be the third time he's seen the video. Am I getting paranoid, or does Designer Woman always find a reason to prise my grandchildren away from me?

"Danielle, I want to apologise for what I said yesterday morning. I should never have suggested you're after my money. It was unforgivable."

Tears well up in the woman's blue eyes, and her delicately-drawn lips press one another convulsively.

"Please, don't say anything. Just accept that I appreciate your heaping me with coals of fire in the shape of this tray of tea, and all the fruit salads and coffees and other things you have been making for me. I promise to try to be a less tiresome mother-in-law for the rest of your stay."

Danielle laughs, a tremolo on the violin D string. "Oh, Irene. It's difficult to stay cross with you for long." I grin and bow my head. "Enjoy the tea, it's not intended to burn."

She makes her way back up the sloping paths bordered with flowers, and I watch her stop, caress lacy blue hydrangea heads, the bright flame of *crocosmia 'Lucifer'*, brush her hands along the herb bed to release the aromas, and bend to sniff the scentless rose *'Bobby James'* rambling up the rowan. Then she shakes her head, moves swiftly up beyond the fuchsias, out of sight.

I drink the tea, and note with gratitude, she has added some of the locally made biscuits I bought for their visit. As I have not eaten since eleven this morning, a sweet, crisp biscuit scented with cinnamon is exactly what I need right now.

A jangling attempt at a tune starts up in my pocket, and vibrates against my thigh. A call transferred to my mobile. By the time I've put down the delicate china cup, scrabbled in my pocket with bent painful fingers and managed to find the green button, the jangle has become loud enough to stop all birds singing.

"Mother?"

"Yes, David."

"Thought Danielle might answer."

"Did you?"

"Look, would you tell her I had a puncture? I didn't mean to be so long."

"Very well."

"You sound very strange, Mother. Is something up?"

"Nothing I wish to talk about on the telephone."

"Oh, right."

"See you soon, David. Bye."

I fumble for the red button. What has he been doing?

Belinda's unexpected visit to her uncle can hardly be a coincidence. I gathered from that fragment of conversation I overheard last night that he does not want me involved (assuming, of course, that it was Belinda who phoned). But I shall be distinctly annoyed if he is using his visit here to make an assignation because that involves me anyway. Not to mention the fact that Norman is an old friend, and might well take exception to being used – not to say abused – by my son.

I'll finish this very welcome pot of tea, then go back to the house. Cancel Call Divert. Let David and Danielle talk things over between them - it's really nothing to do with me. Dear God, if you exist: help these two restore their relationship, and stop my son behaving like a fool.

***

The sun is still hot on the terrace, and up on the balcony, the *surfinia* in the hanging baskets are drooping. Dammit, I forgot to ask Ivor to check their reservoirs.

I collect the upstairs watering can from the guest bathroom, then raise the green parasol. I will sit up here for a while as the children are watching a video. Danielle is better off without me. The sea is a wide expanse beyond the treetops from up here, pale ultramarine melding into the colours of ripening fruit – blue-berries, peaches, apples - as the sun moves down the sky.

A sudden drum-beat startles me, and I turn to see Simon in the doorway, still rapping on the wood though halfway onto the balcony.

"Hello, sweetheart."

The boy leans on the balustrade and points over the garden. "Did you know there's a buzzard in those trees, Granma?"

"Yes, I've seen it."

"I think it's after the baby songbirds. Why do big birds eat little ones, Granma?"

"That's how living things evolved, Simon. They prey on one another. Nature is rather brutal."

He turns away from the garden, and confides quietly, "I wanna get a gun and shoot it dead."

Not a gun. Please. "I don't like guns, Simon. They're dangerous."

"Daddy said it wouldn't be a good idea, 'cos then I'd be the killer. "

"Best not to go around killing things, I think."

"You kill slugs and snails in the garden, Granma."

"True. I do." Tricky one. "By the way, I got some special ice-cream for your visit. Would you tell Mummy? Chocolate and strawberry, so you could have some of each."

"Yeah. Cool." He grins. "I'll tell her you said we have to have both."

I watch him scamper through the door, and pray to the God I don't believe in to watch over him and keep him safe. Safe from men playing macho, shooting animals for sport. I couldn't bear for it to happen again.

19

Danielle

The sun had moved to the west, gilding the tree tops and throwing long shadows across the garden. Beyond the tall beech and ash on the boundary, the sky over the sea was streaked with crimson, but dark storm clouds were gathering from the north. Inside the house, no lights were yet on; the candles Irene always left on the sideboard would have given a welcome glow to the room.

Danielle sighed, and chose to leave them unlit. She looked down at the debris from the meal she had cooked, the roasted vegetables uneaten that now needed a home, the pottery plates smeared with gravy that had to be washed up. In a hotel, that would all be someone else's job.

"We used to watch the setting sun fall through the branches of the pine trees," David said. "Why have they all disappeared?"

"Age, darling. They'd had their time and were becoming dangerous. Had to be cut down."

"Does age make people dangerous?" Danielle asked. Forty, the male menopause.

"Some of us are just pussy cats."

I didn't mean you, you silly woman, Danielle thought. My world doesn't entirely revolve around you, even if you have put me in an intolerable position with your damned stubbornness. She couldn't decide whether to let her anger out, or to weep. Probably neither. Good old controlled Danielle. Always rely on her. She was a brick. That some day, someone would find crashing through their window.

"Perhaps middle-aged men are the real danger."

"What can you mean, Danielle? Surely not the lovely David. He's such a sweetheart."

David shoved his chair back, his face a granite cliff. "I'll fetch another bottle of wine."

"Go on, walk away. You always do. Your mother should know, you're not the sweetheart she thinks you are. You're a lying, cheating, self-centred bastard."

Now I've gone and done it, Danielle thought. I knew I'd throw that brick sometime. I didn't intend to, it just burst out. But you shouldn't take me for granted, David Harper. I really don't care what your blasted mother thinks.

"I thought you said you were concerned for my mother's health," David said with a quiet malevolence that chilled her heart. "This is *not* the way to show that concern. Bitch." At the door, he turned. "Sorry, Mother. A private matter, nothing to worry you."

Danielle leaned her elbows on the table, and sank her chin in her hands, staring out into the darkened garden. All that self-control came to nothing, she thought. I'm such a fool. Now everything I've struggled to protect is ruined.

Irene put her misshapen hand on Danielle's. "Would you like to tell me?" A tear trickled slowly down the younger woman's cheek, bleak despair seeping through the cracks in her carefully enamelled façade.

"I'm sorry. I shouldn't have said anything." She pulled her hand away. She couldn't compound her idiocy.

"Don't worry. I've had a lying, cheating, self-centred husband myself. Makes you mad, doesn't it?"

Don't say any more. "It's just, well, I think he's having an affair. And yes, it does make me mad." So I'm joining the club, letting it all hang out, she thought. Irene, if you sympathise with me, I'll end up a sodden mess. I bloody well refuse to weep.

"I've been there too."

"It seems so unfair. I've never even *looked* at another man." Irene raised her eyebrows. "Well, all right. I might have looked. But I certainly didn't *do* anything about it."

"You could now, of course. Even things up."

"Oh, Irene. As though that would make things better." Sex for its own sake was not to Danielle's taste and never had been. Perhaps she knew too much about the human body to find exchanging bodily fluids with a man she didn't love appealing. In truth, she didn't even care that much about David's infidelity as such. It wasn't the sex that mattered: it was the sense of betrayal that really upset her, the realization he could treat the love they had shared so casually. She could see no way round that.

"Do you want to fight back?"

"I tried. Even thought I'd join the dramatic society too. I've always loved acting, and I'd have been a much better Gwendolyn in *The Importance* than that brain-dead Barbie."

"So, why not, Danielle?

"We can't *both* be out every evening, we've got children." She sighed, a shuddering wind across unshed tears. "So I'm the one who gets left behind. Naturally."

"Hells bells. This is the same battle we were fighting when I was a young mother. I suppose he tells you, you don't understand, don't appreciate all he has to do."

She laughed then, with a sudden sense of solidarity. "Worse. I don't sympathise enough when he tells me he hates teaching and wants to take up this film contract."

"Tricky one. But maybe that's what he should do."

"That really would be the end of our marriage. I know I make a decent salary, but we couldn't pay the mortgage if we had to depend on that alone. You don't know what it's like, Irene."

"Believe me, I do. I was on my own, remember? Five years, with two small children and mortgage interest not five or six percent as it is now, but nearly fifteen, if you can imagine. But there, it's not a situation I'd recommend."

"Anyway, in the meantime, I'm bringing in as much money as he is, *and* I'm feeling abused, unloved, unappreciated, and I think I want to scream."

David marched in, waving a bottle. "So. Washed all our dirty linen? Told my very frail, elderly mother what a shit you think her beloved son is?"

"David, please don't be an ass. I have a decrepit body, but I'm not senile. Danielle has a perfect right to be upset if you're having an affair. And to tell me if she wants to."

"Thank you, Irene."

Danielle didn't know you could pull a cork with venom. But it was almost a relief to see the bottle opened in front of them, for an urge to fill it with poison darkened the air, and a tinge of sulphur wafted in the room. His mother watched him pour the wine with ostentatious care and courtesy, and tried to catch his eye. He filled his own glass to the brim, strode over to the far window and stood staring at the fading sunset, drinking steadily.

"Why are you so angry, David?" Irene asked. He said nothing.

"Could it be shame?" Flame accelerant? But I'm tired of silence, Danielle thought.

"You bloody women!" He turned in a violent movement, and wine splashed like blood on the floor. "Do you *really* subscribe to the St Bernard Fallacy? Do you imagine that supposed saint was *right* to claim it's impossible for a man to be alone with an attractive woman without having sex? A bloody insult." He moved towards them and stood for a moment, watched Irene put out a hand and cover Danielle's clenched one on the table. "I see. Apparently you've made up your minds: I'm just like my father, and my stepfather. So I must be having it off with that blasted woman, just because she helped me get a film role."

"I don't know what you're talking about, David. Your father is irrelevant. How about considering your wife's feelings instead?"

Danielle's breath was rasping in her throat, and her hand was trembling.

"I don't need anyone to tell me how to behave, thank you, Mother." He poured the last of the wine in his glass down his throat. "I am now going out. Don't wait up for me."

Danielle gazed at the Paul Jackson jug streaked with congealed sauce, the tall wooden pepper-mill, the crumpled blue napkin. Then she turned to look at Irene, before gently removing her hand.

"This is the end, I suppose."

"Not necessarily. It wasn't infidelity that made me leave Martin."

"I don't know if I could ever forgive him."

"Depends on what else there is as compensation."

She grunted. "At the moment, not a lot." Standing up, she began to clear the table. "I shall go to bed, Irene, when I've put everything away in the kitchen. Don't bother about David. He's got the key you gave him." What happens now is up to him, she thought. I've made my position crystal clear.

Irene followed her to the kitchen, hampered by a stick and a physical unsteadiness, put away small items like salt and pepper. "Is there anything I can do, Danielle?"

"No, no. All under control." She rinsed dishes under the tap, packed the dishwasher, avoiding the older woman's eyes.

"I really meant, can I help at all with you and David?" Danielle looked at her at last, gave a wry smile. "I know we've been at odds, you and I. But this seems to change things, don't you think?"

"Maybe." She shook her head, sighed. "Lordy, I don't know, I didn't want to upset you, Irene. I just wanted to help you see what a vulnerable position you're in. Before it's too late, and you're stuck in the kind of nursing home you'd hate. But as Dave tells me, I'm not your daughter. No reason why you should listen to me."

"I know you mean well, Danielle."

"Sorry. Road to hell, and all that."

They looked at each other, and both started to laugh. It didn't last, though, and tears were seeping from the corners of her eyes before Danielle turned away.

"Forget about me, Danielle. I really don't need your concern, truly I don't. Sorting out a bloody-minded old woman is not nearly as important as what's happening in your own life."

Danielle poured powder into the dishwasher, turned it on, wiped down the counter, rinsed out the cloth, carefully dried and hung up the rubber gloves. The other woman stood beside the dresser, watching, waiting with an empty tumbler to draw water before going upstairs. I know I shouldn't say this, Danielle thought, but if she really wants to help ... In for a penny, in for a pound.

"You are part of the difficulty between Dave and me, I'm afraid, Irene. I know you don't want to be, but you are. No getting over that."

20

Irene

I am now on the horns of a dilemma: a notoriously uncomfortable place to sit. I make my way up to bed before, like Anita Loos's heroine, it tosses me into the street.

What am I supposed to do? Drop dead? One solution, of course. Or be docile and move away from everything that matters to me, so that they won't have to worry? Or insist on my right to choose how I live out the last of my life, and contribute to the disintegration of my son's marriage?

I never expected to be overborne by a Trojan horse.

That night, Arthritis holds Carnival: Catherine wheels toss stars from my knees, shoot rockets from my hips. Despite feeling too tired to remain awake, my joints have called in the night shift miners, and my brain refuses to stop.

A kaleidoscope of muddled thoughts, fragments of memory: David shining with pride as he told me of the film; a different David, spewing malevolence at his wife after dinner; Belinda, long and blonde, draped over a gravestone while Joseph was buried; Danielle, convinced I refuse to recognize my frailties, telling me I'm part of their problem, I must give in, or their marriage will fail.

No, she didn't. Not exactly. Be fair. But that's what it adds up to.

I have to do something. My son is behaving like a spoiled brat. Which he never was, he was a lovely little boy. Now men are running across fields, firing wildly, children are screaming. Blood. No, no. Remember Danielle, sad, controlled, edges sharp as shards of glass. Simon talking of birds. And guns.

Oh, dear bloody God, I hate this decrepit body.

I raise the head and foot of the bed until I'm propped in as comfortable a position as the blasted chassis permits, shoulders, neck, arms cushioned against goose feather pillows. Glass of Laphroaig from the bottle kept upstairs for just such occasions. Smoky fire-water for the privileged arthritic.

How can this terrible situation be resolved? It's painful to know your child, even an adult child, is unhappy. And I find I care about Danielle: she really doesn't deserve to be treated so badly. Not to mention the children. The usual dark pain grows in my chest as I think of their glorious self-confidence being shattered like glass. Leave it. Take your angina spray, think of something else. Clarity is required.

David's volatility concerns me. Loving father, irritable husband, frustrated teacher – all that's fairly normal. But why does he veer so quickly from delight in his success at landing a good part to anger and then depression? Is there something in the idea that manic-depression can be inherited? That's what they said afflicted Martin's poor mother when she was sent to the asylum.

Martin was only nine, and his brother Graham just five, poor little lads. Their mother wasn't so much violent as unstable. She veered between high good humour, creating fun, and explosive anger, vicious verbal attacks on everyone, even her children, ending in dark depression, and a refusal to get out of bed for weeks at a time. Martin said she wanted to be a music hall artiste, but married his estate agent father instead. Perhaps that's where the musical gift came from. Perhaps the poor woman really was both talented and deeply frustrated; as is David, her grandson.

Lights flash across the window, and I hear the car. Then silence. The sensor lamp on the corner of the house goes on, and the front door clicks. I listen for the creak of the stairs, but instead, a light goes on in the sitting room.

Would it really make a difference to them both if I agreed to sell up? Perhaps after all, I'm just being selfish, hoping to remain independent until the end.

Maybe Danielle has been right all along to try and pressure me into moving nearer to them, so that when I have the next heart attack, there's someone around to pick up the pieces.

Not that I'm entirely alone here. They seem to forget the years I've lived in this house: you can't help out as a school governor or with various

94

charities without making friends; not to mention our music group - Michelle, Cheryl, Norman and Leonard. My children don't realize I have a life of my own. I *would* be lonely if I moved away, leaving everything I've built up over a lifetime. Leaving my souvenirs of a happy marriage.

Strange that David should talk of his stepfather as a bad influence. If Jeff were unfaithful during those early years, how would a young boy even have known? And if he were, it wasn't that important. I knew that my enrolling at university at forty disconcerted him, and that my studies left him feeling neglected. But we rediscovered each other and were happy. So what was David talking about?

I reach for the blue stone I keep these days beneath my pillows. Proof I'm no princess - a pea is nothing to this. A smooth piece of blue Serpentine rock that nestles in your palm, demands to be stroked. Not round, but curved, rather as though a part of the moon were fallen to the earth and polished to a midnight sheen that glows, as the moon glows, with reflected light. Jeff kept it always in his toolbox, up to the day he died. A secret talisman.

I bought it while we were alone in the Scillies, the children delighted to stay with Grandma and Brian. Part of my post-graduation celebrations. I gave it to him as we sat together on the soft white sands of a hidden beach on St Mary's. He caressed it the way it asked to be caressed, and then he kissed and kissed me ... Flashes of memory. How frustrating the mind is. We made love, I remember that, on the beach: it was evening and no one was around. How we managed to avoid the abrasive effect of sand on intimate parts, I can't recall. Just the warmth of love, the delight of shedding clothes and his skin against mine, and a vague, oh, so hazy recollection of the glories of passion.

Whatever David thinks, Jeff loved me. And if he did have an affair, I didn't know and it couldn't have mattered, there was no sign anywhere after his death of the existence of any other woman. Just a secret cache, in a locked drawer, of every letter I wrote to him, every card, every note, and every small gift I gave him that was not in everyday use. Part of me was flattered to discover he had secretly been so sentimental. But the greater part of me teetered on the brink of a black hole, where the light of life is lost. How could he abandon me so soon, when his secret hoard said he wanted to keep all of me safe? I didn't want to be kept safe. I just wanted him. Jeff, my darling. You should never have died. Not without me.

I slip the blue stone beneath my pillow once again, try to believe that he is still with me in some sense, because his talisman is here, recognize that the wound of his death has healed over. Touching the scar re-awakens pain, but these days it has become tolerable. Time brings that benefit.

The light in the living room goes out, and I hear the stairs. Good. David's coming up to bed at last. Perhaps I can get some sleep.

Would it help if I sold this house, and gave David part of his inheritance early? The place must now be worth a great deal more than I really need. I'll ask Charles on Friday to arrange for a valuation. If only I had not lashed out and accused poor Danielle of being after the money I am now contemplating giving them.

Yes. Why didn't I think of it before? I'll move, save Danielle all that worry about the dangers of the garden - for which there may be an element of justification - and find a smaller place locally. In the village. Then I won't have to abandon everything Jeff and I created, I can see friends, keep the same doctor. Maybe even get out a bit more, go to concerts further afield. And they can carry on without fears for their mortgage, Danielle can sort out her promotion, and David can sign this film contract without risking his marriage.

Perhaps it's as well you're not around, Jeff darling. I know you wouldn't approve.

"Aha," he'd say, whenever I chose to consider my children's needs and change my own priorities. "Being a pious pelican again. Thought you were giving it up."

"That's what mothers do," I'd tell him. "They're not feeding off my liver, or drinking my life's blood. They're my children and I want them to be happy."

He'd laugh then. "OK, you protect your babies, even though they're adults, and should be able to cope on their own. I'll just try and protect you from yourself."

If only I could have done the same for him.

21

Irene

Drowsing in goose-feather pillows, and listening to the birds churr despondently in the early morning rain, I notice the door inch open. Fair curly hair peeps round the edge, followed by two mischievous bright eyes and a wide gap-toothed smile.

"Good morning, Tanya."

"You awake, Grammar?"

"No." The night was too short.

She giggles and comes right into the room, pink pyjama top riding up, hair tousled. "You're naughty, Grammar, you're not s'posed to tell lies."

I make a rude face at her, and the little girl clambers onto Jeff's side of the bed. I'm so used to sleeping on the half next to the window, I rarely move more than an arm or a leg onto where he used to be. His side is useful to set a tray on, or leave books. His pillows come in handy too, when the pains get overwhelming and soft goose-down beneath the joints helps. I move the books to one side, and Tanya bounces across, leans elbows on my midriff, plonks a wet kiss on my mouth.

"To what do I owe this honour?"

"Daddy told me to go 'way. He's grumpy."

I look at the alarm clock with its large clear face. Quarter past six.

"Not surprised. It's much too early to wake up."

"Grammar. I'm hungry."

I laugh, and realize I need to get up anyway.

"Is Simon awake?"

"He's reading. He's always reading. He's boring."

"I'll get you some breakfast when I've been to the bathroom. Tell Simon."

"OK." She bounces back to the floor.

"I'll be downstairs in a few minutes."

***

We sit at the long table in the conservatory, and watch the rain drip from shiny leaves. Occasional gusts are thrown against the big plate-glass windows, spatter like handfuls of gravel, and sudden bursts of rain samba noisily on the slate paving. The roses droop, their petals sodden.

Tanya decides to draw pictures, so I provide her with paper and a box of new felt tip pens. The child's face glows as she tries out each unused pen, and she draws a rainbow, then a meadow of multi-coloured flowers. Every pen is sampled, and I remind her to replace the tops so they don't dry out.

Simon joins us, fair hair standing up in spikes, garish green and red short pyjamas. He asks me to cut bread, and makes himself a plate of toast with peanut butter and Marmite, topped with wafers of cheddar cheese. There's a family tradition that lasts. Susan still likes that combination.

I 'invented' it after Davey's accident. Susie nearly died after catching a 'super-bug' brought home from the hospital in late 1963, and both children became emaciated. So to build them up, once Susie could take solids, I would pile butter, peanut butter, Marmite and cheddar cheese on wholemeal bread. As many calories in body-building protein and vitamins as I could manage. A delicious combination, but to be used with caution.

"Can I draw a picture, Granma?"

"Of course, darling."

"I'm using these pens." Tanya gathers them close, eyes her brother with defiance.

"That's not fair."

"It's not. Tanya, there are a lot of pens there, you can't possibly use them all at once. They *are* supposed to be shared." My reasonable tones appear to have no effect on this strong-willed child, and I wonder if it's worth a fight. "I do have some new gel pens," I tell Simon. "You might like to try them out too."

"OK."

As I take the pack from the desk drawer, I bless my squirrel-like desire to collect coloured pens of all sorts. I like to write notes to myself in different inks, and doodle little sketches when I write letters to friends. Amazing to find ball points in orange and mauve, gel pens in pink and lemon.

"What shall I draw, Granma?"

"You could do a picture of your family, for me to remember you when you go home."

He frowns. "I don't think I can make people look right."

"*I* can," says Tanya.

Silent laughter floods my heart. "Perhaps you might draw your family as animals, Simon."

His eyes widen. "Yeah. I can make a family circus."

The last of the tea is stewed. David appears, barefoot, in a towelling dressing-gown.

"Morning, Mother. I'm sorry about last night."

I watch him bend and kiss Tanya's curly head, then ruffle Simon's spiky one. "How's Danielle?"

"Asleep. Shall I make coffee?"

I nod and he disappears. That's why I'm awake, of course. How is this dreadful situation to be resolved?

"Pity we were interrupted Sunday night," he says, as he carries in two mugs, steam trailing dispiritedly, like a sodden flag. "We need to talk about the accident."

"If you wish."

He looks startled, stares at me for a long moment, as though I've stopped him saying what he intended to say. "I want you to tell me everything."

"Everything." I sip the coffee. He hasn't sat down. "Well, I can do my best. When and where shall we indulge in this jolly trip into the past? Should we perhaps get dressed first?"

"More delays. You're stalling." He's standing over me, like the heavy in a B-movie interrogation scene. The children look up, stare at his grim expression.

"David, stop being such a ninny!" Simon giggles and puts a hand over his mouth. "I'm perfectly happy to talk about what happened, but

99

perhaps not with an audience?"

David shrugs, pulls out a chair, leans elbows on the table and puts his glossy head in his hands. A grand performance, aimed at the gallery.

I sigh, and stand up. "I do need to go upstairs, David. I'll be back."

He raises his hand. "Right. We'll talk later. Without the kids."

I nod. As I move towards the stairs, I hear him say: "Simon, I'm going to leave you both for a while. Just make sure everything is good while I'm gone. I don't want either of you getting up to mischief."

"Okay." The boy sounds so nonchalant, I wonder if he has registered what his father said. He's eight. I hope he's old enough to be left in charge for a short time. Heaven knows what Tanya might get up to if left alone for long.

My progress up the stairs seems to take longer than ever, and I feel tempted to lie down on the bed. No. I collect clean underwear, a purple silk shirt, light-weight grey trousers and matching grey wool waistcoat, take them to my bathroom where I can be reasonably sure of being undisturbed.

Why has he brought up the accident again? Surely, after yesterday's performance, his own bad behaviour is enough to be going on with.

Martin, you tiresome man. Unreliable to the last, are you behind the distorted notions your son has created about the accident? For there is one thing I never told either of my children: that accident shattered more than my little boy's face. It destroyed my marriage.

Two Tramadol from my daily allowance. Glass of water from the sink.

Let me find the right words to satisfy my unhappy son. The damage to his eye was traumatic, and I did my best to help him live through it and grow strong. I had not expected him to harbour anger nearly forty years on.

22

Irene

On the landing, I meet Danielle, in a robe, her head wrapped in a towel.

"Hi, Irene. You're bright and early."

"Thank Tanya for that."

She raises an eyebrow. "Oh? Sorry. Be downstairs in a minute."

"No hurry."

The woman is surprisingly cheerful. Perhaps they've kissed and made up. Dear God, please let that be so. Except, they haven't had much time. Perhaps she's so used to dissimulation, after last night's brief lapse she's back on automatic. This woman could give master classes in self-control.

In some ways, Danielle and I have quite a lot in common. Not that I would ever have meddled in another woman's life, not until asked. The Mediation Service might have been thought meddlesome, but at least we only intervened in response to a request for help, whereas Danielle keeps trying to interfere, even when asked to stop. Still, there are similarities between us: both have (or had) two children and an unsatisfactory husband, both show some musical talent, but work (worked) in the helping professions, both are well-meaning, but sometimes get it disastrously wrong. So we should be friends. Alas, an unlikely scenario.

Slowly my querulous hips take me downstairs, and I see David sprawled at one end of the black leather settee, still in his green bathrobe. Tanya is beside him reading.

David grins at me, all hostility apparently evaporated in the company of his young daughter.

"As you see, not dressed. Dani cluttering up the bathroom."

I smile at this incongruous image. "She's emerged now. I met her on the landing."

"Ah, right. Tani, I'm going upstairs now. You can finish reading that to me later." Tanya gazes at him, stony-faced.

"Do you like the book?" I ask her.

"Yeah," she says, with an element of doubt in her voice. "Don't like it when her Dad goes away."

I see David frown as he makes his way to the stairs

"Grammar. Her Dad goes to live with a different lady. I don't like that. Real Dads don't do that. Do they, Grammar? Do real Dads? Dads not in books?"

I lower myself onto the settee beside her. "Sometimes real Daddies do leave their families, I'm afraid. But not very often."

"Grammar. Guess what?" Her voice is almost a whisper, and I lean towards her to catch what she is saying. "Emma – she's my friend - she told me her Daddy did go away. And her Mummy said she mustn't see him, not for ever and ever. I think she's telling lies. Don't you, Grammar?"

"Oh, dear. I think your friend Emma must be very unhappy."

"She was crying. In the girls' toilets. She said I mustn't tell. But it doesn't matter if I told you, Grammar. Does it?"

I put my arm round her. "Of course, not. It's perfectly fine to tell me, or your Mummy, anything. Your friend didn't want the other girls to know. Poor Emma." She snuggles against me, drops the book on the floor. "That book is sad. Why not leave it for another time, and find a different one now?"

Danielle catwalks into the room, in pillar-box red jeans, matching sandals, and a patterned red and white tee-shirt that make her look as though she's stepped from the pages of the FT's *How to Spend It* magazine. Even when wet her hair appears chic. How the devil does she do it?

"Thanks for giving the children breakfast, Irene."

"A pleasure. Truly."

She collects the coffee mugs and moves towards the kitchen. "Time you were dressed, Tanya. Please pick up that book you dropped on the floor, and go upstairs. I'll sort them now, Irene." She smiles at me, and I feel as though the sun has emerged from behind dark clouds.

The phone rings, and I realize it is still where David left it, while I'm buried in the settee cushions. However reluctantly, I shall have to ask for help.

"Danielle," I call. She scurries in from the kitchen. "Would you mind getting the phone? In the music room." She nods, rushes through and picks it up on the fifth ring. I am still so creaky, I stumble as I crank myself up and waddle towards the call.

"Oh, hello, Susan. Yes, we're fine ... Your mother is as well as can be expected ... She's on her way ... No, no problems ... Here she is. Bye."

Danielle hands me the receiver, watches as I perch somewhat uncomfortably on the piano stool, then leaves the room.

"Susie, darling. What a lovely surprise."

"You didn't expect me to abandon you for the whole week, did you?" I laugh. "How's it going? The dreaded Danielle living up to her monster billing?"

"Well, no, actually, I'm relieved to say. She did have a go at me, and I was all set for armed hostilities. But it seems we share a love of music, and that made a difference."

Susan snorts. "Ha! Music has charms to soothe a savage breast. Or is it beast?"

"As it turns out, yes. Whichever. And little Tanya appears to have perfect pitch."

"So you're in your element, Mother dear. Wonderful. I'm so glad. And I have some pretty good news myself."

"Tell me."

"Frank and I have worked out how you can get to our party next month. It's our Silver Wedding, so you *have* to be there."

"I'd love to, darling. But you'd have to move your celebrations to Cornwall, I'm afraid." I feel exhausted at the very thought of the long journey to Richmond-upon-Thames.

"You're a fraud, Mother dear. It's no good telling me you can't travel, because I'm your daughter, and I don't believe anything is impossible if you really want it. So there."

I can see this determined daughter, tall, slim, long brown hair coiled on top of her head, brown eyes steady and chin firm. Happiness flows like golden honey over my wearisome body. Fate must have treated her kindly, for she believes still that we can make of life what we will.

103

"A lovely thought."

"You always said, 'Anybody can do anything', and I believe you."

"Heavens! The unintended consequences of casual remarks. I used to believe that too, before I tried to move a granite gatepost. By myself."

"You did what?"

Her disbelief is almost tangible, even at the other end of a telephone wire, and I laugh out loud. "Just a cautionary tale."

"Go on, mad Mother. Tell me."

"Remember I was only in my thirties."

"A youngster then."

"Our gateway was originally very narrow, so I wanted to make it wider. A granite post being in the way, I attacked the earth around it with a pickaxe and tried to dig it out. Then I remembered Archimedes – with a long enough lever, a man could move the world – but unfortunately didn't locate a lever of adequate length. So I tied ropes around the post, to pull it over with our Land Rover. Total lack of success. In the end, Jeff had to get some men to dig down nearly six feet all round, and then use a tractor and chains to uproot the wretched thing."

"Good God! How did I miss that one?"

"Taught me that determination is not always enough."

"In this particular case, however, it is. You wait and see. We're putting on a really special do at the Silver Fork, and I think, if you wouldn't mind using a wheelchair, we could make it really easy for you."

"A wheelchair?

"Just to make getting around easier. Everything is so much simpler that way. People see a wheelchair, and you get special treatment. And it helps when you get tired."

I laugh. "If you can see a way to make it all happen, I should love to be at your celebrations, darling."

"You will be." Her voice has a happy lilt. "Just put it in your diary. Bye for now."

A wheelchair might make some things easier. When I go to concerts, I'd like to avoid crowded stairs: I've often felt quite vulnerable, not to mention fatigued. Rather a confession of weakness, though. Oh, deary me. Pride getting in the way again. A bit like my earlier resistance to reading glasses. But as I am arthritic and find it hard to move around, I might benefit from any compensations going. Not at home, of course. Not needed here.

This piano stool is not a comfortable seat. I lever myself up, find my stick, walk carefully but perfectly well towards the living room, and my reclining chair.

"I'll take the children into the village, Irene," Danielle says. "That ice-cream was quite exceptional. Where could I buy more?"

"The grocers usually have it in stock, but if not, I can always ask my friends who make it to deliver."

"I know," she says, with laughter in her voice. "You know everyone, and everyone rallies round to make sure you are safe and happy."

Laughter captures me too. "Something like that, Danielle."

"Come on, kids." She herds them through to the back door, where they must change their shoes. Above the chatter of voices, I hear Simon say loudly,

"But I need to tell Granma."

"No, you don't, not right now." Their voices fade and the door slams.

I lie back and close my eyes. What does David imagine I have to tell him that he need send his family away?

23

Irene

"**R**ight, Mother. We are now alone."

David is gazing down at me, tall and dark in a green polo shirt, perfectly presented as the attractive, if well-built, friend of the hero. Whoever plays the lead, I bet he's blond.

"Should I be worried?"

He rewards my facetiousness with a grim smile. "I just want you to tell me what happened when I lost my eye."

No euphemism. No British under-statement. His directness jolts me and I see his distress. "Do sit down, darling. And tell me what you already know."

He perches on the arm of the settee. "All I know is I was cut by flying glass."

"That's right."

"Oh, Mother. How did it happen? Where were you? And my father? Come on, I need to know it all."

"Of course, you do." I take a deep breath, feel my stomach clench. Going back there is like walking into quicksand. "I'll do my best. We flew to Canada the October after you were two, to visit your father's old school friend, Eddy. All of us, you and Susie, and your father and me."

"I don't even remember being on an aeroplane."

"What a shame. You really loved it. And you were so excited before we took off, you could hardly breathe." When the stewardess strapped him into a harness, his body was tense as a violin string: as the plane left the ground, he gasped so loudly other passengers smiled.

"Your father called his friend 'The Dreamer'; they both came from the sooty streets of Wembley, and now Eddy was mortgaged to three hundred acres of apple orchards, a sugar maple wood, fields for grazing sheep and scrub full of deer."

I try to take my middle-aged son back thirty-eight years to 1963 when he was a toddler and I was thirty-two. Dazed by the long transatlantic flight, we were driven in Eddy's enormous battered Cadillac eighty miles from Montreal airport out to the Eastern Townships of Quebec, into wild country ablaze with autumn yellow, vermilion, scarlet. Off the toll road, down dirt tracks, past wooden boards nailed to posts painted NO HUNTING PRIVATE PROPERTY, between gates to a long drive and Eddy's sprawling farmhouse set among tall oaks turning to gold.

There is the big white kitchen where everything happened: long windows above a deep sink, overlooking a yard where logs were stacked under barn roofs; a wood stove with round black chimney rising to a hole in the ceiling; a shiny modern electric cooker insisted on by Erica, Eddy's wife; a big fridge; a long pine table, assorted wooden chairs with patchwork cushions, a green-painted high-chair acquired specially for David; and the big sash window that reached almost floor to ceiling, and looked out past the house, over to the driveway, and fields and scrub beyond. It was here we put the playpen so that David could watch robins the size of English blackbirds toss fallen leaves aside on the lawn, and not be bored.

I attempt to describe how it was on that day, about noon: in the playpen beside the window, my dark-haired toddler sitting like a sultan on his nappy-swathed bottom, playing with his harem of soft toys; his blonde five-year-old sister, kneeling on a chair at the table, drawing, her tongue protruding from the corner of her mouth; Erica and I were upstairs, putting away clean washing; the men had disappeared, Eddy to a far field to mend fences while Martin said he would chop logs.

David gazes at me with unmistakeably patient forbearing as I struggle to convey the reality of that moment, impeded as I am by that English habit of understatement and stiff upper lip. Everything seemed so normal and peaceful. Erica and I were planning a picnic. Then we heard gunshots.

It was as though we had strayed into a war movie. As a schoolgirl, I had watched the Battle of Britain in the skies, and cowered in shelters while bombs fell, but had never been threatened by men with guns. Now suddenly we were under fire and bullets were ricocheting off trees.

Through the window, I saw a deer bounding towards us across a field, chased by a group of men shooting wildly. A series of thumps hit the house. Susie started to shriek.

"So there really *was* shooting?"

"Yes. Alas."

Back in that remote farmhouse, the clothes I'd been folding fell from my hands. I flew for the stairs. More thumps struck the building. Glass shattered. Little David screamed. In the moments it took to plunge down the stairs, I imagined taking the rifle Eddy had proudly shown us, opening the drawer where he kept ammunition, loading the magazine as instructed. If either of my children had been hit, I would shoot those hunters dead.

In the kitchen, both children were hysterical, screaming and incoherent. Susie tried to speak, but could scarcely breathe. A bullet had shattered the window, ricocheted off the table beside her and was buried in the wall behind.

My baby lay in a pool of red, his face a mass of bloody flesh. When I lifted him up, I couldn't believe what I was seeing: shards of glass had flown into his face, sliced through his tender skin and into his eye. I held him close, my child's life spurting scarlet over my shirt. This was the one occasion in my life when – for a moment out of time – I was overwhelmed with panic.

My eyes are shut. David leans forward, touches my hand. "Go on, Mother. Please."

I swallow, take a deep breath, relive the frantic moments as I grabbed towels, tried to pick out the glass and staunch the bleeding. Erica called an ambulance, found my bag, passport, coat, and promised to look after Susie. My little girl's eyes were wide with terror, her skin the colour of paper ash, and she kept asking over and over, 'Why are men shooting us, Mummy? Why? Why?' I could barely do more than kiss her and hug her tight, for I had to leave.

I ran to meet the ambulance. It was a long way to the road, maybe a quarter of a mile. Men were blocking the drive with the body of a deer, about six of them, laughing and joking, two on the ground, gutting the carcass. I shouted at them to move the deer so that I could get past. They were so high on testosterone, I don't think it registered, even when I told them my baby was dying because their bullets had shattered the window and cut his face. My desperation seemed to wash over them, like a voice on the radio easily ignored. Only when the ambulance turned in at the top of the drive did the enormity of what had happened hit them, and two of the men helped me by.

"Bloody hell. What a nightmare."

"Yes. It was."

"And where was my father in all this?

Martin? Cowering in the corner of the kitchen. But I don't tell David this, nor that his father was no bloody use to anyone, not to his wife, not to his daughter, not to his injured son. In a foreign land, frightened of men with guns, afraid he might be expected to do something to help, wallowing in useless grief for a baby who needed action to save his life. When we met in the hospital, he wept in my arms, said he had never realized how much he loved his little boy.

Somehow, when it came right down to fundamentals, I expected my husband and the father of my children to fight back instinctively, to protect us all. He called Eddy a dreamer, but Eddy knew that a man defended his own: when he returned to the house, he went out to confront the hunters, wrote down the number plate of the truck that came to collect the meat. How could Martin stand by, doing nothing?

I had already begun to feel Martin was a Hot Air Balloon. His projects always failed. He was stubborn, obstinate as a boar pig in a turnip field, never listened to argument; but once committed to a franchise, a pyramid-selling project, a new revolutionary product, he had no stamina, no gumption, expected others to bail him out. I knew he was no businessman, just prayed that he would discover his niche before every penny I inherited from my father was gone. But when even his concern for his children dissolved into hot air, I could take no more. My heart believed he was a fool, and I could no longer love him. I never wanted my children to know that.

I look up to find David staring at me. "Have you got problems,

Mother? You suddenly disappeared. It's a bit worrying when you do that."

"Sorry, darling. This was a dreadful experience. Just going back and feeling some of the emotions, well, it's not surprising if I seem a little distrait. I feel a trifle disoriented, to tell the truth."

He nods. "Yes, I can understand that. I keep thinking, what if it was my son? I'd want to kill them too."

There's irony. I try to drag myself back to the present world where the fall-out from that far-off hunting incident in a different country still has power to distort perception today. My unlucky son lost an eye because a group of hunters trespassed on posted land, shooting indiscriminately. They were never brought to justice. The police delayed their arrival until all signs of the kill were cleared away, did not examine the farmhouse, were not interested in the bullet dug out of the kitchen wall, claimed there was no evidence the injuries to my child were caused by hunters. Eddy approached the 'Hunting Correspondent' on the *Montreal Star*, who did write up the incident, but said his readers would see it as 'just another hunting accident' and 'they happened all the time' in the North America of 1963. I was so angry I felt like shooting the hunters all over again.

"I can see this would have been difficult to explain to a small child," David says. His brows crinkle, and I'm oddly aware of long lashes as he turns the full wattage of his dark eye on the current suspect. Forget romantic comedy: this actor is playing a detective. "But when I was older, why didn't you tell me then?"

"You didn't ask. And I had no sense of having kept anything from you." What else is there to say? "It was a miracle you didn't die before we got to the hospital, though it was too late to save your eye. You were six hours in the operating theatre before they finished. Later I was allowed to stay with you, because you were blindfolded and frightened. They thought I'd saved your life, so we were given special treatment."

"Blindfolded? Why?"

"Your other eye was still in danger, and they didn't want you to move it."

"Christ." He stands up, walks over to the bay window and gazes out

110

at the wet garden. "Part of me always blamed *you* for what happened, Mother." He turns, and I see tears on his cheeks. "I'm really sorry about that."

"And I'm really sorry, David, you felt angry when you were little."

"Perhaps I didn't then. Not when I was young." He perches on the arm of a chair near the window, and looks up at the ceiling, where memories are so often stored. "It was really when I was a teenager. When I went to that theatre-training week in Cheltenham, remember? Everyone there wanted to go on the stage or into films, and the competition was fierce. And cruel. That was when I realized I could never hope to succeed as an actor because I had a glass eye, and these scars. It was so bloody unfair."

"That's certainly not what the tutors told *me*. I thought you won some award."

"True. But what I remember chiefly is the bitching. You can't imagine the vicious things the other kids said, and when you're only, what? fifteen, sixteen? you believe it. I guess everyone got ragged, even the best-looking got told they were too fat or saggy or something horrid. But when I kept being told I gave the girls nightmares, I decided I didn't want that. Imagine what the gutter press would make of my eye-less scarface if I landed a decent part."

"They were clever, weren't they? Got rid of some strong competition."

He laughs at that. "Oh, you're good, Mother. Perhaps I should have told you about it years ago. But I was a teenager, and I actually felt ashamed."

I lean towards him, put out my hand. "My poor darling."

He pats my hand, and smiles in a manner intended to convey stoical acceptance of his fate.

The prosthetic has been changed many times, and is remarkably like his real eye. His scars are faint lines across his face: a long curve on his forehead, across one eyebrow, down through the bottom of his right cheek; shorter curves round his left cheek, one curling under his chin. So near the jugular, but blessedly not quite. Thanks to that brilliant plastic surgeon, the scars are there, but do not distort. Just pale threads running through his skin.

111

"Have you looked in the mirror recently? To me, your scars *add* to your charm, they don't detract. Rather distinguished, in fact."

He grunts. "That's how *you* see them, but you're my mother. Don't worry about it. I've learned to live with the Damaged Look."

24

Irene

"Daddy, you know what?" Simon's voice startles us as he calls from the garden, evidently wanting to convey something too exciting to wait. David stands up in one fluid movement, strides out into the conservatory, while I lean back against the cushions, relieved that our painful journey into the past is over. Through the window, I see Simon pull open the screen door, hold it with his elbow as he manoeuvres a heavy plastic bag inside.

"Daddy, we passed a lady walking up Granma's lane. And guess what?" The boy giggles. "Mummy said, 'I think I shall run her over,' and do you know? I could tell. She really, really wanted to. But she didn't. I asked her why not, and she said it would be too messy."

Simon looks at his father, hoping for a response, but from where I sit, David's face appears grim. "There were puddles on the road, and Mummy drove through them. On purpose." Still his father neither smiles nor expresses shock. "*I* thought it was funny, anyway."

Stern *paterfamilias* is not quite it. Anger certainly. Surely not anger with Danielle for such a trivial, if silly, joke? My son appears to be developing into a humourless pain in the neck.

Most unfortunate that simple expressions like that can have a physical outcome. I find I *have* a pain in my neck, and I rub it with my tiresome fingers, remembering. Jeff would talk of a difficult client as 'a pain in the back teeth', and with a really bad one, usually ended up with toothache. Martin's language was cruder: he'd call anyone who failed to live up to expectations 'a pain in the arse' and suffered accordingly. Simon would love that. But I doubt if I shall tell him, in case he repeats it to either humourless parent.

Danielle and Tanya arrive with more shopping. Good heavens. I thought the larder and fridge and freezer were already all stocked for a siege. What more can they need?

"Barbie is apparently coming to visit," Danielle tells her husband, and I can feel the sharp edges from where I sit.

David shakes his head. "Seriously, Dani. She's not supposed to."

"Quite."

The shoppers greet me, then take their purchases into the kitchen. What am I supposed to do with enough food to feed an Olympic village for a week?

"I'm gonna have an apple, Mum, and read my book."

"So'm I."

"You're such a copy-cat, Tani."

"I'm not."

As the children clamber up the stairs, I see Belinda through the bay window. She is approaching the house, stepping daintily across the terrace in wedge-heel sandals, red and white patterned knee-length skirt flowing, blonde hair bouncing as though in a shampoo ad.

This is my house. I must go to the door.

I push down the leg rest, and drag my tiresome body upright. Where's my damned stick? My feet have joined the chorus of niggling complaints, and I glare down at them. Behave, blast you. Do your duty. Padded sandals are meant to cushion, stop these wearisome and unnecessary criticisms from my nether regions. Forget aches and pains. You are a hostess.

I hear David sigh heavily, before he goes outside.

"Davey, dahling. Surprise!"

"What the devil are you doing here, Belinda?"

"Oh, dahling, I have to say hello to your dahling mother. How *is* she? Such a wonderful lady, I love her so much."

"What do you think you are doing?"

"Oooh, Davey, sweetheart. You're being quite a pig." Her voice changes from sultry to childish. "Don't you want your contract then?"

"Christ, woman, stop playing games! It's come after all?"

I have reached the front door at last.

"Belinda, what an unexpected pleasure. Do come in."

"Reeny, dahling. How *are* you?" She minces inside, flashes a brief kiss in the air somewhere in the region of my cheek. I see she takes as much trouble with her appearance as does Danielle, with painted toe and finger-nails, lipstick, eye-shadow. But the effect is not the same, and the difference has nothing to do with the odd muddy splash on her ankles. Danielle looks expensive and dependable, like *Vogue* or *Harper's Bazaar*. Belinda puts me in mind of *Hello! Magazine* - glamorous and trivial.

"Naughty Davey didn't tell you, but I call myself Linda these days. *So much more sophisticated*, don't you agree?"

"Can I offer you some coffee, *Linda*? Or tea?" I must be hospitable. But if she says yes, I'm not letting Danielle make it.

"Oh, too much trouble, Reeny dahling. Why don't we sit down?" She parks herself in one of the wicker chairs in the conservatory. "What a lovely, lovely view you have."

The rain and mist have gone at last, and a watery sun shows that the roses were battered in last night's downpour. I must get out later, and rescue what I can. Carefully, I lower myself into another chair, prop my stick beside me. I'm feeling breathless and pray I'll not need to use my angina spray while she is here.

"You've really got it?" David looms over her.

She looks up at him, flutters mascara-laden lashes. "What do *you* think?" She strokes the shiny red bag beside her with shiny red nails - one of those high-fashion two-handled handbags which, to me, are nothing more than my mother's shopping bag with studs on.

"Yes!" David punches the air, like a triumphant athlete. "My God, at last!" He grins at me, turns to Belinda, holds out his hand. "Give it to me. I *must* see what it says."

"Dahling, so impatient. Where are your manners? I'm visiting with your mother."

American locutions must be 'sophisticated' too.

He glares at her. "Do you mind, Mother, if I take *Linda* into another room? I believe she has the contract I mentioned. Perhaps you could be one of the witnesses?"

"Of course, darling. But I just wonder – as I'm your mother. Doesn't that matter?"

Belinda leans back and smiles.

"Good point, Mother. Damn!" He looks so downcast, I feel I must help.

"Why not try Alex and Joan next door? They know you, but aren't family. I'm pretty sure they're in."

"Lucky people," Belinda comments, frowning slightly. "Not at work, then?"

"Retired, my dear." She looks dispirited, and I wonder if she had been imagining more disruption to David's home life when he found his mother's witness was not valid. What's her game, then?

"Excellent idea, Mother. Come on, *Linda*. We'll go next door and sort everything out round there."

"Dahling. I want to meet your little children."

"And you know, I don't want you to. So come on." Putting on an act of putting on an act, he takes her arm masterfully, pulls her out of her chair, and she mocks, "Oh, you big stwong man," gazing into his eyes. He laughs. "We'll go and get that contract signed, and I will drive into the village and post it. Then it will be finished."

I hope Danielle is aware of all this.

Anyway, I have decided. I shall sell, so there will be money to help them through.

"Bye, bye, Reeny. Sorry it's been so short." She waves, like a child.

"Lovely to see you. Give my love to Norman."

David keeps his hand on her arm, guides her towards the door. "Excuse us, Mother. Would you mind very much telling Dani where I've gone? She'll understand."

25

Irene

The screen door bangs. Danielle reappears. My blasted heart is thumping, and I put both hands to my breast, for a moment, trying to find enough breath to speak.

"So he's got his contract after all. Last night he said it had come to nothing."

"Come and sit down, Danielle. You look as though you've been in a car crash."

"That's just how I feel." She sinks into a chair, closes her eyes. "That Barbie is like a hyena." Evidently, she no longer feels under any compulsion to hide her feelings. "Only interested in what she can steal from others." Belatedly, she adds: "I hope she's not a friend of yours."

"Her uncle is my friend. She's a young person I've known since a baby. Always was a bit manipulative, to my mind."

"Men seem to fall for her tricks, while most women see through her like glass."

"I don't think he's enamoured. Do you?"

She shakes her head. "No. I suspect he's tired of her supposed kittenish appeal. It's just that he's anxious to fulfil his dream, and she's willing to help."

I stare at her. She's gazing out of the window, looking sad. "Are you suggesting that my son, your husband, is just *using* this silly woman to get into films?"

"Oh, I don't think it started like that." She turns to look at me, and her lips curve in a grimace. "My guess is he fell for her when he had to kiss her in the play, and she responded. Perhaps he thought it was *lurve*. So she might have *some* acting talent."

I laugh. An understandably bitchy comment. "Perhaps she fell for him."

She laughs too, and we look at each other like old friends. "Perhaps.

He *is* good-looking, and a charmer when he tries. But what can he offer her? He's a schoolteacher, married, with children and a huge mortgage. No, I think she sees him as a means to an end."

"What end? I shouldn't have thought he had much influence anywhere."

"Ah, you underestimate my husband there. He's very well thought of by everyone involved in theatre around the Home Counties, and trains drama groups all over the south." How odd to find I know so little about my own son. He did mention teaching summer schools, but I hadn't realized quite how significant his extra-curricular activities seem to be. "If Barbie wants to get into film, she needs to learn to act. That is the one thing Dave could do for her. He helped her get the part of Gwendolyn, you know. I bet he had no idea how bad she'd be."

"Danielle, you sound wonderfully acid."

She shrugs. "Do you blame me? She's so shallow, she'd be out of her depth in a puddle. And she hasn't any clout with the film company. She did tell him about the screen test, but anyone could have done that. She's just a glorified typist."

"That I believe."

"Right now, he's like an intercontinental missile, carrying a nuclear warhead. Once it's taken off, there's nothing you can do but wait for the devastation." Danielle looks at her watch, and sighs wearily. "Lordy, the day is disappearing, and we haven't even had lunch."

"You look tired, my dear. No one seems ravenously hungry at the moment. Why not relax for a bit?"

She raises an eyebrow, then smiles, leans back in the chair. "You're right. All this drama with Dave leaves me feeling flat as a hospital trolley."

I too am feeling weary. Some music would help.

"Would you mind if I put on a record, Irene? It might be soothing."

I gaze at my elegant daughter-in-law, smiling. "I was thinking the same thing, Danielle. Please do."

To my astonishment, I hear the unmistakeable notes of Helen Reddy singing '*Oh, so peaceful here*' on my rather scratchy LP. Surely that record was made around the time Danielle was born.

118

"Hope this'll do for you, Irene," she says as she returns. "I heard a track by this woman on Desert Island Discs, and thought I'd like to hear more."

"Suits me beautifully, thanks."

We're both silent as we listen to the inspiring words of "*I am Woman, hear me roar...*" When I was in my thirties, I sang along with this album, day after day, I too was determined never to allow anyone to keep me down again.

Clomping sounds of a child rushing downstairs accompany the next song, and I wonder if Danielle chose this record because she had heard the track about trying to talk it over, but words getting in the way. All the songs I bought during this era spoke of the pain of lost friends and lost love, and of the resilience of women.

Tanya gets as close as she can to the record player, despite the high volume which allows Danielle and me to hear the songs in the conservatory.

"Tani, come and sit on my knee," Danielle calls, as Helen Reddy begins the last song on Side 1. "We can hear the music out here."

"Ohohoh." Reluctantly, the little girl retreats towards the door, her eyes still on the now distant record player. When at last the arm of the player lifts and automatically moves back to its rest, she turns to her mother. "I'm hungry."

Danielle and I both laugh.

"'S not funny, Grammar. We got Cornish pasties. I want one."

"Manners, Tani. You don't ask for anything in that rude way."

She glowers at her mother.

I look at my watch. The hands are blurred, but I think it says nearly three. What a day.

"Perhaps we could all have what's called 'tea in the hand' down here?" I suggest. "Combine lunch and dinner, save a bit of work, Danielle."

"You mean cakes and scones with jam?"

"Yeah." Tanya nods her head vigorously.

"No, no." I don't imagine Danielle considers that a proper meal any more than I do. "True farmhouse 'tea in the hand' is more like a picnic.

A selection of goodies that can be picked up in your hand – pasties, pies, fruit, whatever is convenient."

"And of course, a pot of tea?"

"Absolutely."

"The children would love that." She smiles, while Tanya frowns. "I can rustle up a good variety. Lots of food here now."

"Yes, my dear, and I need you all to eat it up before you go. Don't leave me with food to go off."

She gives me one of her glittering smiles. "Don't worry, Irene. I do hear what you say."

"Why don't I put a cloth on the table out here? Then it will feel more like a picnic."

"Lovely idea. Come on, Tani. Let's get this picnic ready."

I do feel David is right to quit teaching and go for his dream before it's too late. Pity Danielle doesn't yet understand that urgent desire to fulfil your dreams that can overwhelm anyone when they approach forty. But acting is a notoriously chancy profession; the poor woman is bound to be worried. Perhaps I should let her know that I've decided to sell this house. I wasn't going to say anything until I had told both my children, but it might ease one aspect of her anxieties.

I'm not the least surprised she's infuriated by my single-minded, not to say ruthless son. I'm not very pleased with him either. If I allow myself to think about the situation, I find I am very angry indeed. And that does the pain in my chest no good at all.

26

Irene

The rest of Tuesday blurs out of focus. A combination of having to relive that terrible day of the shooting, distress with David, anxiety for his family, annoyance with Belinda, and just plain lack of sleep, leaves me limp and exhausted. Everything aches - my head, my chest, my back, my legs. I climb the stairs to the bathroom yet again, and the thought of traipsing down once more is too much. I simply go to bed.

Danielle comes to find me, and I realize I should be grateful for her concern. But I want to sleep.

"Let me call your doctor."

"No need, Danielle, truly. Sorry I just disappeared, but this is exactly what I should do if I were alone. I'm not ill. Just tired."

"If you're sure." I nod into the pillow. Then wish I hadn't, as it makes me dizzy. "Can I get you anything?"

"Some water would be good. Thank you, Danielle."

I wake later for the usual bathroom visit, and find I must have fallen asleep before she returned. Angina keeps me awake for a while, and in the end I take an aspirin dissolved in water to help fight the blackness in my breast. No. It's not a heart attack. But this slow encroachment in the capillaries of my heart is painfully tedious.

I'll speak to Susan tomorrow, let her know I'm planning to move somewhere smaller. Pity she lives so far away. She was here only three weeks ago, so she won't be down for a while. If I do manage their anniversary next month, that's not the occasion to talk of my selling up and her inheritance.

Just so long as David sorts out his life, and makes things right with Danielle. Oh, I do hate feeling this way about my own son.

Lie still, breathe slowly, deeply. Let it all go for now. The moon is a slice of honeydew behind coiling smoky clouds. The world is sleeping. Only the wind sighs as it passes the window. Yes, Death is out there still, leaning against the apple tree, but she must wait. Don't beckon her in.

I smile to myself as the pains subside, and I drift into sleep. Perhaps I'll outwit you, Death, and move on.

***

The telephone rings. I struggle out of sleep, reach for the receiver. What time is it? Gone nine. Morning. Wake up.

"Mother?"

"Susan, darling. I've been thinking about you."

"Oh, Mother. Please tell me you're sitting down."

"I'm lying down actually. In bed." My heart is thumping like the drum-beat in *Aida*. "What's happened?"

"You're in bed? You sure you're all right?"

"Course I am, darling. Tell me, what's the problem."

"It's Alicia. She's perfectly fine, really. But I think she's about to land on your doorstep any minute."

"Right." I scrabble for the wand, patting the bedclothes all round. Can't find it. Give up. "And what's so terrible about that?"

"I thought you should be warned." I close my eyes, wait. "Well, she's not fine, really. Actually, Mother, she's pregnant."

"Oh, my darling." Now I *am* awake. "How did that happen? Sorry, incredibly stupid question." That poor darling girl.

"I can't believe it," Susan wails. "Eighteen, brilliant A-levels, university place waiting, and now she's damn well mucked it all up. God, Mother. What did I *do*?"

I don't remember hearing my daughter lose control like this for a long time. Not since she was fired from that whiz-kid job in the city. For being pregnant. With Alicia.

"Darling. It's not *your* fault. Try to keep calm, and tell me what you know."

"Unfortunately, we don't know much at all. It just exploded around us yesterday, like a terrorist bomb. I mean, Frank's absolutely furious, which is stupid. But Ali won't tell us who the father is, *and* she won't even contemplate an abortion."

"So she'll have a baby. Not so terrible, surely?"

"The problem is Frank. I do love my husband, Mother, but he's a Neanderthal where his daughter's concerned. We were up all night, no one's had a wink of sleep, Frank ranting on until, I tell you, I could scream."

"Fathers often do, don't they? When it's their daughters." I remember Frank when Alicia was born, gazing at her crumpled face as though at a miracle, playing with her as she grew, indulging her whims even as her mother tried to enforce some discipline. This year, on their holiday in this house, I saw no sign of teenage tantrums. Just a proud father who delighted in both his daughters, and who saw rainbows encircling Alicia's head as she danced to some musically-challenged rock band.

"Poor Jilly was dragged out of bed, because she knew and had promised not to tell, so both girls were shouting at their father. I started to cry, which just made things worse."

"Darling, how dreadful for you." I imagine her thin pale face with its steady brown eyes and firm chin, mouth set, trying to hold it all together, and her control crumbling like a sandcastle overwhelmed by the sea. And Frank, a deceptively quiet, gentle man with a will of steel, his power hidden, like a Porsche engine under the bonnet of a Mini.

"And then Frank went into overdrive," Susan wails, unconsciously picking up my simile. "First, he said she'd got to get married, pronto, and she said, No way, then he threatened to throw her out and never see her again. Of course, he doesn't mean it. But she says she won't let the father of this baby even know. So she and Frank had a blazing row about fathers' rights, at three in the morning. And now she's gone." Her voice has risen to top D.

"Gone? What do you mean, gone?" My voice too seems to be hitting notes normally reached only by trained sopranos.

"She told me that she was going to visit you, because you wouldn't nag her into doing anything she didn't want. I do hope she does, because I don't know where else she could go."

"I hope so too."

"But you've got a house full already. You don't need a pregnant teenager too. Specially when you have dear Danielle to cope with. Oh, Mother, I'm so sorry, getting you involved. I just thought you'd better know before she turns up on the doorstep. If she does."

I take a deep breath, reach for the spray on the bedside table. Listen, heart, no more angina until this is over. Behave, damn you. "Susie, darling, calm down. If she said she's coming here, she will. And she'll be welcome. Do you know how she'll be travelling?"

"It'll be by coach. She doesn't have much money. I gave her what I had in the house. She was planning to sell the pearls Granny gave her, and I didn't want her to do that."

"Good. That's easy then - there's a bus stop at the end of our lane. She can just walk up."

"Oh, Mother. Thank you. A sensible reaction at last."

I replace the receiver and breathe deeply, waiting for my heart-beat to slow. The lovely Alicia pregnant... I thought modern girls – well-educated girls – knew better. But nature has ever been a cruel master and rampant hormones make fools of us all.

I need tea, medication, and to get dressed. As I slide my legs round and struggle to get out of bed, the wand having yet again fallen to the floor, Danielle knocks and enters with what has become her ritual cup of tea.

"Beautiful timing, Danielle. Just what I need. Thank you."

"I heard the phone. Knew you'd be awake." She places the cup on the table, stoops to hand me the wand, and I return to bed to wake a little more slowly. "How are you this morning?"

"Rested, thank you." I sip the warming tea. "Dare I ask? How are things with you and David? I confess I was a bit cross with him yesterday."

She laughs. Alas, the cracked tambourine has returned. "Yes, so was I. Still am, to be truthful. But we'll sort it."

"Children all right?"

"Perfectly fine. Not bad news, or anything? The phone, I mean? It was a bit early."

"Just Susan. She knows I'm usually compos mentis by nine."

She raises an eyebrow, smiles. "Oh, right. Good."

124

So why not tell the woman Alicia is on her way? No particular reason. Perhaps I don't feel it's her business.

This is certainly becoming a jolly family visit.

***

Washed, creamed, powdered and dressed, I venture downstairs, where Danielle offers me yet another bowl of fruit and yoghurt.

"I shall miss your ministrations when you go," I tell her.

She smiles at that. "Happy to be of help. Coffee? With milk?"

"Please, you generous woman."

David and Simon are playing football on the terrace. Don't you dare damage my plants. Nature's depredations are enough to cope with.

I need music: the one way human-kind touches immortality.

My clarinet case lies invitingly on its shelf in the music room, but as so often, I feel inhibited when other people are staying. So I open the piano, and my crooked fingers caress the keys, find they can play today.

J. S. Bach will restore my mind to order. *The Well-Tempered Clavier.* I open Book One, begin the *Prelude and Fugue in C.* The regulated cadences calm the anxiety that aches at the back of my neck, soothe away the fears that have inevitably prickled my skin. Music floods the room.

Like a forest creature summoned by Orpheus's lute, my granddaughter creeps round the door, sidles up to the piano, watches my fingers as they find the notes, press the final chords. She says nothing. Just leans against me once I have stopped playing, gazes at the music.

"Did you like that, Tanya?"

She smiles up me, still dreamy. "Can I play that, Grammar?"

"One day, my darling, if you really want to. You'll need to practise."

"I can't hear all the notes in my head. It's too hard for me. Are you reading it in the book?"

"Yes. Would you like to read music?"

She frowns. "Can I learn this one what you did play?"

I laugh. "Too difficult for a beginner. It's by someone called Johann Sebastian Bach - he wrote lots of wonderful music. One day, when you can read music properly, I'll give you the book for yourself."

"Okay," she says briskly, and to my surprise, marches purposefully from the room. "Daddy," I hear in the distance, "Daddeee!"

Chuckles fizz in my throat. I had thought she might ask me to teach her, but evidently what Daddy started in a desultory way, Daddy must make haste to finish.

27

Irene

"Ali! Ali! You're here!" Simon's excited voice penetrates through to the music room. "Mummy, guess what? Ali's come!"

Children's feet drumming down the hall, clacketing across the slate floor in the conservatory, cymbal clash of the screen door, metronome click of Danielle's heels as she strides out to deal with another unwelcome guest. I follow them in my mind as I stand up, manoeuvre in my habitual molasses-slow way towards the front door.

Alicia is on the terrace, laughing, embracing Simon whose face is pink with pleasure.

"Simon's got a girl-friend," Tanya chants. "Simon's got a girl-friend."

"Shut up, stupid."

"Course he has, Tani. Simon's my best boy, aren't you?" He grins up at her, brown eyes adoring: two Christmases ago, he announced he was going to marry her.

She looks lovely, vibrant: long, untidy, curly black hair, glowing skin, gentle smile. She is wearing a multitude of garments, in what I suppose must be the latest "layered look": something that looks remarkably like a long nightdress, in a garish print, over various bits of underwear, black bra straps, lilac vest, two thin cardigans of different lengths hanging off bared shoulders, long scarves entwined with beads round her neck and waist, and sandals on rather grubby feet with chipped purple nails. She reminds me of the Sixties when I was still young, Flower Power, Rock 'n Roll and the sound of Indian sitars.

"Grandma!" She disentangles herself from her adoring swain, rushes over to me, envelops me in a powerful hug. "Bestest Grandma. Please can I stay?"

"Of course, darling."

"I knew you'd say yes."

"Where's your luggage?"

"Right here." She indicates a lightweight pack. "Don't need much."

"Come on in, then. Let's find you a place to put your stuff."

"Hi, Tani. Hi, Aunt Dani. Good to see you."

I see Danielle raise a shapely eyebrow.

"Lovely surprise, isn't it, Danielle? I'll give Alicia the futon in the upstairs study, and she won't be in anyone's way. Fine with you, darling?"

Alicia nods. "Yeah, like, perfect. Thanks, Grandma. Hey, Simon," she adds, turning to the boy who's followed us in. "Will you carry my bag up for me?"

"Okay." He takes it, watching her, and then turns his gaze on me as I click clack with my stick through the inner door. "Guess what, Ali? Granma is a tortoise, aren't you, Granma?"

I laugh, call, "Quite right, Simon."

Danielle says crossly, "Simon, please. That is not acceptable."

"Why isn't it? Granma said it herself. Didn't you, Granma? Oh, she's gone." Their voices carry clearly to where I move, exactly like a tortoise, towards the stairs. "Ali's a swan. Aren't you, Ali?"

Alicia giggles. "I geddit. Ugly duckling made good, right?"

"Don't argue, Simon. I won't have that sort of talk. And Alicia." Danielle's voice drops, but its clarity carries her words through to me, despite her best intention. "Do I gather you plan to stay?"

"Yeah, Aunt Dani, I do. Grandma said it's OK."

"Of course, she did. What *do* you expect? But she has quite enough on her plate, without another granddaughter turning up on her doorstep."

"Hey, don't worry. I'm here, like, to *help*. I know the situation."

"I doubt it. However, we can talk about it later. I'm sure you don't plan to stay long."

Oh, deary me. Doesn't take much for Danielle to revert to form. Let's get upstairs, and allow the poor girl to settle in. As I start the long trek up the stairs, I hear Alicia add:

"My mother warned me you'd interfere. I *know* my grandma has, like, heart trouble. Whatever. I'll *enjoy* looking after her. So there."

Another strong-minded female in this house. What a recipe for cacophony, when all I really crave is peace.

"You better go back down, bestest boy," Alicia tells a reluctant Simon. "We can play chess later, right?"

She and I collect a duvet, pillows and covers from the airing cupboard, and I sit on the futon as she puts the bedding in order. I need a rest before venturing back downstairs.

"Grandma. Could we talk? Before Aunt Dani, you know, has another go?"

"Of course, darling. What is it?"

Having commanded my full attention, she is silent. Best let her tell me herself. I look at my granddaughter in what I hope is an encouraging manner. So young. So ignorant of the ways of the world.

She starts to speak, but swallows the words. Does so again, and coughs.

"Grandma, I'm ... like ... I'm gonna have a baby." She's gazing at the floor, waiting. Then she looks at me out of the corner of her eyes.

I smile at her, coaxing. "Are you, my darling?"

She stares at me. "Aren't you, you know, upset or anything?"

"Darling, I just care about *you*. Are *you* upset? Why don't you tell me about it?"

"Well, I mean, I might be a *bit* upset." She sits on the carpet, cross-legged, looks up at me. "It *is* definite. Oh, bloody hell, Grandma, I'm pregnant."

"Oh, my darling." I hold out my arms, and she makes a tentative move to come closer, but only near enough that I can stroke her arm a little.

"I don't know what to do, Grandma. I really don't."

"Come here." She moves so that we can put our arms around each other, and I feel her shaking. "There, there, my darling. Have a damn good cry, why don't you?"

She laughs, and then bursts into sobs. "It's all such a big, big mistake. Like, who wants to be pregnant when they're s'posed to go to university? God. I don't want this."

I hold her tight and she begins to weep in earnest. When Nature gets you in its clutches, there's no way out that does not bring tears.

Eventually she quietens, hiccups a few times, and smiles at me. "God, I didn't cry before. That was a bit of a surprise."

"I expect you needed a good cry, darling. Getting pregnant can be a shock."

"Yeah, right." She wipes her face with tissues and blows her nose. "When I told my parents, they both had hysterics, and Mum burst into tears. So I s'pose I didn't, just to show her. She wants me to murder it, you know."

"I beg your pardon."

"You know, have an abortion."

"Isn't that a good idea, if you don't want a baby? It *is* legal these days." She shakes her head. "Oh, no. I won't do that."

"What about your father? What does he say?"

"Huh. Dad was just unbelievable. I mean, I know it was a bit seismic, but still. He went completely ballistic. He seemed to think he was trapped in the worst kind of nineteenth century novel. You know, pregnant daughter's turned out into the storm, and banished for ever."

We both laugh at that. "I'm so glad you're not stuck in the Middle Ages, Grandma. You're older than my Dad, but he sounded like one of those men, you know, who kept nunneries going by incarcerating their daughters."

"Gracious me, Alicia. I'm not that old."

"No, bestest Grandma, I know. So I thought you could help me."

"Tricky one, Alicia. I don't want to go against your parents. But I'll help if I can."

She finishes pulling on the duvet cover, presses the snap fasteners, then folds the duvet in half beside her on the carpet. She looks up at me, and I raise an eyebrow.

"Well?"

"See, I was thinking on the bus, maybe I could, like, move in with you. In Hart House. I'd shop and cook, make you really, really happy to have me. Then I'd, like, have the baby. And you could tell me how to look after it." She peers at me, trying to gauge my reaction. "It'd be so cool, Grandma. Just think, a baby here in this house, and you wouldn't need to do anything. I mean, you know, you could play with it when you want. But you don't have to."

"I agree, darling. It sounds lovely."

She smiles, and I hear jubilant trumpets.

"The difficulty is that my ancient body is letting me down. I can't inflict my increasing debilities on you."

"Yeah. Mum said you'd say that. But actually, you know, me being around'd be a really, really cool idea. I did a St John's Ambulance course, remember? So if you have a heart attack, I wouldn't be useless, see. I'd know what to do."

"Yes, very good. Except I might not want to be rescued."

"Grandma, don't worry. I mean, I know you don't want to end up helpless. I promise, I would *not* 'strive officiously to keep alive', as the saying goes. Not my Grandma, not if you would end up a vegetable."

"That's fine, Alicia. But not quite what I mean. I don't want you, or anyone else, to make the decisions. I want to choose, myself."

She nods her head, and grins at me, eyes gleaming. "Yeah. I can identify with that."

"Excellent. Look, let's just say you can stay here until things calm down. We can decide what's best when everyone's had time to think."

Perhaps it's just as well I didn't speak to either of my children about selling up.

"What about the father of this baby? What is he doing?"

"Nothing. He doesn't know, and I'm not telling him."

"Really? Why is that?" I rub the painful swellings on my finger joints, and wonder why one worries at small aches, provoking them into bigger ones, after repeated experience of this phenomenon. The cavity in tooth syndrome.

Alicia frowns, and shrugs, gazing at the carpet. Don't probe, that's unkind.

"I think you'd better let your parents know you're here, don't you? Use the phone in my bedroom."

"Thanks, Grandma."

My progress downstairs is unexpectedly wobbly, and I'm relieved not to have an audience. Other people seem to make me more aware of my increasing disabilities, and I'm not convinced that's a good thing.

"You *are* having a busy time, Irene," Danielle comments as I reach the kitchen.

"So, indeed, are you, Danielle. Are you cooking?"

"Just a lasagne. I think everyone likes that. And David is cutting a lettuce from your garden. Hope that's all right."

"Of course. Glad to have them eaten before they bolt." I watch her as she briskly moves around my kitchen. She has truly taken over. That's fine. Allows me to conserve my energies to cope with all the crises converging on this house.

My legs are aching more than usual today, and even my feet feel swollen. Dammit. I was going to play the piano again, but I think a rest in my recliner might be a better idea. The dreadful size of my ankles. That's why I don't like wearing a skirt any more. A repulsive sight.

I lurch a little as I move into the sitting room, bang my arm against the door frame. These silly little giddy spells are so annoying - I'm covered in bruises.

***

"Grandma." Alicia appears, smiling. She's discarded the scarf round her neck and both cardigans, looks gloriously young and sexy. "Can Simon and I see if there are any raspberries down the garden?"

"Good thought. There should be some Autumn fruiting ones."

"One of my best memories, you know. Collecting raspberries from the fruit cage. Much easier to pick than, like, blackberries. No prickles. *And* they taste good."

Such pleasure to share her pleasure. She's a delight. Perhaps she and I could live together happily, if that's what she wants. So long as a professional nurse is called in, when nursing becomes necessary.

"Just tell your aunt. She's getting lunch ready."

Alicia stares at me, frowns. "It's late afternoon, Grandma. You've been, you know, asleep."

"Oh." I look at my watch, but the hands are a bit difficult to make out. "Didn't anyone think to wake me?"

"Doesn't matter if you sleep, does it? I did, like, try to tell you lunch was ready. But you obviously didn't want to wake up."

"Where is everyone?"

"Well, they've all been for a swim, and now Tanya's in the bath. Simon and I were planning on picking raspberries for dinner. If that's OK."

"Of course. Um, Alicia. What time is it?"

"Just gone six, Grandma."

"Goodness, I had a long sleep."

She laughs. "Yeah. See you in a bit."

Half a day, melted into nothingness. Annoying. And what day is this? I seem to have lost track. Charles is coming on Friday. Is that tomorrow? Or the day after?

28

Irene

A jubilant gladiatorial victor strides into the room, inches above the carpet, and Grieg's Triumphal March shakes the walls, rattles the windows. Dark bedroom eyes, long lashes, blue chin, seductive smile, these will be the next 'must-have' attributes of the aspiring star.

"You're awake, Ma." Never one to avoid stating the obvious.

"And you can walk on water."

We both laugh, and his joy rings like a church bell. "Yep. It's done. And confirmed. I phoned to say the contract's in the post, and they're sending the script right away. Filming starts the week after next."

"Heavens. How exciting. I bet you can hardly believe it, after all these years."

"Yeah. I confess I was afraid it might not happen. God, it feels good, Mother."

"Savour your achievement, my darling. We really should celebrate with a bottle of champagne." I sit up and glance at those tiresome ankles stretched out in front of me. Much improved, thank the Lord.

"Mother, would you think it too rude if Dani and I went out this evening?"

"Of course not. Lovely idea. Have you and she resolved your differences?"

"Not entirely. Hence my suggestion. I want to sort things out with my wife, make sure she's happy with the arrangements." He strides over to the bay window, stands in the late afternoon sunlight, stretches out his arms. "It's going to work. I know it."

"Dare I ask? Belinda?"

He turns, frowning. "What about her?"

I stare at him. "How can you ask?"

He gives a short laugh. "Oh, Dani's notion we've been having an affair. Good God, Mother, my judgement's not *that* cock-eyed. I enjoyed meeting her again - she can be charming and was a link with my childhood. And we had to play together in *The Importance*. But really, she's rather a silly woman, don't you think?"

Does he believe he is that good an actor? Or is the world of dramatic fiction so powerful its aspirants no longer discern the borders between it and reality?

"You don't believe me, do you? For Chrissake, Mother, didn't you have men friends when you were young? And did you hop into bed with them, just because you could?"

"What has that to do with it?"

"It's the same thing. People seem to believe that if a man and a woman spend any time alone together, they must be having an affair. Like that ghastly St Bernard, who claimed that no man could be in the same room with a woman without jumping her. Just as well he retired to his mountain fastness with his dogs, I'd say."

"So why does Danielle believe you were having an affair?"

He looks down at his hands. "I feel rather ashamed of that, to tell the truth. Most actors tend to flirt. Flirting makes my women students feel good so they work well, and normally no one takes it seriously. Unfortunately, Belinda imagined it meant something. Dani got angry, said I needed to stop her coming on to me whenever we met. I *told* Dani she had nothing to worry about. But she didn't believe me, and that made me mad. Really mad. Over the top. If she wouldn't listen to me, I didn't care what she thought. I've been like the Incredible Hulk for the past few weeks."

"The last bit's true." But my eyebrows are raised.

"I'm not usually like that. I just couldn't bear the thought I might lose my one last chance to do what I was destined for."

"Sounds as though aspiring actors can be intolerable people."

"I know, Ma." He is oozing contrition. "And I'm sorry I let you know how I've suffered with my glass eye over the years."

"Darling, you do need to find a way to live with it."

"I didn't want to upset you. Truly. Permit me to grovel."

I laugh at that. "Oh, David, you're incorrigible. I'm not upset. Just try to make things right with your long-suffering wife."

He flashes a white smile, and shakes his glossy dark head at me. "Yes, she's very good at the suffering in silence bit. Got it down to a fine art."

"*David!* You don't sound very penitent, and you jolly well ought to."

"Quite right, Ma. And I am." A shadow of anxiety falls across his face. "So will you be all right if we leave the children with you, just for this evening?"

"Gracious me, of course, I will. *And* I have Alicia to help."

A smile chases away the brief moment of tension. "True."

"Just have a lovely time. See you tomorrow."

What day *is* tomorrow? And when Charles comes, am I going to ask him to arrange a valuation on the house? Or is Alicia going to play happy families with me? It would be a relief to know that I don't need to move into a smaller house to help save David's marriage.

The truth is, I begin to feel as though any move, into a smaller house locally or into Danielle's so-called sheltered housing, would be too much. This house is so full of *things* – furniture too large for most other places, several thousand books on shelves in every room, CDs that take up an entire wall, sheet music that fills a cabinet, not to mention all the paintings, sculpture, glassware, pottery, fine china I have accumulated over a life-time. How would I ever sort out what to keep and what to get rid of? The whole procedure would give me another heart attack.

Oh, excellent thought. Let Danielle cope with that one.

Except, you stupid woman, moving to release some capital was your own idea.

Which gives me a brainwave. God, Irene, you're clever! I'll ask Charles to arrange what I believe is called 'equity release'. That way I get the best of both worlds: money to help my ambitious son while I remain here. Brilliant!

***

"You're a rotten sod, David. How dare you pretend to your mother that you haven't been having it off with that slut?"

David would have been wise to remember that acoustics in this house have always created problems: for some reason, the wooden panelling seems to carry voices through the ceiling. Poor Danielle sounds as though her self-control is breaking.

"Hey, Dani, hush. You can't believe I ever slept with the silly bitch, and now I don't need to see her at all. She wasn't important.""

"My God, how can you *say* that? You really think being unfaithful isn't important? Don't you even *care* how I feel?" Danielle's lovely mezzo voice sounds as stretched to its limits as Susan's did – goodness me, was it only this morning?

"Of course I care, Dani. You're the only woman who has ever mattered to me, you know that. Come here, come on, let me show you."

"For God's sake, let me be. Don't imagine for one moment I've forgiven you, because I haven't." Sounds of scuffling feet drift down to me, and a muffled bang as one of them collides with a piece of furniture.

"Come on, Dani." His voice is a mixture of impatience, and seduction. "Do let's be friends. We mustn't fight now, not again."

"I'm not the one that brought that slut here."

"You *know* how angry I was, even if she *did* bring my contract. I've told the silly girl to stay away, and this time she knows I really mean it. Forget her, and think about us."

"Christ. Would have been nice if you had done that earlier."

"Hey, that's not fair. I *have* been thinking about us, all the time. I mean, you can't have a very glamorous lifestyle on a teacher's salary, can you? But now, things are going to be different."

"That's right. Even *more* difficult to make ends meet."

"How can you believe that? I mean, I've got a contract for my very first film and I'm a *co-star*. Think, Dani. I'm on my way up."

"Dave, you're bloody impossible. Acting is littered with break-out performances that fizzle to nothing. And they'll give your teaching post to someone else, and then where'll you be?"

"No, Dani, think. You know I'm good, you know I should have gone to RADA."

"Even so."

"Just think what we can do with the money they're offering. We can go on that cruise around the Bahamas you always wanted. Imagine that, eh? Swanning around on a luxury yacht, blue skies, sunshine, sandy beaches, palm trees, glorious stretches of turquoise ocean, and the swish of the waves, the gentle sound of wind in the sails, while you lie back and sip champagne."

She surprises me by laughing. "Yeah, right. Bribe me with a fantasy of sailing in the Caribbean, why don't you?"

"Now I'm gonna hit the big time and it won't just be a dream. It will be a reality."

"Why *do* I put up with you? You live in cloud cuckoo land, you know that?"

"Mmmm. Come on, give us a kiss."

This last demand is followed by silence, which may possibly mean that she has succumbed to his indisputably sexy charms. If I am amazed at how easily she gives in to his blandishments, I should remember my own idiocies when Martin turned the honeyed talk on me. In my experience, both personal and professional, a husband who sets out deliberately to coax an angry wife usually knows exactly which buttons to press. To resist requires total disillusionment.

I confess though, his overt manipulations are beginning to alienate his mother. Who should *not* be listening. Unfortunately, I want to know the outcome.

"Now look, David," Danielle says eventually. "You want us to be friends. And I realize that nothing I say will make you change your mind about this crazy film idea ..."

"Crazy? It's not crazy. It's cool, as my students say."

"Yes, yes. But if you want me to stick around, and pick you up when you fall on your face, than I have to stipulate: *no more fucking affairs!*" The last phrase is expressed with such emphasis that I imagine David leaping backwards to escape the venom.

"Dani, my love. How can you say that? I don't *have* affairs. Truly, you have nothing to worry about."

"Yeah. Right. Well, bear it in mind, because I'm not Patient Griselda. You can't keep fooling me for ever."

"Look, why don't we go out? Have dinner somewhere to celebrate."

"Hmmm."

"Oh, do come, Dani, please. I *need* to celebrate, this is so important. I'd really rather celebrate just with you. I don't want anyone else. Just the two of us, my love, the way it used to be. Before I felt shades of the prison house closing upon me for good."

She laughs. "You never stop, do you? What about the children?"

"No problem. Alicia and my mother can look after the children together. They'll be fine just for one evening. So. All sorted."

"Well, all right." Her voice sounds cool, detached, but there is amusement in it too. "I shall enjoy watching you try to cajole me."

She is rather like a cobra seduced by a snake charmer's tune. But I feel he should be careful, for even a dancing cobra will bite if provoked.

29

Danielle

Prevailed upon once more, against her better judgement, to believe in her persuasive husband, Danielle decided to enjoy an evening off: put aside her worries for a few hours at least. Like Christian in Pilgrim's Progress setting down his burden. That's what it felt like – as though she'd been carrying a heavy load on her back. Except, of course, poor Christian had to wait until he reached the end of his journey, because he was burdened by his sins. As most of her worries were created by other people and she had no need to feel sinful about that, surely she could put her anxieties aside for just this one evening? It would be so deliciously restful not to think about finances and mortgages or turning down a coveted promotion or dealing with her bloody-minded mother-in-law; to forget her absurd notion that this damned Harper family could be different, that they might be induced to face facts and not fritter away time and resources on impractical dreams. She'd been wasting her efforts. Arguing with any of them was like pushing water uphill with a rake.

Not that she had forgiven him. He needn't think that. But as she renewed her make-up, sitting at the tiny dressing table in the guest bedroom, darkened her almost invisible brows, brushed brown mascara on her ridiculously pale lashes, a gentle throb of excitement grew inside her. Just as it used to when they were first together.

She contemplated the limited wardrobe she had brought with her, wanting to find something a bit dressy, a bit nicer than everyday jeans and tee shirt, to complement this pleasurable sense of anticipation. Not that she really expected much. But she'd like Dave to think she'd made an effort, to please him. To help him celebrate.

Celebrate? The *film* contract? sneered her Inner Critic. You're going to celebrate his goddamn *contract?*

Oh, shut up, she told him. This is my husband, and the contract is an achievement. He might even succeed. Though I do think it somewhat

140

unlikely. But you never know. And I'm glad he wants to share his triumph with me.

She slipped on the blue silk-and-cotton mix dress that matched her eyes. Somewhat ancient now, but she couldn't bring herself to discard it because it looked good on her, which was why she brought it to Cornwall. Genuine blonde with blue eyes – she might as well make the most of her natural assets.

She noticed Dave's eyes open wide, take on that dark, smouldering look he always used to have when he saw her, as though fires were being banked up inside him. She was pleased. So long as he remembered to whom he was married, she'd acknowledge his victory over the odds. And try to avoid all discussion of ways and means until tomorrow.

"Have a lovely time," Irene told them, "And don't worry about the children. They'll be fine."

"Course they will, Mother." David bent to kiss her wrinkled cheek, and she smiled into his dark eye. "Let Ali do the work. You just supervise."

"You won't let them go to bed too late, will you, Irene?" Danielle was suddenly unable to leave her children in such incapable hands – an arthritic old woman and an irresponsible hippy teenager. "Perhaps we should wait a bit, until they've eaten and got undressed."

Irene laughed, and David grabbed his wife's arm. "Come on, Dani. They'll be fine. Everyone will be fine." Out in the hall, he called, "Bye, kids. We're off now. Be good."

"Byee." Simon called from somewhere. Tanya put her head round the kitchen door. "Oh, bye," she said and disappeared.

"See," said David, laughing. "No one will miss us, we're not needed in this house this evening. Great eh?"

Reluctantly, Danielle allowed herself to be guided out of the house, across the terrace, into the car. As her husband started the engine, and moved up the drive, she asked: "So where are we going?"

"I have no idea. Mother didn't know of any decent restaurants around here, because every year they all seem to change hands. So I thought we'd stop off at The Red Lion, have a drink and see what the locals suggest."

"Oh." A pub. Beer and canned music. Crisps and pork scratchings.

Other people being raucously jolly. She was not a pub person, Dave ought to know that by now.

"Cheer up, Dani," he said as he manoeuvred into the last marked space in the car park. "This was my local, aeons ago. Just a bit of nostalgia. We won't stay long."

***

She had a confused, ill-lit impression of low shadowy ceilings with heavy dark timbers, tankards and Toby jugs hanging from the joists, plaster walls covered in horse brasses, flags, pennants and photographs, and people. Crowds of people, sitting at dark wooden tables, standing in the way wherever she tried to move, talking, laughing, shouting, "Hey, Dave." "That you, Dave?" "Where you bin to, matey?" And David, grinning, trying to steer her towards the bar, the only brightly lit space in the room.

"Over here, David, old mate." A stocky man with short red curly hair and designer stubble was gesturing from behind the counter.

"Barney. What're you doing here? Thought you'd gone to Oz with Shell Oil."

"So I did. And now I'm back. What'll you have?"

"Dani?"

"White wine, please. Preferably New World." She was beginning to wonder if they'd ever escape this place, where Dave had been so warmly greeted.

"Good choice, ma'am," said Barney, and winked. He handed her a large glass of chilled Australian Chardonnay. Which turned out to taste a lot better than most house wines in London or Oxford.

Realizing he'd a good half hour chat ahead of him, given the numbers of old acquaintance he had inadvertently run into, David ordered a beer. Long and wet. Gave him something to do while others caught up with him. But to his surprise, Barney insisted the drinks were on the house, and after being introduced to Dani, told them he was now the sole landlord. His wife, Margie, was in charge of the restaurant, which they only started a year earlier, and was now so popular, people booked up weeks in advance during the summer.

David and Danielle looked at each other, and nodded in agreement. If you can't beat 'em, join 'em, Danielle thought. Maybe the food was as good as the wine. One could hope.

"Any chance we could get a table sometime this evening, Barney?" But even as David spoke, Danielle realized the place was far too crowded. How disappointing.

Barney laughed. "On a Quiz Night? You're joking."

"Pity. You'll have to suggest somewhere else for us to eat, then, Barney. We're on a mission to celebrate my breakthrough into films, so we need somewhere decent."

"Dave, old mate, you haven't! That's absofuckinglutely wacko! Always knew you could make it, if you wanted to. Just wait here a mo." Barney disappeared through a door in the back. David was accosted from behind by two men in their forties, both dressed in football singlets and dark running suit trousers. Danielle sat on the barstool and sipped her wine. Not quite what she had in mind when she envisioned this evening's entertainment.

Barney returned, a wide grin on his stubbled face. "Put that poor fella down, Jake, you old sod. You too, Kev. I need him." Amid a chorus of joking insults, the two men returned to their table, and Barney leaned across the counter. "I've sorted it, mate. Margie has a special corner for our special customers, so when she signals to me, you can go on in. How's that for service, then?"

"Bloody marvellous, Barney. Thanks. I won't forget it."

"Just send me a coupla tickets for your world premiere."

"Sure thing, pal. While we're waiting for the signal from Margie, tell me, Barney, what's this about a Quiz Night? That's a new one down here."

"Oh, they love it. Locals and visitors, everyone loves it. So do I, to tell true. I set the questions, and it's the greatest fun you can have with your pants on, trying to find stuff to fool the local pundits."

"Do you have a theme?" asked Danielle, her interest awakened.

"Basically it's ten questions on each of five categories also chosen by me, and tonight we have science, geography, theatre, sport and medicine."

Danielle and David both laughed. "Sounds tailor-made for us," David said.

"You can take part if you like. You have to pay for an entry form – that's how we support Air Ambulance. But if you want one, I have a microphone, so you'll hear the questions when we start. Maybe you'll win our bottle of bubbly."

"Maybe we will. Maybe this is our lucky day."

When Margie came to lead them to their table, set in an alcove just beside the restaurant door, they were startled to discover that Barney's wife was Chinese: short black hair, skin the colour of ground almonds, flat cheeks and Oriental eyes that glinted with humour as she registered their surprise. Her voice was soft, her accent Australian.

"Your friend Barney is full of surprises," said Danielle as they examined the menu. "This looks promising."

"He always was a maverick. Probably why we were friends, kept in touch for years. He was Head Boy, you know, won a scholarship to Imperial College. I'd never have thought of him ending up here, in The Red Lion."

They ordered the evening's special – a beef and ale pie, with fresh local vegetables – and crab soup, because so many who came over to the table to greet David recommended it. Danielle was gratified that she, too, received considerable attention: women stared at her when they thought she was looking the other way, and men gazed with unmistakeable admiration, many lingering after they had spoken to her husband to have a word. David made a point of mentioning that she was a gifted singer: several former school-fellows immediately told them of the Friday Night Song Fest, at which locals and visitors were invited to sing along with a group of local musicians. David promised they'd come if they could.

"Well, things have changed since I was living down here," he said. "Occasionally a few old codgers would get together in the Public and sing folk songs - could be quite good, but they only had a tinny upright. Dreary place. Visitors never went in there. And as for food - there wasn't any."

144

The meal turned out to be excellent. And as they were wondering what had happened to the bottle of wine David ordered, Barney appeared with a special bottle of St Emilion from his private cellar. "My contribution to your celebrations," he said, and returned to his bar where ever more customers were crowding in, and existing ones were attempting to stock up on drinks before the Quiz began.

Danielle relaxed. Not quite the intimate dinner *à deux* that she had anticipated, but a pleasure nonetheless. Maybe things would work out after all.

The Quiz began after they had eaten their fill, and were sipping the rich fruity red wine, savouring every mouthful. Not a wine to be gulped down in haste.

"Shall we?" David asked, as staff came round with answer sheets. "It's a good cause."

"Why not?"

The questions were, indeed, challenging, and they were both surprised that such a tricky Quiz should be so popular. However, their own special subjects did not fail them: David was able to answer every question on theatre, as well as most on geography, while Danielle dealt with all the science bar one, plus the medicine. She remembered Simon and the goldfish when they were asked to work out whether a man with O+ blood group could be the father of a child with O- blood, when the mother was A+. How odd to deal with a genetics question twice in as many days. David was doubtful about her conclusion, but she was certain: the answer was Yes, the man could be the father, because Rhesus negative is a recessive gene, and so could have been carried by both parents. At the end they felt they had done pretty well. Their weak area was sport. But they'd done their best.

"I enjoyed pummelling the old brain for a change," David said, leaning back in the hard wood chair. "What about you, Dani, my love? You were pretty bloody good at some of the trickiest questions."

She laughed, pleased. "Thank you, kind sir. Perhaps I have not yet quite dwindled into a wife."

He took her hand and kissed it. "Oh, my beloved erudite wife.

Quoting Congreve without provocation. How I do love you."

"That's good."

"Let us, however," he said, leaning close to whisper in her ear, "be fond and kiss, when we are alone. Very soon." She smiled, realizing that his seductive voice was plucking her nerve strings like a harp. "Shall we go?" She nodded. "Right. Just wait there while I pay Barney."

She handed him their Quiz form. "Take this. If we win, he can auction the bubbly for Air Ambulance too."

"Brilliant woman."

David soon returned, and they left the crowded pub amid farewells and jokes and laughter. Outside, he put his arms round her and kissed her with his cushiony red lips. "Thank you, Dani. That was a good celebration."

"It was, wasn't it?"

"I do understand your concerns, my love, but please don't worry. It's going to work."

"I'm not worrying, Dave. Not tonight." And it was true, she felt relaxed. For the first time in months. Worries could wait.

In perfect harmony, they drove back to a quiet house where the only lights were those to guide them inside.

"How about a night-cap?"

"A bit exaggerated, don't you think?" She felt as though she had drunk quite a lot, and the rich Bordeaux remained, spread like a soft feather duvet in her taste memory.

"Mother has a really good cognac, and I know she won't mind if we have a small one. Let's take a glass up to bed. What do you say?"

She smiled again. Why not, after all? "Sounds lovely."

"Good. Come on, Dani. Let's see if we can remember how to make love. As we used to, before the world was too much with us."

That would be nice, she thought, but felt too mellow for the usual acid comments to make much headway. Perhaps he means it, after all. Perhaps I'm not past it, not about to be supplanted by a younger model. She didn't want to pursue that notion. Too painful. She had abdicated, no longer needed to take decisions, was happy to let him take the lead.

They looked in on the children, both asleep and apparently well, then made their way to their own bedroom.

Dave threw off his jacket, took her in his arms.

"Let's contend no more, Love, Strive nor weep. All be as before, Love."

"Only sleep!" Danielle completed Browning's verse.

"Dammit, Dani. You are far too well-read. How am I to seduce you with other men's words if you know how they go?"

She laughed. "You're too good a teacher, David. I listen to what you say to me, and remember. My memory, that's your downfall."

"I can see I shall have to use my own poor words, and how can they be effective with a woman as clever and as beautiful as you? Oh, Dani. I looked at you this evening, and realized I am the luckiest man alive. No woman in that crowd tonight was as good-looking as you, and I'd be willing to bet none of them was as intelligent or knowledgeable."

She smiled, pleased. "Just because you hoped to win the Quiz."

"Don't be daft, woman. I know you're clever, and brilliant at your job. Where do you think our children get their brains? Not from their father."

"How true."

"But what I like best ..." He kissed her eyes, her cheeks, and she felt the music swell inside her. "What I really appreciate ..." He kissed her throat, and her bones melted. "... is your glorious golden beauty." He undid her buttons, and she slid the dress off her shoulders, down her body till it crumpled on the floor, then he unhooked her bra, gazed on her firm, uptilted breasts. "How do you do it? Mother of two, thirty-five ..."

"Forget my age," she interrupted, feeling chilled.

"My darling, darling Dani, you're not a youngster who knows nothing, you are a mature woman in her prime. Be proud. You should be."

"You sure? Don't you think perhaps I'm getting past it?"

David spluttered with laughter. "My God, woman, don't you realize? Other women envy you, and it isn't because you're married to this gorgeous hunk of manhood. It's because you're so extraordinarily beautiful, and don't even seem to realize it."

"Well, I do take care of myself. Bodies are my profession." She looked

147

down at herself, tried to cross her arms across her breasts, but he took her hands.

"Dani, darling. Please stop being an idiot and come to bed." She allowed him to embrace her again, and she rested her head against his shoulder. Slowly the old magic returned. She loved his musky honey smell, mixed with a sharp tang of aftershave, felt the warm pulse of his blood beneath the skin. He kissed her again, gently exploring her tongue with his, and she delighted in his taste, unbuttoned his shirt.

At last they were both naked and lying together on the sheets and she knew that he could not have betrayed her: he was an actor, but surely not this good, not when there was nothing between them but the softness of their skin. Her nerve endings responded singing to his touch, and she played his body like a cello, rich, deep mellow notes that harmonized with her own, and she knew that he loved her still.

***

As he entered her at last, David mentally breathed a sigh of relief. He loved his wife, of that he had no doubt, but he had feared he had lost her. What did it matter that the world did not love him? He had always felt this need to woo those who mattered least, as though being admired by those who saw only his public face would compensate somehow for the father who had abandoned him and the eye that had been torn out. Deep down, he imagined that universal adulation might assuage his rage at feeling worthless. So he had always been a fool.

Now he knew he was the world's luckiest man. For he felt through every pore in his skin that this beautiful woman beside him was loving him as she always had. As they came together at the climax of this momentous day, he gave thanks to that mythical Guardian Angel that must watch over him. The two things he wanted most in the world were now his: an acting career and his wife.

30

Irene

Alicia makes the dinner, a large and delicious omelette stuffed with vegetables, garlic bread, raspberries and ice-cream for dessert.

"I was going to make pasta and salad, but that's what we had for lunch, Grandma."

"This is very good."

"Yeah. Ali's the best."

Alicia laughs. "Oh, Simon, I've got to learn a few more recipes, I'm afraid. Not the best yet. Just wait."

"I like it," Tanya adds, contemplating her almost empty plate. "Specially the bread."

"I only know three recipes, Grandma. So I think I shall have to take lessons while I'm here. 'Cos you're a brilliant cook."

"I'd enjoy teaching you."

As my eldest granddaughter clears away, and enlists the help of her cousins without any sign of an argument, I can see that having Alicia here could be very pleasant.

Tanya and I cuddle together on the settee, and she reads to me from *The Flip Flap Body Book* - a funny and informative publication that explains how the human body works. I do enjoy children's books, of all kinds, and tend to buy them for myself, then pretend they're for my grandchildren.

Does my darling Alicia really comprehend what it might mean to be here? If I were to die? I don't want to be the cause of a miscarriage brought on by an unpleasant shock. I only want to help her do what she wants.

We take the children upstairs, and they settle down peaceably, perhaps because we allowed them to stay up long past their usual bed-time. I don't feel repentant. This is holiday, and I'd allow some leeway if I were in charge.

"Can I read, Granma?"

"If you need to. Just for a short while, please, Simon. Let's make sure your lamp doesn't shine on Tanya."

"Can I read, Grammar?"

"Nope. It's time you were already asleep, my darling. It's very late."

"'S'not fair." The little girl snuggles into her pillow. "Night, night, Grammar." I kiss her soft cheek and she smiles, closes her eyes. "Night, Ali."

"Night, Ali. Night, Granma."

We leave the door ajar, and go back downstairs. I have a brief dizzy spell half-way down, and crash against the banister. Fortunately, Alicia is ahead of me, at my insistence, and turns only when she hears the bang. I am holding on tight to the hand-rail, aware that I could have fallen.

"Just slipped a bit. Don't worry. All's well."

She nods and waits for me at the bottom.

"You know what, Grandma?" she says, once we are installed in the sitting room with a welcome glass of wine. "I think your house could be much easier for you if you had a stair-lift. Don't you?"

"Quite unnecessary. I manage perfectly well."

"OK. If you say so."

No argument. No attempt to persuade. What a relief.

I've never thought of a stair-lift. It would make climbing those damned stairs a darned sight quicker. But I need the exercise. Can't give up completely, or my heart will simply stop.

"Grandma, do you think a child needs its father?"

She is gazing into a far-off place, mouth half-open.

"Perhaps it depends, not all fathers are good to have." She turns to me, green eyes troubled. "Most children seem to want their fathers, even the bad ones. So it's difficult to think they don't. Need both parents, I mean."

"You left Mum's father. Didn't you?"

"I did, sweetheart. But it wasn't easy."

"Mum said she much preferred her step-father. He was like a real father should be."

Ah, my Jeff. "That's true. Your Grandpa Martin, your mother's father, was fine with his children when he was there, but when he wasn't, he seemed to forget them. Your mother would write to him, and sometimes he'd send her a postcard. But mostly, he just forgot she and your Uncle David existed. Even forgot their birthdays. So Grandpa Jeff was definitely an improvement."

"Yeah. I don't think she suffered not having her real Dad."

"Actually, darling, she was very unhappy when he disappeared." She frowns, puzzled. "She didn't say? I talked to him about a divorce, and the next thing anyone knew, he'd just gone. To Canada, it turned out, to his old friend Eddy. It was a bit of a shock."

"How could he do that?"

I shrug. "I suppose he thought it the easiest way."

"There you are. The biological father's not necessarily best."

"True. But I don't suppose your friend is the same sort of person as Grandpa Martin."

"Who knows? How old was Mum then, anyway?"

"Five. And Uncle David was two. So we had a tricky time."

"Yeah, 'cause he let them down." She looks at me, and sees my frown as I remember our struggles, and Martin's total lack of comprehension. "I bet it was difficult for you too, Grandma."

I smile at that. My guess is that the stress of trying to make ends meet, in an era when women were supposed to stay home when they had children, was the origin of my current heart troubles. But lots of mothers in the world have to cope with a great deal worse than I ever did. At least we had a roof over our heads, and no bombs dropping.

"Are you ready to tell me about the father of your baby, Alicia? Maybe that would help you decide what's best."

Her creamy brow furrows like corrugated paper. "If I tell you, Grandma, will you promise not to tell my parents?"

"Of course, I won't. Not if you don't want me to." But I might try to persuade you to tell them yourself.

"He's, you know, too gentle to deal with this. I mean, he's a bit like Simon. You know? All cuddly? Mum and Dad really like him."

151

"Sorry, I'm having a problem. He's a darling, and you don't want to tell him you're having his baby?"

"Exactly. I want him to go to Cambridge, like he's supposed to. I don't want him to give it all up just because of one stupid evening. Just the one time, Grandma. It's so, so stupid."

"But still. You have a university place too."

"The thing is, we didn't plan to have sex. We just, you know, got carried away. He was so ashamed. He didn't have a condom, and neither did I. I mean, everyone knows you should always have protected sex. No one wants to get chlamydia, or herpes, or gonorrhoea, that sort of thing. We were just so, so stupid, I can't tell you."

I missed sex for a long time after Jeff's death, but I'm glad to be out of the running these days, when sex outside marriage is so risky. Chlamydia? I'd never even heard of it before reading that poster last week at the surgery.

"In my day, all we worried about was getting pregnant."

"Guess what? I never even thought of that." She stands up, and wanders about the room, picking things up, but not seeing them. Tension grips every pore. When I was young, someone in her situation would have been chain-smoking.

"Would a glass of wine help, darling?"

She raises her hands in a gesture of helplessness. "Maybe. Oh, it's so difficult, Grandma. He was so upset, and it wasn't his fault, I wanted it too."

I pour some wine, put it on the coffee table.

"Thanks." She drops back into the chair, takes a sip. "See, I told him I was on the pill, and we both must be clean 'cause we'd both been off sex for ages. So there was nothing to worry about."

She remains silent for a while, staring into the middle distance. I say nothing. Eventually she continues: "But I wasn't. On the pill, I mean. I did take it when I was going out with Keith, but I didn't like mucking up my body like that, so when we finished, I stopped. I don't want Pete - I don't want my friend to know I lied to him."

I gaze at my beautiful, muddled granddaughter, remembering that time of youth, when we feared the unknown yet knew we were immortal and could change the world.

"A baby is rather a big thing to hide, just for one small lie."

"Yeah. Okay, it's not just that. If I tell him, he'll want to get involved. Do The Right Thing. I don't want him to."

"Poor chap. Sounds as though he'd want to know about his own baby."

"Yeah, right. But it's not going to be his baby. It's mine." I look at the set of her chin. She appears such a sweet, gentle girl, but those curls and dimples conceal a core of steel. "I really do like him, Grandma, but I couldn't live with him. Let alone be married. He's just a lovely friend."

"So what would you want in someone you married?"

"I'd want someone more like my Dad. Or Uncle David. You know, someone a bit dominant, who'd take charge in a manly way, not leave it all to me."

I have to laugh at that. All these feisty females seeking a dominant male. May they be preserved from the bully.

"Anyway, I do know non-biological Dads can be good. Grandpa Jeff was the father Mum always loved."

"Is that what she said? I'm glad of that." My head is filled suddenly with the glorious music of a tenor singing the Master Song from *Die Meistersinger*, Wagner's paen to poetry and love. My beautiful, funny Jeff, with his lop-sided smile and curly hair. "He was a lovely man. Have you any memories of him? You used to stay with us every summer."

"He had this big workshop, and we had to be very careful 'cos the tools were so sharp. He'd let me watch him plane wood. I loved the smell of wood shavings, but he wouldn't let me play with them. Said I might get splinters." She laughs. "I wanted to, they looked so soft and beautifully curled. Was that how he made a living? As a carpenter?"

"He was a skilled carpenter, among other things. In Cornwall, he was in great demand, and started his own building and joinery business. He was a tough boss - he'd never tolerate laziness or incompetence. But people said it was a privilege to work for him. So he got it right."

I never did fathom his secret, but almost everyone seemed to like

153

him. I was fortunate to have him, though not for long enough.

"Mum was really sad when he died. I remember her lying on the sofa, tears just pouring into her hair, soaking the cushions. I must have been, what? five? six? How did he die, Grandma?"

"He drowned, my darling." I'm back on that beach, watching that foaming, turbulent sea, and my husband flying on the waves as they sped to the shore. After being tumbled over and over, I'd given up,, and was not surprised to see the red flag being hoisted, and life-guards converging to call the swimmers back in. It was becoming dangerous.

Jeff turned back. I saw him, and shouted. But he'd seen the boy being dragged out to sea by a rip. He was there, so he had to go to the rescue. Even though lifeguards were rushing out with their superior equipment.

"He was trying to save a young boy trapped in a rip current." I could see them both, then massive rollers intervened, and I could see nothing. "The lifeguards saved the boy." Beyond the crashing foam, the boy was dragged onto the guard's big yellow board. I still couldn't see Jeff. I ran towards the sea as it surged in, but a guard held me back. I screamed, "My husband is out there!" The powerful young man just held me, while his companions dealt with the boy, and a power-boat searched the bay. When they found him, it was too late. "The sea demanded a victim."

"Oh, Grandma. How horrible. Why did he go, if the guards were there?"

"His automatic response. If anyone needed help, he'd always give it."

"So he was a hero."

"Yes. But I do wish he weren't." We smile at each other, May and December, each with our own grief. The pain has dulled considerably over the years, but I still mourn my lost husband.

31

Irene

I wake to the rattle of china, and a soft knock on my door: neither Danielle's peremptory drum beat, nor Tanya's cheeky entrance.

"Come in."

Alicia appears, in a baggy pink tee-shirt decorated with teddy bears, and long, skinny fuchsia pants, black curls tangled. She carries a tray, with cosy-covered teapot, two cups and saucers, milk jug, slop basin and strainer, which she plonks on the chest at the foot of my bed.

"Good morning, bestest Grandma. The sun is shining, so here's some tea to wake us up."

"What luxury." My legs feel blessedly free under the duvet. I scissor them gently, enjoying the smooth coolness of fresh sheet against skin. But my right hip wrenches, and the deep seam miners restart their drilling.

"I bet your silly control has fallen on the floor. Always does, doesn't it, Grandma? Here." She turns to pour the tea, and I'm able to breathe away the worst of the pain before raising the head of the bed.

Blasted, blasted body. Now my damned legs are jagging. Next time around, I'm choosing parents who don't have arthritis in their genes. You hear that, Mother, wherever you are? You didn't like it much either.

"I thought teenagers slept in till all hours," I say, when the aches have subsided to a dull throb. "We shouldn't see any sign of you until mid-day."

She laughs. "I know. It's weird, but since I got pregnant like, I feel alive. Like I want to be doing things. So I thought I'd show you, you know, how useful I can be." She sits on the window seat, legs curled under her, gazes out of the window. "I do love being here, the garden, the sea, and everything. It's, like, a wonderful place to be."

I smile, happy to see her so happy. "I'm glad. What day is it, Alicia? I forget."

She turns back to me. "Thursday, I think. Oh, oh. Look who's here."

The door opens wide and two young children leap on Jeff's side of the bed.

"Ali's naughty, Grammar," says Tanya, leaning on my chest and looming into my face.

"Careful," I tell her, as I try to place my cup safely back in its saucer. "Why is she naughty?"

"Mummy said no one must come in here 'cos you're in bed. Ali did."

"So did you, young lady."

"Only when Ali came. I sawed her."

I laugh. "So you knew it was all right. Morning, Simon."

"Can I do the bed control. Please, Granma?"

"You can use the wand on Grandpa Jeff's bed. But I need mine just as it is."

The two children first sit, and then lie on the mattress at either end, and push the controls to make the head and the foot rise and fall, giggling as they feel it move. Ever since buying this wonderful bed, designed to help arthritics but a boon to all who enjoy comfort, young children have revelled in the sensation of a moving mattress. I feel secretly glad these two found a way to circumvent their mother's well-intentioned directive. I'm happy to be visited in bed by my grandchildren.

Alicia pours us both a welcome second cup of tea, and I start to take my morning medication.

"Can I do that, Grammar? Can I push the things out?"

I consider the probability that many of my tablets might disappear into the bedclothes or onto the floor, and shake my head. "Sorry, Tanya. I have to do this myself."

"Why do you have all those things, Granma? What're they for?"

"All these bumpy bits underneath the foil are different medicines that I need to take because I'm old."

"Why?" The eight-year-old is puzzled and can't find the right question. "You're still old."

I laugh. "Yep. They're to keep me functioning even though I'm old."

"Mmmm." He nods, judiciously. "Hope they do, Granma. You're not gonna die, are you, not yet?"

I laugh, and Alicia cries, "Simon! That's an awful thing to say."

The boy looks so downcast, I put out my arms to him. "Come here, Simon. It's not awful at all." He looks hard at me, and then snuggles up. "We all know I am going to die one day because I am, very old. But we don't have to worry about it, do we? Let's just enjoy being together."

"Yeah. Right," he says in a low voice, and we sit together on my bed, my hip and back grumbling away in the depths, not quite near enough a lift shaft for their complaints to reach the surface and require attention.

The sound of a woman's voice singing some pop song I have never heard before flows into the room.

"That's Mummy!" Tanya scrambles off the bed, flings open the door, scampers from the room. "Mummee!"

Simon leans against me, and we all listen until the song is complete.

"Mmm. Aunt Dani seems to have had a good evening." Alicia grins at me. "You know that scene near the end of *I Capture the Castle*, where the older sister has run away with her lover? Do you think she's read that and is trying to tell us something?"

I laugh. "Oh, Alicia. Such a lovely thought. And such beautiful singing – I wish she could be as happy as that all the time."

A brief but sharp tap on the door heralds the arrival of an unexpectedly tousled Danielle. "Did you have a lovely time last night, Danielle?" I ask.

She smiles. "Yes, it was a good evening. Thank you, Irene. Sorry about my children. They know they're not supposed to disturb you in the morning."

"No, no," I protest. "They weren't in the way. Not in the least. And we loved your singing," I add, with the teensiest touch of malice.

She blushes. "I thought you must be awake. Sorry, if it disturbed you."

"It didn't. I was beautiful. I love to hear you sing, Danielle - it could be the perfect way to be wakened in the morning."

She smiles at me in some confusion. "You're a dreadful flatterer, Irene. Come along, Simon. Time you got dressed." She glances at Alicia, raises an eyebrow, then ushers him out.

Alicia and I look at each other, and she shrugs. "Oh dear, I think I'm

157

definitely in Aunt Dani's bad books."

"She does seem to be in a good mood, though. Have you decided when you'll tell her why you're here?"

"You think I should?"

"Having a baby is not something that can be hidden for long. And I didn't think you were ashamed of it."

"I'm not. It's just – well, I don't want her to tell me what to do."

We both smile at that. "Let's try to keep things friendly. She's worried about me. Seems to think I'm a lot more fragile than I think I am, and tries to protect me from myself. She means well."

"Yeah. She's halfway down the road to Hell."

"Alicia!"

"Sorry. Anyway, I'm here, and like, if you need looking after, I'll do it." She grins at me. "Don't worry, yeah? I'm not the bossy type. You don't want me to care for you, just say, see? And I'll leave you alone. Your choice."

"Could you be the answer to an ancient's prayer?"

"Hope so." She waltzes to my bedside table. "You finished your tea? Right. I'll take the tray. See you in a bit."

***

I find for the second day running I dare not climb into the bath in case I can't lift myself out again. I'll have to consider more than the strong bars I have to lever myself up. What a nuisance. All the aids to the decrepit I have read about are making sense. I wash as well as I can, and resolve to telephone the plumber this morning.

Getting dressed is more difficult than usual too, which is odd. Perhaps my mind is elsewhere, worrying about Danielle and the children, and whether David will be a success; and the lovely Alicia, taking on a new life when she has barely started her own. I feel so breathless. Perhaps it's the weather.

I put on a long, full skirt that I have loved for years, a creamy background with flowers in blues and greens. The hem is slightly torn, but I don't think it shows. A green blouse to pick up the colour, and green sandals. And because I have no pockets, I decide to use the clever spectacle case that hangs on a cord round my neck: made from a soft, velvety material, with a slot for glasses and a zipped compartment for my angina spray. From the window, I see Simon and Tanya playing among the trees. It must be later than I thought. Perhaps it's as well Danielle has taken charge. I take considerably longer to get things done than she does.

Halfway down the stairs, I slip slightly, and sit down. Deary me, decrepitude is increasing. Perhaps Alicia's stair-lift would be the answer. What a lot of expense this crumbling frame is creating. Never mind giving money to David, I shall want that equity release myself to pay for all the aids I appear to need.

Alicia and Danielle are in the kitchen, and their raised voices carry quite clearly up the stairs. Oh dear. I did hope that Danielle's happiness this morning would help them get on. Perhaps Alicia is not always as tactful as she might be.

"What's your problem, Aunt? If I'm here, Grandma's gonna get more care than she does now, not less."

"Look, Alicia," Danielle says, in a voice as sharp as a chef's chopping knife. "I know you mean well, but you're a different generation, and have completely different values. It's just not suitable for you to live with your grandmother."

"How do you know? Grandma likes me being here."

"Oh, for heaven's sake. Just look at this morning. You think it's acceptable to lounge around her bedroom in your pyjamas. You incite my young children to disobey my strict instructions ... "

"That's not true!"

"And now you tell me you're expecting a baby. What on earth makes you imagine you're a suitable carer? I don't know how you dare inflict such a burden on an old woman."

"Grandma said it's good. She's happy about it."

"Of course, she'd say that, wouldn't she? She wants to help you, and she wants you to be happy. Have a bit of sense, young woman."

"For chrissake, get out of my face!"

"Bad language doesn't help." Danielle sighs with impatience. "Pull yourself together, Alicia. You need to realize, your grandmother is fragile and getting worse. Her mind appears sound enough, but her body certainly is not. I recognize the symptoms: she'll become weaker and weaker, until she has no choice but to go into a care home."

"You're such a sodding know-it-all. We don't need you to interfere."

"My God. This family drives me mad. Are you trained in care of the elderly? Don't bother to answer. Your grandmother imagines she'll die before she needs professional care, but she won't. Basically, she's too tough, too bloody-minded, like the rest of you. She'll just end up helpless, and her failing body will probably survive for years."

"Why don't you fuck off? You're absolutely horrible." Alicia is in tears. "No wonder no one in this family likes you. I'm gonna tell Grandma you're a right bitch."

I hear her run off. How can I possibly retrieve this situation?

But my malevolent body must always have the last word.

Hells bells. Not another one, not now.

32

Irene

I hear heavy footsteps crossing the hall below, and will them to go away. I don't want anyone to know. The spray is in the spectacle case, but I can't move the zip as the harpoon enters my breast. I clutch my hands against the centre of my ribcage, trying to breathe, knowing my face must be contorted. The pain is spreading. Left breast, left arm, left shoulder, up into my neck. Dammit. Dammit.

The spread of the ache releases the sharp harpoon, and I scrabble at the zip for the spray, remove the cap while rocking against the pain. Two, no, three squirts under the tongue and it tastes bitter. I close my eyes, feel the chemical unfold into my blood.

"Mother. Mother! What's the matter? Why're you sitting on the stairs? Oh, dear Lord, let me help you."

I gaze at my son, bent over me with prompt concern, his brown eyes gentle.

"Mother. Are you ill? Can you move?"

The pain is not subsiding. If anything, it's stronger. "Angina. Please get me an aspirin."

"Of course."

He runs up to the bathroom cabinet, returns swiftly with a glass of water already dissolving a large tablet. I swallow it with distaste - it's now my best protection.

"Let me carry you downstairs." He manages somehow to scoop up this bedraggled chassis, holds me against his breast as he carries me down, and I smell the faint honeycomb of his skin mixed with the tang of old spice. He places me carefully on my reclining chair, pulls out the lever so that my legs can be supported. "Should we get help?"

I smile, for I had thought he might automatically phone for an ambulance. I won't need to fight him.

"No, not for angina. It should go away soon."

It catches me again, crushing my ribs. Perhaps this is a heart attack. Eyes closed, I rock against the chair back. Please God, if it is, do the job properly this time.

"I'll fetch Danielle. She'll know what to do." He sounds tense but in control, not panicking. I had wondered how he'd behave in an emergency.

Dear Lord, this feels bad. I recline the chair until head and shoulders are just higher than my feet. The blood, thinned by aspirin, struggles to make its way through clogged capillaries in the heart, and I imagine it slowly silting up, like the bed of a sluggish stream. A clot occurred at some time in the past within the heart itself, and ever since, the heart muscle has been dying bit by bit. Not much can be done. Tiresome, but a fact of my life.

I hear feet clattering across slate tiles in the conservatory, and children's voices jumbled, "I wanna see Grammar", "Why can't we? 'S not fair," and Danielle issuing edicts: Keep Quiet. Go Back in the Garden. Leave Your Grandmother Alone. A cacophony of voices raised in anger, and Alicia clearly: "Tight-arsed bitch. Come on, kids. We'll see Grandma later."

Professional persona carefully adjusted, Danielle is bending over. "How do you feel, Irene?"

A single bubble of laughter jumps in my throat, but it's not enough. "Angina, Danielle. It'll pass."

"I think we should call your doctor. Can you give me his name?"

"No need ... only angina."

"Please. Tell me anyway, just in case. It might be a good idea for us to know who's familiar with your case."

Good point. "My G.P is Patrick Carr ... Details are in ... plastic container ... in fridge." My breath runs out and I don't say, I thought you might have noticed the green Emergency Information cross on the door. The pain is not fading. I will her to go, afraid she'll pick up my struggle against this attack.

Danielle smiles her professional caring smile. "Anything I can get you?"

"I'd love ... cup of tea."

"Of course, Irene."

My ears seem to pick up every sound: woosh of water, thud as the kettle settles in its cradle, click as it is turned on.

"She's not going to die on us, is she, Dani?"

"Your mother's far too bloody-minded to let death win yet."

Laughter. The pizzicato notes of footsteps across a slate floor. Mmnaah as the fridge door opens, bnnagh as it is closed again.

"Have you seen this, Dave? 'THIS PATIENT DOES NOT WISH TO HAVE HOSPITAL TREATMENT' in large capital letters. What does she think she's at?"

"She did say something."

"And did you know she took all this medication?"

The spray is still not working. I need to take more. Bitter taste, burning under my tongue, ache all down my left side, and up into my neck.

"Suffering Thespis, three printed pages of prescription. Mean anything to you?"

"Looks like stuff for her arthritis and just about everything you could think of to keep the heart pumping. She never let on, did she?"

"We knew she had a couple of heart attacks. But I thought she got over them. I tell you, this is absolutely not the moment for my mother to get ill. She can't wreck my career again."

I thought we'd sorted that, David.

"This is exactly what I have been predicting. For ages. Believe me, I am not getting landed with nursing her, so don't imagine for one minute that you can get round me on that. Specially not now you've committed to that bloody film, my job's far too important."

"Don't worry. I don't need that sort of hassle. Bloody typical. I get my one big break, and a fucking great Deus ex machina descends and puts the kaibosh on everything."

"Right. And you're the tragic hero. I've heard it all before."

"So you say. But I haven't had a big chance to get into films before, have I? I can't let anything get in the way this time."

"Now you know why I've gone on about your bloody mother going into a care home. What're you going to do about it?"

Nothing, I hope. Let me be. Please.

"Doesn't look as though we have a lot of choice. We can't move my mother against her will, that'd be going too far. Susie wouldn't stand for it. So Ali is the obvious answer. She's a good sensible kid. And she wants to stay here, and look after her grandmother."

"She's too young, Dave. And too irresponsible. Did she tell you she's having a baby?"

Oh, Lord. I really don't want to hear all this wrangling.

I close my eyes and my ears, and focus on the physical envelope that holds my spirit: both much the worse for living, worn out. The pain is slightly less intense at last. So not this time, after all. But I'm tired.

When the body finally shudders to a halt, what happens then? I hope I've been right for most of my life, and that God does not exist. Please, dear God, let death be the end. Discovering that You exist would be terrifying, for who could trust the goodness of the Creator of this world?

I'm doing it again, haranging the God in whom I have no faith. Why am I so absurd? It isn't even as though I'm afraid of death. I'm not. I know that Death is there, lurking behind my chair, and I'm ready to welcome her when the moment comes.

Perhaps, though, I might be afraid if I really thought that life does not come to a final end. However warming the thought of seeing Jeff again, or my mother, I've never been able to believe that we all meet up with our loved-ones in a heavenly afterlife. It's so illogical.

Why would Jeff hang around waiting for me for twelve years? And perhaps my mother would rather spend eternity with someone else? If I thought about it very long, I'm sure I wouldn't want to wait around for Susan and David to die too, and how would I deal with the Dreaded Danielle? No, eternal survival of every human that ever lived in some blissful hereafter is rubbish.

Or the Buddhists might have it right. I'd hate that too. I'd rather not have to go through reincarnation after reincarnation. Life is not that precious.

Perhaps, though, I've earned a final ending. Perhaps I shall reach Nirvana. The blissful end to the everlasting cycle of life and death.

Or perhaps not. Perhaps when you greet Death as a friend and she smiles, that is Nirvana. When you go, it's like a candle being blown out. That'd be acceptable.

I quite like the thought of being suddenly not.

33

Irene

Sounds that suggest kissing and cuddling waft through to where I lie in the sitting room, and I smile to myself. An unexpectedly happy ending. And my pains have gone.

I manoeuvre the chair to an upright position. After that bad attack, my body feels as though encased in ice. I struggle to my feet, balance with one hand on the arm of the chair, then totter towards the small cupboard under the stairs, where I keep a spare duvet.

"Heavens, I forgot. I said I'd make her a cup of tea."

China rattles. I bend down to pull out the duvet.

"Dave. I know your mother doesn't want us to interfere. But you've seen how vulnerable she is. Don't you think we should at least notify Social Services before we leave?"

Red heat floods my eyes, and something sharp pierces my skull.

"Why would you do that? My mother wouldn't like it."

"Someone needs to keep an eye on her."

My head feels as though it is separating from my body.

"Alicia will be here. I know you think she's irresponsible, but she's not stupid, and she can use a telephone."

"Bloody hell, Dave! You're still living in cloud cuckoo land."

A strange dark light moves towards me, and I see a light darkness, strangely tinged with red, and strangely I can't see anything else, and I seem to sway and float on a strange soft breeze.

***

David is lifting me, carrying me back to my chair. I'm cold, miss the soft feathers of the duvet cradling my limbs.

"She should be sitting up," Danielle says. I can't see her.

"You sure?"

"Yes. Push it down more than that. The doctor is on his way."

"I don't need a doctor." The words don't sound right. How odd. I try again, and David frowns.

"Sorry, Mother. I can't understand you."

Hell and damnation. I feel all right. No pain. Eyelids strangely heavy. I close my eyes and that floating sensation returns. No. Don't want it.

Patrick appears from nowhere, takes my hand. "Well, Irene? How're you feeling?"

"Fine. Just a bit of a headache." The sounds come out muddled again. Damn.

He pats my hand, then does a series of tests, asking me what I can see and how many fingers he's holding up, which is silly because my eyesight is fine, though my speaking is not. He says half my vision is gone, but it seems all right to me. A swoop of fear follows when I discover my left hand and arm won't obey me. The one thing I dread.

"Your mother has had a stroke," he tells David. "Probably what we call a transient ischaemic attack, and the symptoms should go in about twenty-four hours. We could take her into hospital, but I know she has expressed a wish to remain in her own home." Bless you, Patrick. You remembered. "Are you happy with that? You're her family."

I wait for my loving son and dutiful daughter-in-law to be "realistic" and "practical". A damned stroke, so I can't even argue. And I can't get at my secret hoard of sleeping pills, to end it all. I'm damned well trapped in this useless old body, and I want to scream and yell, and all that emerges from my mouth is a kind of mewing, like a bedraggled kitten in the rain.

"Would it be safe?" David asks.

"Grammar, Grammar. What're you doing?" Tanya runs round the adults standing in a solemn semi-circle before me, like druid priests preparing for a sacrifice, scrambles up to recline beside me. My left arm flops in the way, but the child just pulls it round her, as though she instinctively understands, and snuggles against my breast. I lean my cheek on her curly head, and breathe in the warm child smell. "Stop sleeping, Grammar. I wanna be with you."

"Tanya, get up." Danielle says. Of course. Interfering, possessive bitch. "Your grand-mother's not well."

167

"The child can't hurt her, Mrs Harper," Patrick says. "Could even be therapeutic."

Danielle looks at him, her eyebrows raised, porcelain skin crumpling on her forehead. "Really? I was worried the children's antics might make her worse."

"Not if they give her pleasure."

They both look down at me as Tanya snuggles into my traitorous body. Danielle smiles encouragingly, eyes anxious. I try to smile back, but can't be sure how my mouth is behaving.

"Just treat Grandma gently, Tanya."

"I always do."

"Your mother doesn't need to go into hospital if there's someone here to look after her," Patrick tells David. "I can arrange for an agency nurse. Private, of course."

There's a brief silence, while David and Danielle look at each other. Then David says, "That would be helpful, thank you. We know that's what she wants."

"Um, I'd like to look after my grandmother, if you could tell me what to do." I can't see Alicia, and wonder how long she has been there quietly listening.

"Are you staying here then?"

"Yes, I've come to live with my grandmother." Alicia appears, cheeks streaked with tears, and flashes me a tremulous smile. "So she probably doesn't need anyone else."

Patrick turns to David, but Danielle says:

"Alicia is totally inexperienced, and far too young. She would not do. But I'm a trained physio. I can look after my mother-in-law until the weekend, if you tell me what's required." She sounds breathless, as though she's been running a marathon. "I just want it quite clear. I shall not be staying on after Saturday, so that if further nursing is required, an agency nurse will need to be called in then."

"Excellent arrangement," says Patrick. "It's just common sense really, you'll know what to do. But do call me if there's any change. Strokes can occur more than once, and the next could be serious." He turns to me.

"I'll look in tomorrow, Irene." He picks up his black bag. "Alicia, is it? Come and see me at the surgery, and we'll sort out how to help you to help your grandmother."

Alicia's eyes gleam, and aim a volley of poison darts at her aunt. "Thanks, I will."

While David shows Patrick out, Simon sidles into the room, leans over the back of the chair. I put up my good hand to caress him, and he snuffles his head into my neck, then moves round, perches on the chair arm and leans against me. I'm bracketed by my two youngest grandchildren, cuddling me quietly, as though they know something has gone wrong and they can heal me with their love. Darling, sensitive Simon hasn't said a word, and delicious Tanya is humming a lullaby.

Alicia drags up a stool and sits beside me, strokes my useless left hand, looking distressed. I wish I could communicate with her. Tears ooze out of her eyes, and I can't even squeeze her fingers.

"Thought that was the last thing you wanted," David says to Danielle in a low voice, somewhere in the background.

"Don't start, Dave. Of course I'll look after her while I'm here. But don't you forget. I'm damned if I'll be trapped, just because I'm apparently the only one in this entire bloody family who knows what to do."

"It does help, doesn't it? Knowing what to do, I mean."

"My God!" Danielle sounds as though she might detonate. "Neither you nor your bloody sister has the remotest grasp of reality. Probably get it from your mother."

"Hey, lay off my poor mother."

"Your poor bloody mother my ass! How she ever imagined she could carry on living like this, I fail to understand. The whole goddam bunch of you are all the same. You think you can swan off into the glamorous world of film, and all the bills will continue to be paid, even if your idiot wife has to quit her job to care for your frail, sick mother. Your sister sends a pregnant teenager to nurse said old woman, when the girl needs a bit of care herself. The whole bloody family is just a bunch of impractical dreamers."

"That's a bit strong. After you just offered to nurse my mother. Of your own free will, I might add."

"I suppose that means you think I'm an easy touch. We may have had great sex last night, Dave, but don't kid yourself. You've got away with far too much already, and I'm not standing for any more."

"Hey, Dani. I thought we were friends again. And now my mother's dying, I need you more than ever."

"You're a monster deep down, David. Trying to use your mother's infirmities as blackmail. It's not going to work."

"How can you be like that? What am I going to do now, for heaven's sake? Will she be fit to leave down here? How can I start my new film if I don't know my mother is being properly cared for?"

"Exactly. I might remind you – and your dear sister, if ever she listens - that I told you. And told you and told you. Your mother needs professional care. I am not the one who will give it."

"Now I don't know what's the best thing to do." There is a sob in his voice. A Donald Wolfit in embryo, I do declare. Milking every scene to the last emotional drop.

Danielle sighs, like an Inquisitor who'd hoped that the mere sight of the rack might have sufficed. "Dave, it's simple. Phone Susan, right now. You and she have to arrange for your mother to get round-the-clock nursing care. Either here, or in a home. It's too late for total independence. She'll die if she's left alone."

I was afraid of this. Somehow I had a premonition that this visit would do me no favours. I do wish other people could believe that Death might be a welcome visitor.

"I thought you said she was too bloody-minded to die. I believed you." I hear a tremor in his voice. It could even be genuine. "I don't think you'd care if she did."

"Don't get it, do you? " She laughs suddenly, but her lovely voice sounds like a cracked tenor bell. "I love the woman, or we wouldn't be having this conversation. Even if she is a bloody-minded old harridan."

Deep inside this tiresome body, laughter sparks and fizzes. A good epitaph.

34

Irene

Nature, that degrading old dictator, persists in demands on my bladder despite its recent failure to maintain a decent blood flow to the brain. This is where I need help. But the words that are so clear in my mind emerge sounding like a mewing seagull, and I foresee the ultimate humiliation if I can't drag this inert body off the chair. With my good arm, I push Tanya away from under the useless one, and lean forward, trying to wriggle my bottom out of the corner. Alicia watches, a frown on her face. The foot support wobbles uncomfortably and I haven't the strength to push it down.

"Grammar, stoppit. I wanna sit with you."

Simon slides off the arm, tries to pull me up with all the strength of his sturdy eight-year-old body. "Granma wants to stand up."

"Why does she?"

"What are you kids doing?" David strides over, lifts both children bodily out of the way, squats down in front of me. "What is it, Mother? Can you tell me?"

"She wants to stand up," Simon says impatiently. "I was helping her."

"Don't. You don't need to get up, Mother, just tell me what you want."

More mewing. Danielle joins the gawping throng, and I screw up my face, trying to convey my urgent need to get to the bathroom before it is too late. Even if I can get to my feet, climbing the stairs seems an impossible project. Why did we never install a lavatory downstairs? Two bathrooms upstairs, elaborate facilities outside in the garden annexe, but nothing within reach now.

"I know," Alicia cries. "Grandma needs the loo." Clever girl. I nod, gratefully.

"You need the bathroom, Irene?" Danielle asks, and I nod, more vigorously. "I'll help you."

"Is that it?" David sounds relieved. "No problem, I'll carry you. Much the easiest way." He lifts me into his arms, and I lie against his broad shoulder, smell again his faint odour of honey and old spice as he puffs his way up the rather steep stairs. "You're so small now, you're light as a child."

I don't believe it, but appreciate his attempt to conceal the struggle. Danielle follows, having firmly admonished the others to remain below, tells her husband to wait until she calls, closes the door, helps me pull down my panties without embarrassment. I relax at last into the release, surprised I'm not mortified that Danielle is there. This remarkable daughter-in-law reveals an unexpected talent for knowing exactly what will make things easier.

"Would you be more comfortable in bed, Irene?" I see flash across her face a sudden apprehension I might think she is trying to banish the invalid, hide me away, and she adds hastily, "Or would you feel happier with your family round you?"

What do I want? I want to lie down, certainly. But I'd like the children's company, so no, I don't want to go to bed. How am I supposed to answer? Words are so untrustworthy, I daren't say a thing.

"Bed, Irene?" I shake my head. "Downstairs?" I nod. "Fine." She helps me sit back down on the lavatory lid, opens the door, and calls, "Dave."

He must have been hovering, because he is right there, scoops me up like a young bride. I feel my mouth try to laugh at him, though I have no idea if it succeeds. I wonder what I look like. Lopsided, I suppose. I hope Patrick is right and this paralysis will soon go.

"Ridiculous not to have a loo downstairs," David tells me, as he carries me down. "I think I should telephone your plumber, and ask him to install one as soon as possible. What do you think?"

What do I think? Great idea. One Jeff and I had on numerous occasions. But the question always was where to put it? We liked our big rooms too much to lose any part of them, and the only obvious place – the old larder – had become a laundry room. I didn't want to spoil that either. Idiotic really. The past few days show that a downstairs lavatory should have been high priority. But who, when young, ever believes the infirmities of age will affect them?

172

"Sorry. You can't really discuss it, can you, Mother dear?" He deposits me in my chair, and fumbles with the footrest. A strange sense of floating in space envelops me. "Dr Carr said it shouldn't last too long. So if I phone the chap, see if he can come over before we leave, would that be all right? Just nod. Or shake your head, as the case may be."

"She could have a stair-lift, Uncle. That would do just as well."

"Good thought, Ali. Yes. Might be easier to install. What do you think, Mother?"

I really don't care at the moment. I feel strange, as though my body is not quite part of me, but is there, hovering a little out of reach. I concentrate. Yes, my buttocks are pressing against a firm but yielding surface, and I sense the smooth leather beneath the layers of cotton panties and silky acrylic skirt, and how the yielding surface extends beneath the soft silk of my blouse, up my back, across my shoulder. My right hip creaks and jags, distracts me from discovering whether the left shoulder and arm are back. Jangles of arthritis reassure me. I'm still here, dammit. Just a little disoriented.

"Why don't I get quotes for both? Can't go away and leave you without some extra facilities, Mother, now we've seen they're needed."

"Phone your sister," Danielle says, sharp as a porcupine's quill. "Never mind the tradesmen."

"I'm going to, woman. I can do both, you know. It's hardly what you might call multi-tasking."

"Get her to take some responsibility too." Oh, Danielle.

She has brought down a duvet, which she now tucks around me. I'm not a damned invalid, Danielle. Come on, Irene. Stop deluding yourself. Right now, you are almost totally invalid, and you need to face facts. Bloody hell. This is seriously annoying.

"Would you like a cup of tea, Irene? The one I didn't actually manage to give you earlier?" There is laughter in her voice again, and I hope the smile that erupts in my mind manages to materialise on my lopsided face. I nod, and I think grateful amusement shows in my eyes.

"Grammar. I wanna play music."

"I don't think we can touch Grandma's piano when she's not well,

Tani." Alicia is still out of sight, so I suppose she keeps hovering around my left side. Do hurry up and get better, stupid brain. "Why don't we put on a record? Grandma would like that, wouldn't you, bestest Grandma? Let's see what she's got."

"I know! Wait, Ali." I hear a child's footsteps running into the music room, and then returning more slowly. Tanya appears, clutching the tawny-brown, hard-back-covered collection of J. S. Bach's *Well-Tempered Clavier*, which she lays on my outstretched legs. I can feel the weight on both knees. And I think my left thigh. "See? This is Grammar's music and it's good."

"How do we find what she'd like?" If I turn my head, I can see Alicia peering at the stacks of CDs in the case below the window. That's mainly opera, and cantatas, and an old, wonderful collection of jazz classics. Instrumental – solo, chamber, orchestral – are all over this side of the room, stacked in alphabetical order by composer. Pity. I don't feel much like singing at the moment. "I've found Bach's *Brandenburg Concertos* with Yehudi Menuhin." Serendipity. Misplaced, but welcome now. "Would that do, do you think, Tani?"

"Is it by this man what wrote Grammar's book?"

"I think so."

"Okay." I love the way this five-year-old so casually demands the work of one of music's great geniuses. She climbs onto my chair and inveigles her way under the duvet, adjusting my still useless left arm to her satisfaction, while Alicia comes over to the CD player and endeavours to work out its mysteries. I'm sure she's used it before, and infer that she too feels disoriented by my unfortunate attack.

Danielle brings in a cup of tea, which she places carefully within reach of my right hand, moving the little table, and discomposing Alicia in the process.

"Am I in your way, Aunt? I'm just trying to put on a record."

"Good. Just press that button. It says 'Open slash Close', if you look carefully."

"Yes, right. I can do it."

"And when you have managed to put in the CD, and to press the

'Play' button, perhaps you'd like to pull your weight by starting to prepare lunch? That is if you still imagine you can take over here. And do mind that cup of tea, your grandmother would prefer it not in the saucer."

"Get out of my face! What's so sodding difficult about getting lunch?"

Giggles bubble in my chest and I wonder what might emerge if I let them rise up into my mouth. But the stately opening movement of *Brandenburg No. 1* takes over – too loudly, as the volume control is set high from when we were listening to Helen Reddy in the conservatory. Fortunately, Alicia immediately turns it down. My hearing appears to be the one faculty that has remained unimpaired, thank the Lord in Whom I do not believe. How tortured Beethoven's last years must have been, losing his most important sense.

Alicia stomps off in the direction of the kitchen, and Tanya snuggles against me as we listen to the beautiful cadences of the slow movement. This is the best medicine anyone could prescribe. Clearly constructed, elegant harmonies to put me together again, enjoyed in the company of my gifted granddaughter: love and music, twin peaks of human achievement, where we rise above pure animal nature to as near immortality as human beings can ever be.

"Susan will try for stand-by on tonight's flight, Mother." David strides in, clearly relieved to have found practical arrangements to make. "I'll meet her in Newquay, if she manages to get on. She'll phone from Gatwick to let us know."

Poor Susan. I hope she's not too worried. It's not as though this damned transient whatsit is going to last. Such a lot of fuss.

"I've also got a stair-lift engineer to come tomorrow. I said to bring possible lifts with him, as you need the equipment urgently." I manage to raise my right eyebrow at him, and he adds hastily: "Only if you're happy about it, of course."

Oh, David, David. Carry on. I don't mind you being masterful if it helps you and your wife go away feeling I will be all right. Because I will, for the time I have left.

Wrapped in down, savouring the warmth of my young granddaughter, sensing her total absorption, I cut out every sound but Bach's glorious music, feel tension ebb. The concerns that led to this deplorable episode drip slowly to the floor and evaporate.

When the final chords of the third Brandenburg Concerto have drifted into silence, I remember the tea. It has cooled after more than fifty minutes, but is still drinkable. I sip about half, and Tanya sits up.

"I think I like that music, Grammar." She frowns. "It was a bit funny. I have heared orchestras, but the piano did sound funny. Why, Grammar?"

Yes, indeed. Her wonderful gift of hearing the notes. A piano is essentially a percussion instrument, in which strings are hit with hammers, whereas in a harpsichord, the strings are plucked like a harp. How to tell her? With my right hand, the good one, I imitate writing, then outline a sheet of paper. The clever girl clambers down from the chair, and runs to my desk. "Here y'are." She returns with an armful of felt tip pens and a wodge of paper. I wish I could laugh the laugh that wants to burst its confines in my throat.

I raise the chair so that I am sitting at an angle, and take a pen, indicate I need her to move the paper. Then I print carefully, "It was a harpsichord not a piano."

"What's a harp – thing?"

I have two books which would tell her about harpsichords. In a harpsichord, the strings are plucked like a harp, whereas a piano is essentially a percussion instrument, in which strings are hit with hammers. First, she needs a picture, so we could start with *The Oxford Companion to Music*: a very battered copy, given to me by my mother when I passed the eleven-plus.

So I write: "Big blue book MUSIC on back." With my good arm, I point at the shelves behind me. Unfortunately, all the music books are on the second shelf, so I add: "Get stool. Kitchen."

It's astonishing what a fixed determination can achieve, even at the age of five, but her mission collides with that of the rest of the household, which is more concerned with a late lunch.

"I need the stool, Daddy. Grammar said."

"Come on, Tani." David strolls over, Tanya firmly held in one hand. "What's this all about?" I try to indicate to my disgruntled granddaughter that she should show her father my notes, which she does, eventually, with a theatrical sigh. "I see." He lifts down *The Oxford Companion to Music*, finds the reference to harpsichords, and shows his daughter the illustration.

"Is that what they played, Grammar?" she asks. I nod. "It's got two lines of keys. Why?"

"I've no idea, Tani," says her father. "I have to read what it says in this book."

"I'm gonna wait for Grammar." What touching faith. I too shall have to read it up, see what *Grove's Dictionary of Music* can add, and convey same to the lovely Tanya. Tomorrow.

I lie back, and close my eyes. "You all right, Irene?" Danielle asks, as she collects the teacup. "Can I fetch you anything before I join the others?" I shake my head. "I expect you'd like a nap. I'll come and see you when lunch is finished."

I put out my good hand, touch hers, feel her tremble. Oh, my dear. I take her hand briefly, and squeeze it a little. I do want her to know I appreciate all that she does for me.

"There, there, Irene. I know. But you'll be back to normal tomorrow."

She is difficult and dominant, and sometimes a pain in the neck. But I feel real affection for this much put-upon woman, and hope I can show her before it's too late.

35

Irene

"I wanna go to the beach." Simon's voice drifts through the haze of my drowsiness, and I hear the chink of crockery as dishes are carried to the kitchen. Lunch must be over.

"What a selfish boy you are, Simon. Think of your poor Grandma."

David, David, what a really crass comment.

"That's stupid. Granma can't go swimming, and she likes us to have fun. She said so." These unlucky children. I do wish I hadn't managed to disrupt their holiday so badly.

"Don't dare talk to me like that."

"Come on, Dave. Leave the boy alone. He's just as upset as you are."

"This is my mother, in case you've forgotten, Danielle."

"Lighten up, for chrissake. Frankly, I think Simon has a good idea. The sun's shining, the tide is right, and it would do everyone good to get out of the house for an hour or two."

"What about my poor mother? We can't just leave her."

"Of course not. But Alicia is here. You won't mind being in charge for an hour or so, will you, Alicia dear?"

"No. 'Course I won't. But ... what if ... er."

"Just use your common sense. Your grandmother simply needs to rest, so you shouldn't have to do anything. And we'll leave you our mobile numbers, so you can phone if you're worried. All right?"

"Yeah." Poor Alicia. She sounds very uncertain. But I shall give her no cause for alarm.

"Try it out for a couple of hours. See how it goes. Then you'll know if you can do this, won't you? My dear?"

Well, well. I have to admit, Danielle's idea is good. She's perfectly justified in her scepticism, and a teenager, however well-meaning and loving, should not have to care for a dying old woman.

David tiptoes in to check on me, his exaggerated care reminiscent of the traditional pantomime villain creeping upon some innocent with evil intent, while Simon follows, trying to imitate his father. As I cannot speak, I feign sleep. Danielle and Tanya both visit me in a less theatrical manner, and I do my best to convey the hope they have a lovely time.

Through half-closed eyelids, I see sunlight flickering on the creamy flowers of the oak-leaf hydrangea outside the bay window, hear the bustle of their departure, the slam of the car doors, the sudden roar of the engine and the swish, crackle of the gravel, the faint clang of the drain.

I imagine them walking down the long road from the car park to the beach, laden with swimming things and surf boards, negotiating the rocky entrance that has defeated me now for some years, down beside the rushing stream that has worn a deep gulley through the rock, beside the cliff with its perennial warning of falling stones, out onto the wide expanse of golden sand. No doubt it will be crowded in this last week of August, so they will make their way around the rocky promontory, past the little bay full of rock pools, where small children play, past the steep sloping expanse of rock where we used to take evening picnics and watch the sun sink crimson into the ocean, on to where the yellow sands stretch out and they can feel less confined.

I can see them in their costumes, running down the rippled sands in the sunshine, lithe brown limbs, brightly coloured polystyrene body boards under one arm, splashing into the white surf. The sea will be a wide expanse of blues and greens beneath a cerulean sky, a series of rolling waves breaking just where youthful inexperienced surfers can enjoy them most, not too big, not too dangerous, but exciting and exhilarating as they catch the breaker at the crucial moment that will carry them speeding to the shore. I hope it's like that. And that David remembers about tides and rip currents and how to be safe.

The sound of a clarinet fills my mind: I know it is Gervase de Peyer playing Mozart's *Quintet for Clarinet and Strings*. I love the way music becomes somehow embedded in my brain, and comes back to me complete, out of the blue: as though it is the one creative art that can live for ever. De Peyer is now playing the second movement. I sink into my chair, swimming in the music, floating in sound, drifting with the current created by the woodwind. Then the tempo changes, and I am trying to join in the dancing exchanges with the strings, but I slip and fall, slide full-length down a steep, icy surface, that becomes steeper and steeper, and I don't know how to stop.

I wake up, though I hadn't realized I was asleep. I'm still trapped in the unpleasant sensation of going downhill too fast, and dare not close my eyes again.

"Grandma? You OK?"

"Think I .... want sit ... up." Glory be, I spoke. Was it comprehensible?

"You spoke to me, Grandma. Oh, wonderful!" Alicia drops her book, and scurries over to my chair. "Let me help you. Oh, Grandma." She stoops and kisses my undamaged cheek. "You're getting better. Aren't you?"

I savour the sense of sitting upright, and smile at my granddaughter. At least, I hope I smile. "I did say ... pro pro ... right words... did'n I?"

"That's cool, Grandma. I didn't like it when you couldn't talk."

"No... I not like..." Well, it's a start. Can't seem to get all the words in my mind out into the world, but I shall be normal by tomorrow. I'm not going downhill fast. Yet.

"Shall I get you a cup of tea? You might manage to drink it all this time." She grins at me, youthful vitality restored. That's a relief. It's not part of my End of Life Plan to precipitate depression in any of my grandchildren, especially not this lovely girl has taken on a daunting burden so early in her life.

I must find a way to persuade her to go home. That dream made me realize Death is stalking me for a reason.

36

Irene

We're still savouring the traditional British brew Alicia produces when the others return. I leave it to her to announce, with a soupçon of smugness, that on her lone watch Grandma has recovered her speech. Fortunately, the buzz of excitement that follows allows me a considerable delay before I must demonstrate.

"Great news, Mother."

"Wonderful, Irene. I knew you'd be fine for a short while."

"Guess what, Granma. I did some really good surfing today."

"He did, Mother, he did. Getting nearly as skilled as you used to be at catching the waves."

"I did it good, too, Grammar."

"Come on, leave your grandmother in peace while you get showered. You're both covered in salt and sand."

"Well, Mother, I'm glad that things are looking up." David settles himself on the settee, leans back with one ankle balanced on the other knee. "Can't leave you without making sure you're going to be all right."

"I've told you, get a professional nurse if I'm unable to cope alone." That is what I intend to say. But to my dismay, though the concept is perfectly clear and coherent inside my head, and words do emerge from my mouth, I see him frown.

"Sorry, Mother. I didn't get that."

"Get nurse ... when go." Simple words, simple ideas. Surely those are the right ones.

"You want a professional nurse, is that right?" I nod. Christ, this is difficult. I presume I can dismiss a nurse if I choose. "Makes sense. I take it there is no problem with money?"

Please God, re-cement the connection between mouth and brain in time for me to talk to Charles tomorrow. I may need equity release to pay for a nurse. Not to mention the stair-lift that David has ordered.

"Ali. Wouldn't you like some time to yourself? After all the responsibility this afternoon?"

"Yeah, right." Alicia stalks from the room like an offended cat, and I see her pass the window, walk up and down outside, talking on her mobile.

"Sweet girl. Not quite the right person to care for you, though. She's very young. Very naïve. Don't you think, Mother?"

I nod. "I said ... pro .. pro .. professional."

"Yep. Got that." He sighs, and gazes at me sadly. "You know, there's something I feel I should sort out with you, before we go. There's never a right time, and I never wanted to upset you. But now I realize, one day, it'll be too late. So ... if you're really getting better ..."

Now what? I wave my good hand in a 'whatever you wish' manner.

He looks at me, like a diver about to run up the springboard, hoping the bounce will take him high enough to perform his jackknife dive cleanly. "I need to tell you, a part of me has never forgiven you for sending my father away."

I frown. I can sense it's lopsided. My left cheek feels bruised and stiff. "What?"

"He told Susie and me he had to go to Canada because you wouldn't let him stay."

Gracious. What a distortion. How old were you then? Two. And you've believed that ever since? Oh, David. The absurdities that children nurture in their immature minds.

"Does S .. S .. Suse ... believe ... that?"

He gazes out of the window. "No, don't think so. She's quite hostile about him, I'd say." He turns back to me. "I know this is really unfair, especially now. But I always wondered why you didn't make Daddy keep in touch with me." I shake my head at him in disbelief. How does he imagine I could do that? "He wrote to Susie."

"Very ... rarely. She was ... older ... He saw you ... as baby."

"Didn't you think I needed a father?"

"Yes, David. I did." I thought about it a lot. We look at each other, and I hope his aggrieved attitude is more theatrical than genuine. I really don't know what he thinks I could have done that I did not. "I'm s .. s .. sorry ... you feel like this."

I want to add that, in the light of his personal experience, he might bear in mind his own children's need for a father; given that he appears to be as willing to estrange his wife for his own ends as he is to attack his mother. Perhaps it's just as well I can't yet trust my treacherous tongue. I've no desire to fight my son, especially as I won't see him again before I die.

"I used to adore you, you know. You were just a fleeting vision when I was little, never there. But I thought you were the best Mummy in the world."

Never there? I was always there. What can he be thinking of? Unless he means that I wasn't always waiting at home, like a story-book mother, because I had to go to work. It has to be that. And I'd always imagined that that was one of my virtues, being able to make a good enough living for us all that I could pay the mortgage, buy a car and child care even when Martin refused to contribute a penny. Do all virtues have a down side?

"What threw me into a rage was you marrying that bully Jeff. A rage that has lasted thirty years."

Dear God. Dear, dear God. I didn't know.

"I thought ... you liked him. You s .. s .. said you did."

"Of course, I said I liked him. To please you."

I'd never have married him if I thought you'd be unhappy. "I really ... thought he'd be ... good father ... and what you wanted."

"Don't blame me for your marriage, Mother. I've heard you say it was my fault for years and I don't want to hear it again."

"What? I ... never blamed ... you."

"Oh yes, you did. Time and again you said, I married him for you, David. To give you a father. Well, he wasn't the father I wanted."

Oh dear, so many misunderstandings. I sigh. At the end of my life, I have to face the fact I failed my son. Does Susan feel like this? I'd like to think not, for we've had a good relationship. But then I thought my relationship with David was good too. Still, Alicia does seem to believe

183

her mother loved my Jeff as a father, that's one good thing.

"Mother?"

"Yes?"

"Don't you care?"

I'd like to laugh, but the fizz is not there. Look around you, David, look at the walls, the tables, the windowsills, the shelves. Everywhere, photographs of you and Susan, and your own children. Go upstairs, open the big cabin trunk. It's full to overflowing with albums and loose photographs of you and Susie; old film tapes of you children in the bath, the garden, on the beach, with your friends; school reports, Susie's sports certificates, the theatre programmes every time you appeared in a play. I threw nothing away. It's all there, a haphazard record of the almost forty years you've lived on this earth.

What did I ever do with my life except be a mother?

I worked in public relations, to support my children; I was a School Governor, because I was a parent; I was a volunteer and fund-raiser for Save the Children. Apart from creating a garden, and learning very belatedly to play the clarinet and becoming a mediator, I've done nothing but be a mother.

Of course I cared. Still care. Have never stopped caring. And now I know I failed. Nothing I say now can change that.

He drops to the floor, clumsy and ungainly, like a seal flopping onto a rock.

"I didn't want to make you unhappy, Mother. That's why I never said anything before. But when you had that mini stroke, I realized that one day I'd find it was too late. I just thought you might be able to put things right for me. I've made an awful mess of things up till now."

I stroke his glossy head and he leans against my thigh. "How can I ... put things right? ... Can't change what happened."

"I don't like this anger in me. I don't know what to do with it."

"I remember that feeling ... trying to keep ... volcano ... from erupting."

"Did you? Did you really feel that way?"

"Don't you remember? ... I used to lose ... temper all time ... I thought

I was ... appalling mother ... anger for years."

"No. I don't remember that." That seems impossible. "It's Jeff I remember. Picking on me, shouting at me, talking as though I was scum."

"Darling, surely not ... I thought nice to you ... played games ... encouraged you."

"Why did you marry him, Mother? Really? I'm not attacking you."

"I loved him ... I never good at judging men ... but I did think he was right ... thought you liked him ... He tried very hard .... not to bully like his father."

"Then we saw different things. I thought he was a selfish bastard. And I'm turning out no better, alas."

"You have choices ... David." I'm becoming breathless. Words are starting to flow more easily, but oh dear, this conversation is making me very tired.

"Yeah. I wish I liked myself more than I do."

He takes both my gnarled swollen hands in his, examines them as though he has never seen them before. Then he raises his face and his brown eyes are liquid.

"Susie said your heart is dying. Is that true?"

"Melodramatic... way put it."

"I can't believe it. You're a bit frail, and you did have this attack. But most of the time, you can look after yourself, even cope with the children."

"I'm not ill, David ... It's just ... my heart is ... giving up."

Running feet clatter down the stairs, children's voices chirrup and chirp through the hall, into the kitchen.

"Can't the doctors do anything?"

"Nothing useful. So I don't want ... medical intervention ... Please remember."

"Yes, I did hear you." He gently replaces my hands in my lap, and clambers to his feet. "Maybe that's another reason I feel so angry. You're much too young to die. People are living to eighty and ninety these days."

"Please accept ... I have ... Death is not so bad ... so long as keep ... dignity."

He gazes out of the window, then bends and kisses my cheek.

"Don't worry, Mother. I'll do my best for you when the time comes."

An ambiguous promise. Just as well Charles is coming tomorrow. I'm not relinquishing control yet.

37

Irene

Inevitably, Nature makes another peremptory call. I'm able to manoeuvre myself out of my chair, and hobble as far as the stairs. But the first step defeats me. Once again, David carries me up, cuddling me a little more warmly, if I am not mistaken.

"Glad to be of some help, Mother darling," he whispers. "Sorry I'm taking out my hang-ups on you."

What can I say to that? I shake my head at him and hope I manage a recognisable smile. "Thanks for the lift."

I shuffle into the bathroom, and close the door, decide not to lock it, just in case. My damned left arm is quite useless still, but I can manage with just one hand. Thank heaven I put on a skirt this morning.

Ablutions finished, I examine my reflection in the mirror. A definite sideways tilt, alas. I thought it might go, with restoration of speech. Not yet. My left cheek sags more than ever, and the corner of my mouth is turned down on that side. Ugly. I wonder what the children make of it.

I'm tired. Now I can believe the effects of this wretched mini stroke are disappearing, I think I'll retire to bed. A considerable crowd of people is expected tomorrow, and I'd like to feel more capable of coping with them than I do now.

David is hovering at the head of the stairs.

"Shall I take you down?"

"I'm going to bed."

"Right. I better tell Dani. She'll want to help you."

"Fine." My slow progress into the bedroom would make a slug look speedy, but I get there eventually, and sit on the side of Jeff's bed to recover.

Suddenly David is back. Standing in the doorway. "Susie's on the phone and wants a quick word. Can you pick up that receiver?"

Where is it? The other side, on my bedside table. He grasps the situation, strides round the bed in seconds, hands me the phone.

"Hello, darling."

"Oh, Mother, so glad you can speak. I just wanted to hear your voice. And I'm on this evening's flight, by a miracle. Dave said he'll meet me. "

I try to say it's wonderful to know she's coming, and there is nothing to worry about, but fatigue takes hold, muddles my faithless tongue, reduces my daughter to tears.

"Don't struggle any more, Mother darling. I know what you're trying to say. I love you too. Take care till I arrive. Please."

David replaces the telephone. "The plane arrives at nine, so I'll be on my way soon. Anything I can get you?" I shake my head. "Best leave it to Dani, eh? See you."

I sit on, feeling utterly worn. Waiting for a small surge of energy that might allow me to move. Undress. Actually get into bed.

I have no idea how long I sit there, like a tramp in a dustbin. Waiting for Godot.

Danielle appears. "You tired, Irene?" I nod. "Not surprised. Let me help you undress."

Her hands are firm and gentle. I wonder what made her choose to care for a mother-in-law who was unkind to her. I fought the poor woman off so long, she must have felt deeply hurt. And now, if I had to have a nurse, Danielle would be the one I'd choose. Maybe tomorrow, I'll be able to tell her so, without fearing the words will emerge in a tangled clot.

Her generosity of spirit won't be tested for long now. I don't blame Danielle for wanting to avoid being trapped as carer. In her place, I'd do the same. A fountain of laughter spurts up through the ache in my chest and into my mouth, and as I look at this chic, sleek daughter-in-law folding back the duvet, plumping up the pillows, I realize we have more in common than she will ever know.

Danielle helps me into bed, and I raise my arthritic right hand to caress her cheek. "Thank you ... my dear. This old ... harridan ... recognizes quality."

"Heavens, Irene, you're a one-off." A giggle, like a trill on a cello string. "Now, let me get you some refreshment. I don't believe you've eaten all day."

That's true. I'm not hungry, but now she comes to mention it, I'd like a little something. A Winnie-ther-Pooh smackerel. Almost as if she reads my mind, she suggests:

"What about some thin bread and butter with honey, and a glass of milk?"

"S..sounds ... just right."

"Good. And when I bring it up, I wonder if you might suggest where Susan can sleep? We're starting to run short of beds."

This last comment is made with a trace of laughter in her voice, so I nod. Good question. Only other sleeping place is the settee in the living room. Alicia could move down there, while her mother takes the futon. I've slept on the settee, it's very comfortable. But not really satisfactory. I look around my bedroom, seeking inspiration, and it comes to me: Susan could sleep in Jeff's bed. She's the only person I could tolerate there beside me. I smile to myself. I would take bets that Danielle has been through exactly the same thought process, and hopes I will come up with this solution. Smart woman.

Alicia puts her head around the door. "Can I come in, Grandma?"

"My darling." I don't trust words, so I stretch out my right arm, and we hug each other.

"I wish I was more use," she whispers, and her cheeks shine with moisture. "I will learn, Grandma. Promise."

I pat her young hand with its chipped nail polish. "You are always .... lovely. A real ... pleasure."

"I'm gonna, like, find out what a proper carer should do. I mean, it can't be that difficult. Lots of people do it."

I kiss her soft cheek with lips that still feel unsteady. "You'll be fine," I hope I say. "Whatever you do."

"Get better quickly, Grandma. Love you."

She scurries out as Danielle arrives with a loaded tray and places it, as I would do, on the flat surface of the bed beside me: jug of water, glass, tall tumbler of milk, plate of wafer-thin brown bread properly buttered, honey in a jar, shortbread biscuits, and grapes. Perfect fare to please the uncertain appetite.

"Food to please an old harridan, I hope." She winks at me. Now we're sharing a joke.

"Perfect."

"Good." She smiles, more relaxed than I have seen her this visit. "Have you any ideas about Susan's bed? I think I should get it ready, if I can."

"Danielle ... you are marvel ... S .. Suse can s .. sleep here." I indicate Jeff's bed, and she nods.

"And the duvet?"

"In that cupboard ... she knows."

"Good. I'll leave you now, then. Enjoy the snack."

I take a small wafer of bread and butter, lean back against my pillows, savour the creamy, slightly salted flavour of the butter mixed with the coarser texture of the bread. My taste buds seem to have remained unaffected. Good. The more senses the better. I wonder how my sight is doing. Difficult to tell. What I can see is all there appears to be, but I suppose that's how it is whether one has full vision or only a fraction.

I'm improving. I drink the milk, take the remaining medication that I need in the evening, then lower the headrest. I shall sleep until Susan arrives. I just hope she won't regret her journey too much, for she'll find I'm not ill, not in need of her ministrations. However much I'd enjoy her care.

***

I feel soft lips on my cheek and smell the faint perfume of Estée Lauder Beautiful. My darling Susan is leaning over me, her features taut with concern. I smile at her, or hope that's how it appears to her, and fumble for the wand control. She has switched on the light beside Jeff's bed. It must be quite late.

"Mother, darling. You're awake. Oh, God." She puts her arms round me, and hugs me tight, and I feel her shaking. "You got me quite worried, you know that?" Then she lets me go and I raise the bed until I'm sitting up, while she perches on the side of the mattress, gazing at me. "Let me look at you. How're you feeling now?"

190

"Much better, thank you, darling." And I am. A complete thought, without hesitation. I'm sure it came out as intended. Oh, glory. Try some more. "How was your flight?" There. I'm back to normal. Thank God.

"Very crowded. I was really, really lucky to get on. Seemed as though everyone's coming down to Cornwall for the bank holiday."

"Oh, dear. Bad timing. What about your restaurant?"

"Frank'll cope. Don't worry about that. You're much more important."

"I'm delighted to see you, my darling. But as you see, I'm fine. Just a storm in a teacup."

"You look a bit battered to me."

"That's a nice thing to say to your mother."

"I shouldn't have woken you really. I'll just sort out the bedding and take this tray down, then join you. You are sure you don't mind me sleeping here?"

"Of course. My idea."

She raises her eyebrows at that. "Oh my. An honour."

Speech is back. What about the rest of me? A trip to the bathroom will be revealing. As Susan picks up the tray, I swivel my legs round to pull myself to a standing position. I'm weak and wobbly, but that's probably because I've been asleep. Come on, stupid legs, move. Feet, you're on a soft carpet, stop making such a performance of moving from one spot to another. Slippers? No. Never mind that refinement. Now, one foot and then the other. Good. Right hand holding on to furniture, just as a precaution. Out onto the landing. Shuffling now. Into the bathroom, shut the door. I can manage everything really, except that my left hand still appears resistant. Never mind. Everything else seems fine. And it's not even twenty four hours. What a relief.

I complete my ablutions as well as I can with one adequate and one recalcitrant hand, make my molasses-slow way back to bed. I feel triumphant. I managed entirely by myself. And my arthritic aches appear to be taking a holiday. The proverbial silver lining.

38

Irene

The game of musical tea-cups so recently instituted among my visitors ends in the undoubted victory of the incumbent: Susan, who has a bed in my room, is the one to wake me as she brings a tray of tea for us both.

"You really got everyone worried, Mother dear," she tells me as she pours out. "The Dreaded Danielle seems calm enough, but Dave – he's clacketing on like an old man with half his marbles. I swear he sounds as though he's the one had a stroke, not you."

I laugh, and then wish I hadn't. The arthritis is back, dammit. Every joint is screeching, just in case I might have imagined heart problems gave immunity.

"Susan! What's your poor brother done to deserve that?"

Oh, my bloody hips. Do, for pity's sake, let up for a while. It's a bank holiday weekend, mining should come to a standstill.

She puts the tea on my bedside table, makes sure I have the wand control, and my pillows are adjusted comfortably, then installs herself on the bed beside me.

"Perhaps I shouldn't say anything. But he does go on. I expect he's told you about this film thing of his, has he?" I nod. "Of course it's important to him. But he is being a bit – how should I put it?"

"Single-minded?" I sip the warming liquid, feel an almost imperceptible relaxation of clamorous muscles. I should be accustomed to this tedious morning process. The tangles in my muscles always need time to unwind.

"Maybe. Bloody bossy is more what I had in mind. Perhaps being married to Dani the Diva has rubbed off on him."

"I must tell you, Susie darling, Danielle has been splendid. I really can't hear anything against her."

Susan turns to me, her mouth hanging open in half-genuine, half-theatrical surprise.

"Danielle? Your overbearing, impossible daughter-in-law? You know, the one who wants to hoink you out of this lovely house and plonk you in a nursing home? You lost your marbles too?"

I laugh, and it's not so painful this time. "The same. She's been kind and thoughtful, ever since I had this unfortunate incident. Really she's very generous. Give her a chance. I think you'd like her."

Susan snorts. "Hmmph. I'd never have guessed. Not in a million years. What on earth has been going on down here?"

She gets up to pour us both a second cup. I reach for my medication bag. My left arm aches rather badly, and I don't seem to be able to move it very well. Forget it. I try to push out the pills and capsules from their foil, while Susan settles back again on the bed.

"Here, give me those tablets, your fingers obviously could do with a rest." Reluctantly, I cede temporary defeat on the medication front. "How's my Ali?"

"Lovely, as always. Said she wants to stay here and look after me until the baby comes."

"She can't do that. Now can she, Mother?"

"No, not really. But I don't want her to feel I've let her down."

"It would be easier, Mother, if you would simply refuse to have her here."

"Do you mean that? Isn't it better to let her choose for herself?"

"Yeah, perhaps. It's just..." Oh, my poor Susie. Her lovely oval face is beginning to be filled with worry lines, across her forehead, down beside her mouth, in the corners of her eyes. "If she'd just come home, Frank and I could sort something out. It is our grandchild. And I do really want her to go to university,"

I stretch out my good hand to caress her shoulder. "Darling, that'd be wonderful. Just tell her that and she'll make the right choice."

There's a gentle rap on the door, and I call, "Come in."

Alicia scurries in and pushes the door shut, as though a fugitive from pursuers too near for comfort. "Oh, Mum. I'm so glad you're here. I been sick, and I feel awful." She throws herself into her mother's arms, only missing an embarrassing accident because her mother has finished her tea. The cup wobbles in the saucer, and Susan hastily hands it to me before hugging her daughter tight. Tears cascade down both their cheeks. I feel distinctly de trop.

I turn away, finish taking my medication. Getting up seems like a good idea. Just after eight. I wonder when the stair-lift people will arrive. Patrick will probably come about noon, after morning surgery. And Charles at three this afternoon. There. My memory is good as ever.

"Er, sorry, Grandma. I ignored you earlier. How're you feeling today?"

I turn to see a very tousled, whey-faced young woman, tear-streaked and woe-begone. Morning sickness. Reality is starting to assail her.

"I'm very much better, thank you, Alicia darling. See? I can talk properly and move about. I hope it's all over."

"That's cool, Grandma. I'm so happy for you."

"You feeling under the weather, darling?"

"Yeah, a bit."

"Good thing your mother's here, isn't it? Much nicer for you, when you feel grotty."

She disentangles herself from her mother and stands up. "I better get dressed. See ya."

As the door swings behind her, I manoeuvre my argumentative body to a standing position. "I shall wash and dress now, Susan. Tell Danielle, if she comes to help, I think I can manage now."

"She won't. I told her last night I'd take over. After all, I'm right here."

Through the open window I see a thin veil of white cloud, too fragile in places to conceal patches of speedwell blue sky. Sunshine filters through the trees to the east, spills patches of light onto the garden. No noticeable wind, the only discernible movement a wren in the golden David Austin rose bush. Good weather improves everyone's temper, so, with a bit of luck, we'll get through the next couple of days without too many ructions.

Susan collects my underwear and the cream silk blouse I select, carries them to my bathroom, where I can dress in seclusion. The skirt I was wearing yesterday appears to have been thrown in a heap on the floor. Never mind. I have others.

I try to insist on being left alone, but it soon becomes obvious that I can't manage without help. Not even to take off my night things.

"I could lift you in and out of the bath, if you'd like," Susan suggests, but I'm not inflicting my wrinkled body on her either.

"Don't be absurd, darling. I'd break your back. I think I could do with one of those clever devices with a motor, to lift me in and out."

"I'll get Jilly to find suppliers on the internet, if you like. Get the best deal that way."

"No, no. My plumber can sort it out."

Perhaps Susan or David could try to get hold of young plumber Mike's mobile, while I deal with Patrick. And the stair-lift man. And Charles. Mike's usually helpful, and I really would like him to come up today, if he can, just to assess the situation. Before the holiday weekend shuts everything down.

As my left arm is totally useless, I do let Susan help sponge my upper body, then put on my bra, fasten it at the back. Underwear, blouse, skirt, sandals – all demand some intervention from my willing helper, despite my repeated attempts to prove I can manage alone. This is a damned nuisance.

"You're going to need help like this for a while, Mother."

"No, no. You'll see. It'll be gone very soon. I'm fine now, thank you, darling. I can deal with face and hair myself."

"Mother dear, I am delighted to report you're as stubborn as ever." Susan kisses me on the nose. "I shall go get us both some breakfast."

No amount of Clinique Repairwear face cream will deal with the ravages, I realize. Eyesight is not all it was, but the droop on one side is so marked, I have the horrible notion it may never disappear, and the crevasses down my cheeks are canyons. A horrible sight. Pity I can't wear a mask.

The long mirror on the landing startles me. I look very bent this morning. Like an old woman. And my clothes are draped over me, as though on a washing line. I try to straighten up, but it's an effort, and my back seems to want to shrink down, curl up. Bloody useless spineless spine. Another few days of maintaining the façade, that's all that's required. Surely you can manage that, stupid body. They'll be gone soon.

When I come to negotiate the stairs, I realize that David's – no, Alicia's – stair-lift is exactly what I could do with right now. The banisters are on my left side going down, and that hand is really not to be relied on to stop me falling. I manage the first short flight of three steps to the half-landing, but at the top of the main staircase, I teeter hesitantly. I'd rather not fall, and I don't trust my body not to falter at the crucial moment. Strange to feel so alienated from all the physical elements that make me me. I don't trust them. And yet, that's all there is of me. This useless, failing collection of bone and sinew and flesh and blood and nerve endings. Lots of nerve endings. And memories. Nothing else.

Slowly I sink down, sit on the top step, laughing inside at the discovery: I'm schizophrenic. Must be. To insist on the me that is my mind being separate from the me that is my perfidious body.

I wonder if either of my children would find this situation funny? Probably not. I do. I sit at the top of the stairs, enjoying myself. Really, the whole set-up is farcical and the only thing to do is laugh. As Albert Camus said, life is absurd.

"Daddy! Daddee! Come quick!" Simon rushes in from the garden, and I can hear panic in his voice.

David hurries into the hall below me. "What is it, Simon?"

"You must come. The big cat from next door is eating a pigeon, and it's still alive!"

"Don't be silly."

"It is, really. Really. I tried to make the cat go away, and the poor pigeon was trying to flap its wings and the cat was eating its body." He is near tears now. "Please, Daddy. You need to kill the pigeon. Please."

"Right. Come on, then. Show me where it is." He strides outside after his son. Poor Simon. The more you examine nature, the more cruel you discover it is.

I sit on, consider whether I should try bumping down from step to step on my bottom, like a small child. It might work. You do have to be able to control your muscles to some extent whatever you choose to do, and I am not convinced I can rely on mine to do as I wish.

Alicia comes out of the kitchen and sees me still perched at the top of the stairs.

"Grandma? What're you doing?" She climbs up to me. "Do you need help?"

I give her what I hope is a rueful smile. "I do, rather. I'm a bit stuck." I have a foolish desire to giggle like a silly schoolgirl.

"Hold on to me. You need to stand up."

I look at this slim teenage girl, and envisage the two of us tumbling down to the hard wooden floor below.

"You know, darling. I think your uncle would be the best person. Could you tell him? When he comes back indoors."

She frowns. "I can do it."

"Trouble is. My muscles seem to have seized up and I don't think I can move."

"Oh, dear." She sits on the stair below me. "Good thing, yeah, you're gonna have a stair-lift?"

"As it turns out, it's a brilliant idea. What made you think of it, you clever girl?"

"My friend Julie's Gran is living with them, right, and they got one. I had a go on it. You'll like it, Grandma."

"You feeling better?"

"Mmm. Grandma. Would you, like, think me awful if I, like, go home with Mum?"

I look at her pale worried face, and know that she could never have coped. Her loving offer of care was an adolescent fantasy. Poor darling. I wish I could have offered proper help, and not seen her feel she has failed me. Because it was, strictly speaking, I who failed her.

"Darling, I think you've made the right decision."

"You don't mind?"

"Of course not. I just want you to do what makes you happiest. And I expect your parents will help you to get to university if you let them."

"Love you, Grandma."

"Love you, too."

39

Irene

A sharp ring at the front door makes Alicia and me both jump, principally because the sound-box has been tucked just under the ceiling at the bottom of the stairs, a position designed to allow me to hear it where-ever I am in the house. Where I'm sitting now, it's uncomfortably loud.

Danielle emerges promptly from the kitchen, followed by Tanya and, more slowly, by Susan, who glances up and sees us both at the top of the stairs. She raises one eyebrow, and shakes her head at us with a grin, but says nothing. Voices clash and mingle in the conservatory, like an orchestra tuning up. I hear Simon wail loudly, "But the cat will eat it if you go away." And David reply, "This is important, Simon. I'm sure you can chase the cat away now." The outer door slams.

Then David ushers into the hall a short, dapper little man, with a pink bald head fringed with neat grey hair, a toothbrush moustache, wearing a dark brown suit, shiny brown brogues, a startling multi-coloured tie, and carrying a large briefcase. They walk towards the stairs, and the entire family gathers in an untidy semi-circle, like spectators at a circus, and gazes up at Alicia and me. She waves.

"Hi, Uncle. We need your help up here."

"My mother, Mrs Harper," he tells the little dapper chap. "Mother, may I present Mr Finch of Third-Age Mobility Services?"

"How do you do, Mr Finch?"

He bows in a courtly manner, and slowly climbs the stairs. "Ma'am."

"Please forgive me for not standing up, but I appear to be stuck." A childish giggle struggles to escape my throat.

"I infer that you are nicely demonstrating your urgent need for one of our products, Madam. I shall be very happy to help. May I assist you in descending?"

An educated salesman with an elegant turn of phrase. I shall enjoy this. No doubt it will cost. Yes, I see a Rolex, if I am not mistaken. At least he's not wearing a diamond ring, like that loss adjuster from the insurance company when a pipe burst.

"I think, if you don't mind, I'll ask my son to carry me down. Could you do that, David darling? I don't seem able to move." The giggle has invaded my voice, and Mr Finch smiles involuntarily. David carries me down to my reclining chair, and the crowd follows. "Thank you. Now, Mr Finch, please tell us what you could do for us, as a matter of some urgency."

He places his leather briefcase on the coffee table, snaps it open to extract several large, glossy brochures showing glossy interiors and glossy white stairways carpeted in oatmeal, and smiling faces of extraordinarily well-preserved glossy people beside their neatly-installed glossy chair-lifts. He hands them to me, then perches on the settee, and gently brushes his fingers together.

"I shall make coffee," Danielle says, as Tanya slides round my chair, leans on my thigh, and stares at the top picture. "Would you like a cup, Mr Finch?"

"That would be very welcome, Ma'am."

I gently try to shift Tanya to a more comfortable position.

"I asked you here today, Mr Finch, because we need a lift immediately. That right, Mother?" I nod. I'll never get rid of them, if I can't manage the stairs alone.

"Well now, Mr Harper. And Madam. A straight lift to the half landing, that is, to where you were sitting, Ma'am, a simple straight could be installed within 24 hours. And because I can see that this is a true emergency, I could, if you wish, arrange for work to be done tomorrow. Even though it's a bank holiday weekend."

"Why not today? As I thought I arranged yesterday?"

"Until I have measured the staircase, Mr Harper, I am unable to promise any more. That is to say, at the moment."

"Right. And you are talking about one that would go just up to the half landing, but not round the corner and up the next short flight?"

"Precisely, Mr Harper."

"So what if we need to go all the way up?"

"Ah, then, that would require what is known as a curved lift, and that has to be made to measure. As I am sure you understand, all staircases are different. Nevertheless, we are very prompt, so it would only take two, maybe three weeks." He hands David a brochure. "You will see several illustrated there."

"David, I think time is of the essence, don't you? I mean, it is the steep first bit that is my problem. It would be nice to have a lift that goes the whole way, but you don't want to stay here until it's installed, do you?"

"Well, well, Mother. The first confession of weakness I've heard from you!" I hadn't realized Susan was behind my chair.

I turn to laugh at her. "Your mother is a realist. I did get stuck this morning, and would rather it didn't happen again."

"How do you do, Madam," says dapper Mr Finch, directing a mini bow towards Susan. "I wonder, Ma'am," he adds, addressing me. "I wonder if it might be a good idea if I took some measurements? Then we can talk more realistically about delivery."

"And costs, Mr Finch." He nods. I recognize the symptoms. One does not talk price until the customer is hooked. I hope this house is worth as much as I think it should be.

"Thank you, Ma'am." He extracts from his briefcase a retractable tape measure, a second measuring device that assesses dimensions by laser beam, a printed yellow pad clipped to a board and a pen. He is followed by an inquisitive Tanya, and more slowly, by her father.

"Can I bring you some breakfast, Mother? Danielle has made one of her fruit salads. Looks good. Even Frank would approve."

"Sounds lovely, Susan darling. With some yoghurt, please. And I'll have a cup of that coffee she's making. Told you she came up trumps, in lots of ways."

"Mmm. Got the picture."

Susan disappears, only to be replaced shortly afterwards by a shocked-looking Simon.

"Come here, Simon. Something horrid happened?" I put my arm round the boy and he leans against me, breathing heavily.

"That black cat, you know? From next door? It was eating a pigeon when it was still alive. When it was *alive*, Granma." He breathes deeply, and I can hear the still unshed tears. "And do you know? It wouldn't go away, even when I got a stick and hit it."

"Oh, dear. That is horrid."

"Dad got your axe, and chopped off the poor pigeon's head, and then the seeds in its crop scattered all over the place, and it was just horrible! It really, really was."

"It sounds dreadful. Poor you, to see that."

"Granma, how can a nasty cat eat a bird while it's still alive? It's just ... I can't think of the right words, it's so horrible."

"What did you do after Daddy put the poor bird out of its misery?"

"I put it in a cardboard box. Like a coffin. Cat didn't like that, and it slunk off."

"That's good."

"Yeah." He smiles at last, and then confides: "I gave it a funeral. A proper one. I wanted somebody to care, so I did."

"What a splendid idea. Where did you put the grave?"

"Down in the wood part, near a beech tree. I dug a deep hole, Grandma. And I gave it a slate head thing, too, and I carved its name on with a sharp stone. Didn't have much room, so I just put 'Pigeon'."

"That sounds really good. Do you feel better now you've buried it properly?"

"Yeah." The tension seems to have left him finally. "I knew you'd think it was a good idea. Dad said it'd be silly, but he's wrong. Isn't he, Granma?"

"If you feel good about it, that's what matters." We grin at each other, like conspirators. "I'm a naughty grandma really, but you don't have to let on."

"No," he says in a low voice full of laughter. "Don't worry. I won't."

40

Irene

Patrick arrives while David and Mr Finch are still negotiating: I have the impression that both pride themselves on their astuteness. My task will simply be to write a cheque. I hope my son is as good at bargaining as he appears to believe.

"How're you feeling today, Irene?" I gaze up at this tall, gangly doctor with his wide grin, and his air of striding into the cricket pavilion after scoring a century for his county. He's the one doctor I trust.

"Much better, thank you, Patrick."

"Good. Language back. Any problems?"

I hesitate. But soon, I hope, I'll be on my own, and I do need to know exactly what the situation is.

"Just a bit. With my left arm."

"Yes. And I can see the left side of your face is affected. Can you manage the stairs?"

I laugh at that. "Usually. Funnily enough, my son is negotiating about a stair-lift as we speak."

"I need to examine you, Irene. Properly. In your bedroom, where we can be private. If you want someone to be with you ...?"

"Of course, not." I look around, see Susan hovering near. "Could you tell David, darling? I think it might take me too long to climb those stairs."

I manoeuvre until I'm ready to stand, and realize I haven't got my stick. Nor have I any idea where it is. Oh dear. Not sure I can make it as far as the stairs. Fortunately, David appears.

"You need to go upstairs, Ma?"

"Please."

He lifts me in what is becoming a practised manner, and carries me up into the bedroom, gently lays me down on my bed. "I hope that will be one of the last times you need me to carry you." He grins at me, triumphant. "The stair-lift should be installed today, believe it or not."

"Clever you. And thanks."

Patrick plonks his black bag on the chest at the end of my bed, while I scrabble once again for the wand control. Susan puts her head round the door.

"All right if I come in?"

"If you must." I pat Jeff's bed beside me, and she sits there, clearly anxious. "Don't say a word."

Patrick proceeds to make all the usual examinations: takes my blood pressure, listens to my heart at rather too much length, manipulates my limbs, palpates the left arm, shoulder, neck, finds the deep pain that spreads up into my cheek.

"Right, Irene. You have some residual damage, so we can no longer consider that was a TIA. Obviously you have had a cerebral accident. But I suspect something else has been going on. Did you have any other troubles? A possible heart attack perhaps, just before this stroke?"

I think back. Actually, yes. I remember being on the stairs, caught by an impossible, crushing pain in my chest. I couldn't breathe. David coming to my rescue. Aspirin. Using my spray, several times. Lying in my chair, trying to deal with what I assumed was a very bad bout of angina. It went on for a long time, and I thought then it might be a heart attack. But it went away in the end.

I don't know what to say. This is going to mean I won't be left alone. I can see that.

"Right." Patrick's patience is wearing thin. Oh, Lord. "I'd like you to go to hospital right away. You need immediate drug treatment."

"I hear what you say, Patrick. But I don't want to go to hospital. Ever."

He flashes a smile. "Yes. I know. And we both know you have the right to refuse treatment. But I'd really like you to reconsider this time, Irene, because it looks as though you had another myocardial infarct. And the cerebral accident was probably caused by a part of the infarct breaking away and lodging in your brain."

Dammit, it's happening too soon. How can I get rid of them all before Death finally lays her skeletal hands on me?

"This is serious, Irene. Three heart attacks and a stroke in layperson terms. Even without tests, I should warn you that another attack may be imminent. You need clot-busting drugs only the hospital can give you."

I shake my head and wish my daughter was not listening.

He sighs. Then he takes out what looks like a large mobile phone, or very small computer, on which he presses numerous keys, frowning. "I've told the office you need an ECG and blood tests today. Arrange them with the nurse, please – I assume one of your family can take you in? And I want to see you in the surgery first thing Monday morning."

"Monday? You sure? It's a bank holiday."

"Tuesday then. Be there. Unless you want me to wash my hands of you."

"Patrick! Don't say that. Please. You're the only one I trust."

"Just as well we go back such a long way, or I'd pass you on to one of my unsuspecting partners." He winks. Thank heaven. Back to our old joke.

"Don't you dare. Or I'll tell them I caught you smoking by the dustbins."

He laughs. This is true, though hardly a secret. Everyone knows that Dr Carr smokes, and his partner, Dr Olde, drinks to excess, and the heart consultant is obese. We do have excellent role models in our local doctors.

"I'm glad to see you're being looked after by your family. Goodbye, Irene, I can let myself out." He nods in a friendly manner to Susan, to whom I suppose he was not introduced, and disappears.

"Well, Mother dear. This is serious, isn't it?"

"No. I don't think so."

She stands up, folds her arms and glares. "You are an impossible woman. I'll speak to Dave. We have to do something."

Why do all these middle-aged adults, who are old enough to know better, assume they should take over my life rather than let me decide?

I am just girding the loin ready for battle, and trying to recall where I last had that elusive walking stick, when David knocks and comes in.

"Do you want to stay here, Mother, or shall I take you down?"

"Downstairs, please."

"The contract is ready for you to sign, if you agree."

I discover all the adults gathered together in the living room, drinking coffee. Installed in my chair once again, I gratefully accept the cup Danielle offers, sip the hot, tangy liquid with pleasure. A caffeine buzz is exactly what I need. Life is becoming tediously fraught.

"Well, Ma'am, I have talked to Mr Harper, and I hope we have come up with a pleasing solution to your difficulties. May I show you the contract?"

I smile what is undoubtedly a lop-sided, but, I hope, friendly smile, and Mr Finch places a document of several pages into my hand. Fortunately, I remembered to hang my glasses round my neck, and I scan the details, and the blurb, examine the key questions: cost, installation date, guarantee. The total sum due on completion makes me blink.

"It *is* a lot of money," David acknowledges handsomely. "But it can be installed right away, and you'll be able to use it tonight."

"There is, Ma'am, a premium involved, if I am to arrange installation so late in the day before a holiday weekend." Mr Finch puts his fringed bald head to one side, like a moulted robin watching for a worm. I can almost imagine him whistling chirpily. "I know you will understand that, Ma'am."

"Yes. I understand. Can I put it on a credit card?"

"Could you write a cheque for, let us say, ten per cent of the total? Then we can go ahead with the installation, and I will arrange for the balance to be accepted on your card. Can't say fairer than that, can I?"

I realize the cheque can't possibly be cleared until Tuesday at the earliest, by which time I can have arranged to transfer savings. I did say I could pay for whatever services I might need, though I am quite aware that this, plus any professional nurse that may be imposed on me, will noticeably deplete my savings. So I sign, and write the cheque, and David and Mr Finch are garlanded with smiles. Then the dapper little man struts out onto the terrace and speaks into a mobile.

David lets out a theatrical sigh, raises his arms like an Olympic winner. "What a relief. You'll now be able to manoeuvre the stairs, Mother."

"Yes, darling, thank you for arranging it. I can see it will be A Good Thing."

"Listen, everyone," Susan says. "Before we get inundated with chaps putting up the lift, we have things we need to discuss."

"I don't think so, Susan. My consultation with my doctor was private. Even if you *were* present."

"What now?" David looks as deceived as the England football coach watching his team go down to defeat. My goodness, yet another sporting image. Watching television *is* affecting my brain.

"I thought so," Danielle says, razor-sharp voice returned. "You need live-in help, don't you, Irene?"

"No. I do not." Not really.

"You both need to know that her doctor thinks she should go to hospital immediately."

"He agreed I have the right to refuse. Which I have."

I see them all staring at me. Danielle now looks as though made of marble. If her thoughts were broadcast, I feel sure we would hear over and over, '*I knew this would happen. Bloody-minded old harridan. Fantasy-ridden family. I told them, but no one ever listens.*' David is frowning, probably wondering what more he has to do before he can escape to make his film. And Susan, new to this fraught family debate, wrinkling her brows, expecting everyone to cooperate to find the best practical solution.

"So what are we supposed to do now, Mother?" David demands. "Ignore your doctor's advice? Leave you on your own, when we know you can't cope?"

"Not only that," Susan adds, "she has to have a lot of tests which she should be phoning about right now. At the surgery in the village. And Dr Carr wants to see her first thing Tuesday morning. So how are we going to arrange that?"

"What are these tests? What does he think is wrong?"

"An ECG, I think, and blood tests because he thinks she had a third heart attack. And it was not a transient thingummy, it was a full-blown stroke."

"My God, Mother!"

"A *mild* stroke, David. As you hear, I can talk again. No harm done."

They all stare at me as though I'm speaking some incomprehensible language.

"Have you looked in the mirror?" Susan asks, and she too sounds angry. "*And* Dr Carr said she could have another heart attack any time. This is ridiculous. I'm going to phone right now and make an appointment. I assume you can take her over, Dave?" He nods, still looking shaken, and she disappears.

"Well, Irene. At least you'll have a professional nurse now, won't you?"

"I don't *need* nursing, Danielle. You did a wonderful job, and now I'm sure I can cope. Especially with this stair-lift. So long as I can move around the house, I don't need anyone living here. I have lots of other help, you know, when you're not around."

Danielle sighs and David puts his head in his hands. Sounds of men tramping into the house assail us, and Danielle quickly goes out, apparently directs them to bring the equipment in through the back way. She really has taken charge.

Susan marches back in: she too is exercising her ability to organise. "Right, Mother. I have arranged for you to see the Practice Nurse at three. She'll do the ECG, but there may be some problems about the blood tests, because it's so late in the day, and all the labs apparently close over the weekend. She'll try and sort it out, and let you know when you see her." She turns to her brother. "Would you be all right if I drove your car? That way, you can make sure the lift people do their stuff?"

"Yes, sure. Just don't scratch it in these narrow Cornish lanes."

"Cheek. I drive in London, for heaven's sake. You don't need to worry about little things like that."

They grin at each other, relaxing in the thought that, together, they will manage to sort out their mother.

"There *is* a problem," I venture, but David hastily tells me, "There *isn't*, Mother."

"Well, I think there is. I'm supposed to see Charles Boscawen at three. Here. And it's important."

"Mother, *really!*" Susan says impatiently. "Your tests are important. So let Dave sort out whatever it is."

"He's your solicitor, isn't he?" I nod. "Tell me what you want, and I'll deal with it. Can't be that complicated, surely?"

"Except that he should be bringing papers for me to sign."

"He can leave them, can't he? A few days aren't going to matter."

It's true I have managed to avoid being carted off to hospital while they're all in the house. So far.

"I also want him to arrange for a valuation on the house. I *might* sell, but I'm really thinking about equity release, so you might ask for information about that, if you would."

"Does that mean financial worries?" David is frowning again.

"The stair-lift will make a dent in my savings, which I use to live on. Not to mention if I have a professional nurse. Equity release might be a solution."

"Yes. I can see that. I'll ask him for whatever help he can give."

"Thank you, darling."

"You never said you were worried about money, Mother." Susan sounds like a barrister who has caught out a hostile witness.

"Heavens. Why would I? I'm not destitute, I'm just concerned that all the extra expenses my decrepitude is leading to will deplete my savings, until I can't pay my bills. Surely any intelligent person would take precautions."

"Sounds eminently sensible, Irene." Danielle has returned. Susan glares at her. "I saw the children coming up the garden, and it's lunch-time. Would a scratch meal of bread and cheese and salad suit everyone?"

"Good idea, Dani. I'll come and help you." I have never seen David so eager to assist in food preparation. The two escape to the kitchen.

Susan frowns at me like a stern schoolmarm. "I shall stay on for a couple of days, Mother, and see if you really *can* manage on your own. I'm afraid, right now, I'm feeling a bit cross with you."

I laugh at that. I know my face is distorted, and I look like a haggard old crone. But inside, I am still me: Irene May Harper, *née* Marshall, somewhere in my forties most of the time, happy to live the life I have made here, in this house. You sound just like me, Susan. As I was then. And as I feel, deep down, I continue to be.

I see Death at the window, grinning those tombstone teeth, tapping skeletal fingers on the glass, and I shake my head. No, not yet. Wait till they are gone. Please.

41

Danielle

The children's voices twittered and chirped just outside like frantic nestlings, and their tiresome cousin called through the open door of the conservatory: "Aunt Dani, could you come a moment, please?"

Danielle strode through from the kitchen, anxiety crouched on her shoulders, clutching her hair. "What's happened?"

"Nothing. We just got a bit muddy, so I thought we could clean up in the garden shower room. If you could get us some towels, please, and some clean clothes for the kids?"

Simon and Tanya were giggling inanely, looking as though they'd been on a marine assault course. How dared she? "You two, go and take those filthy things off. In the annex. Your cousin will join you in a minute." They scampered off.

"I'm first in the shower," Simon shouted.

"No, me first!"

Danielle turned back to her irresponsible brat of a niece: "Wait there."

Then she made her way upstairs, past a workman preparing to drill holes through Irene's new crimson stair carpet, collected three beach towels, as well as clothes for Simon and Tanya. Irene wouldn't appreciate having her good towels ruined as well as her carpet: without proper supervision, the children were bound to dry themselves still streaked with mud, and then drop the towels in a soggy heap on a wet and filthy floor. And who was going to clear that up?

Susan appeared to be faffing around in Irene's bedroom, well out of the way of the mayhem caused by her own daughter. Nice for some. Danielle was glad to help her frail old mother-in-law, but she was fed up with being the one everyone else relied on. If she were not here, nothing would get done, no one would be fed at the proper time, no one would wash the dishes, collect the washing, pack the suitcases for tomorrow. She'd like to escape the lot of them. She should be out there, striding along a long, sandy beach somewhere. Feeling her muscles come alive and the blood flow through her limbs. Entirely alone.

"Thanks, Aunt Dani. See ya."

Danielle watched Alicia run round the house. No daughter of mine will ever behave like you, she thought, and her hands wrung her niece's phantom neck.

Sounds of drilling invaded her skull. She decided to set lunch outside, under the awning. It was summer after all, even if the sky had turned the grey of well-used sheets. If necessary, Irene could be tucked up in a blanket. She just hoped the children would not be disturbed by the poor woman's distorted face. And that they knew better than to comment. Who could tell what effect the company of a selfish, irresponsible slut was having on their behaviour?

David was preparing his own version of a vinaigrette, shaking the screw-top jar so vigorously, its contents had started to solidify.

"Who's the villain you're shaking to death then? That brat, Alicia?"

He laughed, briefly. "No, I'll leave her to you, Dani. It's my bloody-minded mother gets me. How can she refuse to go into hospital? Even when her own doctor says she should?"

"I'm not staying beyond tomorrow. I mean that."

"Fine. I heard you. So what are we going to do about her?"

Danielle shrugged, started setting out cold meats and cheese on wine-coloured Perspex plates designed for use in the garden. "Lord knows. Let's get this lunch over, and see what Susan learns this afternoon. I've said all I have to say."

She carried a laden tray outside, started setting the table with cloth, cutlery, plates of meat and cheese, bread and butter. Tanya skipped past, long golden curls now darkened into sodden tangles, followed by Simon with an armful of muddy clothes.

"Put those in the laundry room, please. In a separate pile on the floor."

"Okay."

I'd better just put them in a plastic bag to take home, Danielle thought. No time to wash and dry them now.

Through the open window, she saw Tanya run into the sitting room,

211

eyes gleaming with mischief. "Grammar! Guess what? We ate lots and lots and lots of blackberries."

"Did you? I didn't know they were ripe yet," Irene said, comfortably relieved of any responsibility.

"Not all. We saw lots of green ones, Granma."

So thanks to the Slut, we can expect both children to have stomach ache.

"Where did you go, Simon?" their grandmother asked.

"Up the valley. You know, where the cows are. There's lots of blackberry bushes, and we didn't have anything to put them in. So we had to eat them."

"I can see that. And was it muddy?" Both children looked at each other and giggled. "What have you been up to?"

"Simon made a mud slide."

"You're not s'posed to tell, Tani. Ali said. Grown-ups think it's naughty." Yes indeed.

"Grammar won't be cross. Will you, Grammar?"

Irene laughed, of course. "Oh, dear. I'm not cross. But it was a bit naughty, if your parents would be cross about it." They both looked suitably downcast. That was something. "And did Alicia have a go too?"

At this, they both nodded conspiratorially, and giggled together again. And then the Slut appeared, wrapped in a brightly-coloured beach towel, sarong-style, long black hair half-rubbed dry and in a tangled mess round her head.

"I'll leave our muddy shoes outside."

"For heaven's sake, go and get properly dressed, Alicia. And please don't flaunt yourself in front of the workmen as you go up."

"Never change, do you, Aunt? Perhaps I'll become, like, a streetwalker. You know, give you something real to sneer at me for."

"Ali! Please don't talk like that." Susan had deigned to appear. "Not to your aunt. Not to anyone."

"Oh, Mother, gimme a break. The woman's a bitch. See you all in a minute."

Simon and Tanya were staring at each other, mouths slipped open.

Danielle heard men's voices on the stairs, then Alicia, and laughter.

"Go and sit down at the table," she told the children.

"Simon. Have you any idea what happened to my stick?"

"Yeah, I know. I'll get it."

"It's all right, Irene. David will come and help you."

But no one appeared to be taking any notice of her so far as Danielle could see. They'd soon notice if she didn't make lunch though.

"Did your face hurt, Grammar?" Tanya asked.

Danielle saw the woman try to touch her left cheek with her hand, and could feel her frustration.

"Not very much, sweetheart," Irene said. "It's more that it's a nuisance. And looks horrid, doesn't it?"

"It looks hurt." The little girl reached out and caressed the sagging jaw.

"Oh, my darling," Irene said, and Danielle felt tears welling up in her eyes, in her throat.

"I'm hungry. Come on, Grammar."

"Lean on me, Irene," Danielle said.

Irene gave her a lop-sided smile. "Just as well you're a strong woman, Danielle my dear. In every sense. Thank you for keeping it all going."

42

Irene

Lunch is more relaxed than I expected, principally because we're all outside where the sun has at last found a patch of clear sky. Sitting upright in a chair increases the interminable complaints from back and hips and legs, so I retire to a lounger beside them.

Alicia returns in a startling African-print wrap-around skirt and two skimpy sleeveless tops, neither long enough to cover her bare midriff. Danielle eyes her with unmistakeable disdain. I do hope she can avoid verbal criticism, as Susan would then join the fray; she hates anyone to criticise her children, just as does Danielle.

My colourful granddaughter escapes the otherwise inevitable post-mortem on her muddy excursion with the children when I remember my bath problem and ask David to phone the plumber. This turns the Inquisitors' attention back to delinquent me.

"Of course I'll try to contact this Mike, Mother. But I'd like to know how you imagine we can go away tomorrow, knowing that you have so many difficulties coping?"

"I don't. I cope very well. I'd just like to have a proper bath. That's all."

The two women share a shrug and grimace that says 'Irene/Mother is back with the fairies', two former enemies united in condemnation of this tiresome old woman.

"Please be realistic, Irene. We both know you *couldn't* have managed yesterday," Danielle says. "I know you dislike it if I say things like that. But *really*. We were both *there*."

"Why're you all being nasty to Granma?" demands Simon.

His mother turns to him angrily. "Just stay out of this. Eat your food, and be quiet."

Simon glares at his mother, and Tanya grins.

"We have to go, Mother." Susan comes over to my lounger. "Do you need to go upstairs? Or fetch anything? I don't want us to be late."

Twenty five minutes to three. For a journey that takes five. Ten at the outside.

"I'd like to visit the bathroom, as a precaution. One last time, David, if you could help me?"

"Course I will, Ma." He stands up, leans over me with his dentifrice smile. "Come on, old thing. I might as well carry you all the way. Be quicker."

I laugh. "Muscle Man, eh? Hope I don't break your back."

He lifts me up, and he does seem to have become quite good at carrying me. Practice, I suppose. I can't be that light, even if eating has lost its appeal for a while. I enjoy milk, and Danielle's flavoured milk that she calls *caffe latte*, and occasionally a few spoonfuls of yoghurt and fruit. Oh, and that thin slice of bread and butter. So I'm not starving myself.

"You'll not be needing that hulking great chap to ferry you places for long, Missus."

"Glad to hear it. He's not as reliable as a machine, you know."

The two men laugh as David makes his way past the partially-installed rail.

"Ai offer Modom a Personal Service, don't you know?" David says in a parody of a Hollywood butler, and one of the men responds:

"End Ai'm sure Modom fully deserves it."

"Modom is truly grateful," I call, before I am deposited in the bathroom, and David shuts the door behind him. Won't be long now. Independent living is a boon not always appreciated until it is taken from you. I want my freedom of choice back. Even if I am severely restricted by the realities of old age.

My reflection tells me I am not improving. Everything sags on the right – no, left side. Eyebrow, eyelid, cheek, corner of mouth, neck. I suppose I should be grateful I have my speech back. And I am. Hair looks awful, but I brush it into some sort of shape and give it a quick spray. Skin ghastly. Leave it. Time running short. Glasses? On chain, round my neck. Bag? Ask David to collect from chair in bedroom. Stick? Downstairs. Right. That's it.

May this afternoon not bring any more unpleasant surprises.

43

Irene

"**I** shall come in with you, Mother, if that's all right."

"Oh, darling. That's not at all necessary. Thank you." I see Susan press her lips together. "Turning's just up there, on the right. Parking's at the back."

"I think one of us needs to know exactly what's going on with you, Mother. I don't think I trust you any more."

I look at her as she turns into the driveway. "That's sad. I do hope the feeling need not be mutual."

She pulls up the parking brake, and turns off the engine. "Trouble is, you don't tell *anybody*, not even your own doctor, what they need to know. So how can I trust you right now?"

"Darling. This is me, your mother. I don't deliberately deceive you, I just don't want you to worry when there's nothing you can do."

"Yes. Quite." She opens her door, comes round to help me out. Which in itself is a tedious process. "Come on, you dreadful woman, time to learn the worst."

"Don't be so daft!" It's only an ECG, for heaven's sake.

Margaret, the Senior Nurse, comes out to meet us when Susan tells the receptionist we are here. I'm still creeping in small incremental shuffles from the door. The waiting room is almost empty: just a family of holiday visitors, with a ten-year-old nursing a leg bound in bloody bandages. Poor things.

"Lovely day, Irene. You been sitting in your beautiful garden? Come this way."

Susan follows, ignoring my frown, and my 'go away' gesture as Margaret leads us to her large, light consulting room. She is tall, strongly built, has an open, friendly face, always wears a uniform, and gives an impression, from first meeting, of super-competence that has never been betrayed in our years of acquaintance.

Susan closes the door. Is this *force majeure*?

"Margaret, this is my daughter, Mrs Susan Franklin. I imagine it would be better if she waited outside?"

"That's all right, Irene. How do you do, Mrs Franklin? If you'd like to sit on that chair over there?" She turns to me with her usual warm smile. "I hear you've been having a few nasty turns, Irene." She closes the blinds. "Let me help you take off your blouse, and your shoes. Now we'll get you lying down, skirt up. Yes, like that. Well done."

"You've changed the pictures on the ceiling, Margaret."

She laughs. "Some of my regulars get bored seeing the same old faces."

"Understandable." And some of us are bored just by cute little puppy dogs. Still, it could arguably be better to have something irritating to look at than just an unexceptionable white ceiling.

She trundles a machine over to the trolley bed, smears jelly on various places across my chest and arms and legs, and sticks different coloured electrodes on these smears.

"Ready? Just lie still." The machine springs into action, recording the various signals sent by my unreliable heart. Then it stops. Margaret tears off the printed sheets, examines them for a few moments. "Hmmm. Better do that again."

She adjusts two of the electrodes, checks the rest. "Right. Still as you can." The machine whirrs again, and the pens inscribe busily until it suddenly stops. Margaret tears off the sheet, compares the readings with the previous ones. "If you would excuse me for a minute." She leaves the room.

"What's going on, Mother?"

"I've no idea."

Margaret returns, followed by a thin, pleasant-looking but tired teenager.

"Mrs Harper?" enquires the adolescent, whose hair could do with a shampoo.

"Yes. And you are?"

"This is Dr Rosemary Richards," says Margaret hastily, "our new practice partner."

"How do you do, Dr Richards." They say doctors seem to be getting younger, but this is ridiculous. She doesn't look any older than Alicia.

"I understand from your notes you have recently suffered a cerebral accident, probably an embolism from a recent infarct."

"Apparently."

"From this," and she waves the ECG, "it seems clear you did indeed have a myocardial infarction within the past few days, and that there is a strong likelihood you will undergo another without immediate treatment."

"I see."

"So I shall arrange for an ambulance to take you to Derriford Hospital right away."

"Dr Richards, I'd rather you didn't do that." She raises an untidy eyebrow. "I have explained to Dr Carr, I don't wish to go to hospital. Under any circumstances. Dr Carr fully understands."

"I also see from your notes," says this child, "that you resist medical advice on occasion. But please don't. Not today. You need immediate hospital treatment in a specialist unit, and that is all there is to say."

"I do have the right to refuse. I'm sure you recognize that."

"Mrs Harper, I have given you my medical opinion. If you refuse to take it, then I shall have nothing more to do with your case. It's up to you."

She looks at me, her grey tired skin making her look more like a victim than a medic with power over life and death, and I smile at her, not wishing to offend more than I need. She turns and strides out of the room.

"Mother!"

"You really determined not to go to Derriford, Irene?" Margaret exclaims. "It's a dangerous decision."

"I'm not going. If I die, I die. Doctors have been making predictions like this for years. It'll happen when it happens. I want to die in my own home, preferably in my own bed."

"I see. We'll file this for Dr Carr. He'll be in Tuesday morning. So if you are still with us, Irene, I may see you again then."

We both smile, as she pulls away the electrodes, and cleans up the jelly.

"Is it really a dangerous decision, Margaret?" Susan asks.

"Could be. No one knows for certain. Dr Richards couldn't risk not sending your mother off to hospital, not given the ECG. But it doesn't necessarily follow that what is *likely* to happen *will*. If you see what I mean."

Susan nods. "Yes, I do see. Thank you. Come on, Mother. Let's go somewhere where I can explain to you what a really dreadful mother you are!"

Fortunately, she winks, and we're all able to laugh as I tick tock tick tock over to the door. "She should have a wheelchair, don't you think, Margaret?"

"Would be easier, wouldn't it?"

"Bossy pair! Bye, Margaret. See you Tuesday."

"Goodbye, Irene. Good luck. And goodbye, Mrs Franklin. Good luck to you too."

"Thanks," says my daughter. "I think we're going to need it."

44

Irene

Susan helps me into the front seat again. On the outward journey, David insisted on carrying me, and his extra muscle made it simple to lift me bodily into the seat. But I discover it's become difficult just to climb into a car. My uncooperative limbs make me feel almost frantic. The most effective way, we find, is for me to back in with my bottom aimed at the seat, with Susan guiding me until I can actually sit, and then swivel round. Fortunately, this damned paralysis has not reached my left leg, but I begin to feel worryingly helpless. If it doesn't leave me soon, my freedom of movement will be horribly impaired. And I won't even be able to play music. Dammit. Dammit all to hell.

Susan fixes my seat belt, closes the door, and climbs into the driver's seat. But instead of starting the engine, she sits gazing into the middle distance beyond the escallonia hedge, slim hands gripping the steering wheel, features taut as a leopard watching its prey.

"I know I said I understood when you told me you didn't want to be sent to hospital, Mother. But now I find I don't"

"Why is that?"

"*Why* do you refuse even when the doctor says you'll die if you don't?" Her thin face looks almost haggard. "It's as though you want to commit suicide."

"Not suicide, darling. I just don't want to be kept 'officiously alive' when Death comes to call."

"Oh, my God!" She puts her head in her hands. "That doesn't tell me a *thing*."

Several cars drive in. Afternoon clinics have started. "Are we going to sit here long?"

She raises her head, and gazes into my face, her brown eyes aching pools of disenchantment. "It really would help, you know, if you would explain so that I understand. Preferably before we go back, and you have to face the others. If you want me on your side, that is, because I'm beginning to develop quite a sympathy for Danielle's position."

"Oh, my darling." I put out my good hand to caress her pale cheek.

"Don't, Mother. I'm serious. Explain now. Before it's too late."

My future in the hands of my thin, over-worked daughter, imprisoned in this ancient Volvo, in the car-park of a medical practice in a seaside village at the edge of civilisation? What a splendidly absurd situation. Because I have to admit, without the cooperation of my children, I could find myself carted off who knows where, against my will. How *do* I explain what it's like to know that medical intervention can change nothing, would simply make everyone feel better, because they' d done their duty.

"Can you give me my bag, please, Susan?"

She raises an eyebrow, then leans into the back, hands me the Italian leather shoulder bag Jeff and I bought together in Lucca, and which I have used ever since. What joy we had on that holiday, up in the Tuscan hills ... the castanet clicks of cicadas, and the smell of wild thyme ... watching villagers shake the olive trees, and the fruit cascade onto the harvest nets ... the taste of sun-blessed tomatoes straight off the vine ... and the delights of *limoncello* made by our landlady from lemons that ripened outside our window. Irene! This is not the moment for nostalgia.

"I carry this as a sort of insurance policy. Just in case I have to argue with medical men, who think I don't show the right symptoms."

I hand her the photocopy of the consultant's report on my coronary angiogram. Patrick gave it to me to carry as a precaution, after I was carried off to hospital and my notes were unavailable. One thing Patrick and I agree on, bed rest is the last thing I need given the state of my heart muscle, and in hospital, bed rest is exactly what every cardiac patient is prescribed.

She looks through the three pages, now slightly tattered despite being inside a plastic sleeve. Her brow is wrinkled like sand at low tide.

"This is just medical mumbo-jumbo. Explain in your own words. What am I supposed to understand?"

"It's just more of what I told you earlier this summer. A blood clot got trapped inside the left ventricle, and stopped the flow, so part of the heart muscle died. No one really knows when."

Except that I remember an exceptionally bad night in Chertsey, when all I could do was walk the streets under the lamps, ignoring the world, hoping the pain would leave me. I didn't dare stop, because that made it worse. So I called a friend to look after the children, then walked for hours. I had no idea what was happening. I was too young, still in my thirties, no one thought of a heart attack. It must have been then. The damage I saw on the angiography screen was so great, I couldn't possibly have missed its happening, and that was the only occasion, until recently, I endured almost intolerable pain.

"Right. And what have they been doing about it?"

I shrug. "You've seen all the pills and capsules I take every day. That's what's being done."

Patrick was the first doctor ever to take the pains around my left breast seriously. I was lucky to find him, especially after Dr Olde, the senior partner, told me I was "too intelligent for my own good" when I asked for explanations. But as a young woman, I learned that when a female asked for help, the first assumption was that she was neurotic, so I chose to make my own decisions.

"Mother. Please. Stop disappearing. I still don't see why you refuse to go to hospital, if the doctor thinks it will help."

"Because there is nothing they can do. Really. They can give me drugs to prolong the process, but in hospital they always insist on my staying in bed, which makes me that much more likely to die."

"Why?"

"Because I have to keep moving as much as I can, or my heart will give up. Every time I'm incapacitated and *can't* move around, I have bad angina."

"And that signifies?"

"Well, Patrick – that's Dr Carr – thinks angina indicates more clogging in the heart."

"So... it *isn't* exactly what you said, is it? She hands me back the letter. "You just told me angina means a bit more damage to your heart."

"Which, in my case, it does. Because of the original clot, you see?"

"Which you didn't mention. So what you're saying is, nothing I found out about angina on the internet is relevant, and you're just a freak."

I laugh. "Probably."

But she doesn't even smile, and her thoughts appear gloomy. Just like the sky. Dark storm clouds have blown in from the sea, and covered the sun. "When *was* this investigation?"

"What's the date on the letter? Goodness, nearly seven years ago now."

"I see. And why didn't you tell me and Dave about this before?"

"There didn't seem much point, really. When nothing could be done."

She rocks back and forth, eyes closed, apparently trying to deal with a problem that I can't see. Then she opens her eyes, and they have turned chasm dark.

"You know, what I *really* find difficult about all this is your attitude towards us. Your children. You appear to imagine that we don't *care*. Which is the most offensive thing you could think about us I can possibly conceive."

"Darling. I don't think that at all. I just – well – I didn't want to worry you. You have enough to cope with, running your restaurant and looking after your own family. Especially now Alicia's pregnant and Frank's upset, and Jilly's presumably upset too. You don't need to add me to your list."

"I'm not just talking about *now*, I'm talking about seven years ago. And all those other occasions you were taken ill, and insisted on being left alone. I'm feeling – oh, I don't know - bereft, I think. As though you've already died to me, before your actual death."

We look at each other for a long moment, and then I turn away. I want to weep. I thought I was doing the right thing, *not* adding to their anxieties.

But I suddenly remember Norman telling me about his mother:

"She had a major heart attack on holiday in Scotland, Irene, and we weren't told till after they returned. She'd made my father promise, if she did die, he'd have the funeral up there, and only tell us – my sister and me – when it was all over." Norman shook his head in disbelief. "Can you credit it, Irene? She thought it would save everyone heart-ache.

Our father wouldn't have to transport her body home, and her children wouldn't have the bother of attending her funeral. She was surprised that we were angry. I've never understood what made her do such a cruel thing."

And I had agreed with Norman. It *was* cruel. Is my own daughter thinking that I've been cruel too?

"I'm sorry, Susan. I'm really, truly sorry if I made you think that. Darling? Please?"

She looks at me with such a sad face, I feel a lance piercing me to the heart. That damned, vital, hectoring organ. What am I to do?

"Darling, tell me. What do you want me to do?"

She shakes her head, gives a brief bark of a laugh. "I've no idea. Don't you *know* I love you? And would do anything for you? I just need to feel you realise that."

"I never doubted that. Not for an instant."

"Good. Though it would have been more convincing if you'd confided in me earlier."

"Don't you ever want to protect your own daughters from painful realities?"

She snorts. "That's hardly the same. They're still children."

"Alicia is officially an adult, and allowed to vote. And she's about to have your grandchild. So, differences not *so* great, Susan darling." She grimaces and shrugs. Clearly, I've failed to convince. "Anyway, Susan. I've now told you everything I have to tell. Except that I really do prefer to be left alone, to make my own stupid mistakes. But that doesn't mean I don't care about you. Because I do. From the bottom of this faltering heart."

As she ponders, brows still wrinkled, I think: if they won't leave me alone, I'll just have to make sure I carry my cache of sleeping pills with me. I'm not going to accept being chained like a run-away slave, however benevolent the enslaver may intend to be.

I wonder how Death would greet me, if I were to go to her uninvited. Desperate measures for despairing thoughts. Oh, Susan, I did think I could rely on you.

She turns the key in the ignition. "We'd better get back. Don't worry, Mother. I can see how you've been thinking, and I do vaguely understand." She backs the car, and drives round to the road. "I hope you won't object if I tell Dave."

"I doubt if he'll want to know details, Susan darling. He wants to be able to start filming with a clear conscience."

"*Does* he?" Her jaw looks uncompromising.

"I'd like him to do that. Really."

Why, oh why does everyone fight over my failing body?

45

David

"Uncle Dave, why did you marry Aunt Dani?"

Danielle had taken her children upstairs, and David was relaxing under the awning, having had the briefest of visits from Charles Boscawen, who all too clearly felt he had wasted an afternoon by not being able to see Irene. Alicia had been texting on her mobile for what, to her uncle, seemed like hours.

"What an extraordinary question, Ali. You *are* an odd girl, aren't you?

"Not really. I just, like, want to know. You know."

"Articulate, too." David laughed. "I guess I married her because she's beautiful and clever and wonderful at her work, and we both wanted to. What else?"

"Did you, like, love her?"

"Of course, I loved her, you daft girl. Still love her, infuriating as she can so often be. Are you asking because she's mad at you? Is that it?"

"You know, she's not very nice to me."

David looked at his tousled niece, and smiled: in her own youthful way, she was a lovely girl, but he was not surprised Dani found her hard to take. What had they in common? "I'll let you into a secret, Ali. I expect you remind her of my First Love. You're a bit 'alternative', as she was, if you see what I mean."

"Not really." Alicia frowned, as though her uncle had the weirdest ideas, and talked a different language. "What the heck is 'alternative' when it's at home?"

"She had long hair, and long drapey clothes, and scarves and beads, just like you. *And* she wouldn't let other people tell her what to do."

"That's 'alternative'? Sounds modern to me. I mean, like, I'm with it. Dunno what you're talking about."

David laughed again. "Ali, you're priceless. Well, I fell for this girl, Jodi, when I was at university. It was the Thatcher era, so let me assure you, long skirts and beads were definitely 'alternative', a badge of defiance of authority. They signalled a different approach to living, a rejection of money as a prime motive, two fingers to a prime minister who said there was 'no such thing as community'. So there was a political dimension too. Don't suppose you've got into that sort of thing yet, but give it time."

Jodi, Jodi Walters. Took him a long time to forget her.

"What did this Jodi person do then?"

"She persuaded me to join the protests in support of the miners. On one occasion, we were with a large group of students and strikers picketing a mine near Wakefield. There were scuffles and, I may say, a considerable amount of unnecessary police violence. And Jodi and I were among the dozens of peaceful demonstrators dragged off in police vans. Not my idea of fun, I can tell you. Put me off activism very effectively, I'm afraid."

"But why did you do it?"

"Why? Just think of all the men whose livelihoods were being destroyed, all those families with nothing to look forward to and nothing to live on but the dole." He saw his niece frown and shake her head. "You must have heard about the clashes between the miners' unions and Mrs Thatcher, and how the coal industry was almost wiped out. Surely?"

Alicia was puzzled. "I've heard of Margaret Thatcher. She was the first woman prime minister ever, everyone knows that. And coal is dirty and pollutes the atmosphere. So if she closed the coal mines, she did the right thing. That's what I think."

David sighed. It didn't take long for life-shattering struggles to become fodder for old men's memories. Not that he himself was very good at taking part in political struggles. He'd rather direct a play that made sharp political statements, like Brecht's *The Resistible Rise of Arturo Ui*. He was a sad disappointment to Jodi, and in the end, she left him for the Greenham Common Women's Peace Camp encircling the U.S. Missile base. No wonder she didn't manage to get her degree. At least the nuclear warheads had gone - she must have cheered when the Americans finally departed. He wondered where she was now.

"So you didn't want to marry your first love, then?"

227

"Not after we ended up in court for affray. No." David laughed. "She thought I was a wimp. Different values, I guess." At least she waited to tell him it was over till after Finals. So she cared for him a bit. "I'd rather fight tyranny with drama, because that I understand. Every man should do what he can in his own way."

"And woman."

"Of course, and woman." He thought of checking on the workmen, because he could hear very little activity, but his niece appeared unusually on edge. Had Dani really upset her? "What's on your mind, Ali? It's not my early life on the picket line."

Alicia shrugged. "Oh. You know."

"No. I don't know. Why not tell me."

The girl gazed out over the garden. "See, my friend Pete keeps texting me. And I just don't know what to do."

"Is he a good friend? A nice chap?"

"Oh, yes. He's lovely. You know, like Simon really. Only older." Her eyes remained unfocussed, turned away from her uncle.

"Lucky you," he said, watching her.

"Yeah, but, you know, I don't think I should tell him ..." Her voice tailed off, and David nodded, light dawning.

"I see. He's the father, is that it?" His niece bit her lip. "I think, if he's a nice guy, he might be peeved if you don't tell him. It *is* somewhat major."

"Would *you* want to know if you had a place at Cambridge?" she demanded belligerently.

"Yes, I can see it's tricky. However, if he hears about it from someone else ..." He broke off, as he saw the two workmen apparently piling packing cases in the conservatory. "Excuse me, Ali. Looks as though I have to sort things here."

He stood up, and accosted the red-haired one, who appeared about to carry a tool-box back to the van. "May I ask what is going on?"

"Nearly four. We're packing up, and should be back first thing Tuesday morning. All being well. So your Mum will have her stair-lift in good time."

"Oh, no. You can't go now. The arrangement was that you'd complete the installation today. No matter how long it took."

"Can't be done, mate. Can't be done."

"But it was all agreed with Mr Finch. We've paid a massive premium to ensure my mother gets her stair-lift working before the weekend."

The man shrugged. "Dunno nothing about that."

"Didn't Mr Finch tell you?"

"Listen, mate. We knock off at four. After that, it's overtime. *And* it's a Bank holiday."

"Yes, I understand. But as far we're concerned, we've paid for your overtime, plus. Mr Finch should have told you this."

"Why don't you phone the office, mate? Better hurry. They'll be knocking off work soon too."

"Right, I will. Tell you what. My wife will bring you and er, Lenny, a pot of tea, and you can both relax here on the terrace while I go sort things out with your company. How about that?"

"Cuppa tea'd go down a treat," Red conceded handsomely. "Then we'll see. Here, Len." He signalled to his partner, who had sauntered outside and lit a cigarette.

Danielle, who had noted the change in activity and spoken to Lenny, appeared promptly carrying a tray loaded with tea and a cake she had intended for this evening's celebrations. Worth sacrificing, she thought, for the sake of having something *to* celebrate. Let's hope they, like most men, can be seduced with rich chocolate cake.

"Here, chaps. I could see you need a decent tea break."

"Hey, Missus. That cake looks something." The two men settled comfortably into the wide wooden chairs, feeling appreciated at last. Danielle poured out, cut each one a very large slice of sticky cake, told them to help themselves to more. Simon, who realized the chocolate cake was likely to disappear before he had any, joined the men at the table, helped himself after his mother returned to the house. He giggled at their jokes, and Red and Lenny were pleased to have an admiring audience.

David phoned Head Office, left an urgent message with a secretary, who promised her boss would call back within half an hour.

46

Irene

The big white Third-Age Mobility Services van is still in the driveway when we get back, and the two workmen are under the awning, drinking tea and eating chocolate cake. Simon is kneeling on a chair, elbows sprawled across the table, apparently enthralled by their company.

"Nice place you got here, Missus."

I intend to answer, but find I've become breathless just shuffling across the terrace from the car. Making a temporary stop on my recliner seems a good idea. Somewhat awkwardly, I sink onto the cushion, manoeuvre my legs round and lie back, good hand holding my chest. Simon rescues my stick from where I drop it, and props it against the table.

"You all right there, Missus?"

"I think you should fetch your Mum, young feller. Your Gran looks a bit done in."

"Come on, Len. Let's get that stair-lift fixed for this little lady."

"Right. Thank your Mum for the tea, Simon."

The two men return inside, and Simon squats down beside me. "Whatsa matter, Granma?"

I breathe out slowly. "It's all right, sweetheart. Just a bit tired." Lack of breath still assails me. How tiresome this ageing body can be. "You been doing anything interesting, Simon?"

"Those men are funny."

"Are they?"

"Yeah." He grins to himself, but apparently is not going to share his amusement. I could do with a laugh.

David joins us. "They're back to work. A miracle. What did you say to them, Mother?" I shake my head. "You all right?"

Susan comes outside, followed by Danielle, who piles the tea things onto a tray. Then both sit down. If I didn't know better, I'd say they look like conspirators.

A cool breeze is blowing up the valley. Strange how the lie of the land funnels any wind from the east straight at this garden; or would, if I had not planted a thick screen of trees to break its power. I feel it, though. Filtered and chilly.

"You warm enough out here, Mother?" Susan asks. I nod. I don't want to move for the moment. "Right. We need to talk. Out here is quite a good idea, but I think Mother should have a blanket or something round her."

"I'll get something." David goes back inside.

"What's all this about, Susan?"

She snorts. "I don't know how you can ask."

"Couldn't we just let things go, for a little while?"

"Obviously not."

Family discussions get so tedious. No wonder I feel tired. I'm fed up with the lot of them. It's like being back at school, and teachers and parents discussing your future and never asking what you want yourself, never hearing what you say.

David returns, with an ancient blanket we always used for picnics when he was young, and tucks it round me. "Thank you, darling." At least it's clean. It was always full of sand, however much we shook it before bringing it in, but hasn't been near the beach in years. What a lot of tatty relics I still hoard in my creaking old house.

"Ali says, could she and Tanya please play your piano? They promise to be very careful and to wash their hands first."

"Does she play?"

"Of course, she does, Mother." Susan looks at me, startled. How could I not know that? Am I forgetting important things now?

"Tell her, yes. That's all right."

David nods. "Come on, Simon. You too. You can tell Ali what Grandma said, and then find a book to read. We grown-ups are busy." The boy doesn't even wail, goes straight into the house. "Right, Suse. So what's the verdict?"

"The doctor on duty told her she needs to go to hospital immediately. Naturally, being our mother, the dear woman refused. So the doctor

231

washed her hands of her."

"Oh, my God. And you let her?"

I have to laugh at that. Susan looks at me, and starts to laugh too. "Let her? Tricky one. Let's say, we arm-wrestled, and I didn't win."

"Are you suicidal or something, Mother? *Why* won't you go to hospital, when a doctor says you need to urgently?"

"Exactly what I asked, Dave."

"And?"

"This is really hard to explain, so it's no wonder we've had a tiny problem understanding what our dear mother is on about. I'll see if I can convey the gist of what I think I was told. It seems that, sometime in the past, a blood clot got stuck inside her heart and stopped the circulation. And now a large part of the heart muscle is dead. All the medication she takes keeps what's left going, but nothing more can be done. Is that it, Mother?"

"Yes. You've got it."

"That sounds absurd, Irene. A block in the circulation around the heart can almost always be sorted, by a stent, or a by-pass if necessary."

"Perhaps you should show Danielle the consultant's report, Mother? At least she'd understand the medical jargon."

I sigh. Convincing my family is just as much hard work as convincing doctors who haven't seen the report. Let everyone look, if it will stop them wrangling over my decaying body. I hand over the photocopy in its plastic cover, and husband and wife examine the pages, frowning, their foreheads like a pair of corrugated iron roofs on adjacent allotment sheds.

"This was seven years ago." I nod. "And you've taken all that time to let Susan and me know? Don't you *care* about us?"

"Of course, I do. What's that got to do with it?"

David leaps up, throws back the heavy wooden armchair, strides away across the terrace.

"I told you, Mother. Keeping important information like this from your own adult children is very hurtful."

A damned pain is developing in my chest, and round my disputed heart. Given the distress I appear to be causing, this could simply be heart-ache of the most mundane kind.

"I didn't want to hurt either of you. I simply wanted to prevent you worrying about me, because that would help none of us. I didn't want to disrupt your lives with my ill-health."

"I'm afraid neither of us can thank you for that. And I know you meant well."

I press my hand against my breast, where the pain is growing, and call with as much voice as I can summon, "David. David! Please come back." He marches towards us across the slates, face like Dorian Grey's attic portrait. "I'm sorry. Really sorry if my good intentions were so misguided, I upset you."

"You know what *really* upsets me about all this? It's the strong impression I get that you think *we* don't care about *you*."

"That's exactly what I said, Dave."

"It seems I got a lot wrong. Of course I know you care about me, and I care very much about you."

Enough of the hearts-on-sleeve stuff. I think we must sound like a rather bad soap opera.

Where do I go from here? I know they care in their own ways. And I love them. They are my children. But I don't *want* them to be concerned about me. In my ideal world, I'd be left to sort out my own life, and they'd sort out theirs, and we'd meet as often as convenient, and enjoy each other's company without anybody trying to run anybody else. Freedom, that's what I want. Freedom of choice.

Death is peering from behind the magnolia, and I see her shake her empty skull, rock with mirthless laughter, mocking me with a clearly audible drawl: '*You gotta big choice there, sister. Daie heere. Daie in Derriford. That's your lot.*' Death as a seedy gangster's moll? How very odd.

And my children continue to discuss my living arrangements without ever supposing I might have contingency plans of my own.

"If Mother's not going into hospital," Susan points out, "we need to sort out how she can be cared for when we've all gone home."

"I take it you no longer imagine Alicia could cope?"

"I never supposed she could, Danielle. She just needed to realize it herself. I don't try to run everyone's life for them, you know."

"I'm sure you know what you're doing." Danielle's voice clearly suggests the opposite. "So what do you propose we do?"

"At least one of us has to stay here, until she's seen the doctor again on Tuesday."

"We really can't, Susan. I have to be back in the hospital on Monday. I dare not risk my job, not now, not with Dave off in cloud cuckoo land. We'd lose the house and everything else if my job went. You do understand, I hope."

"Of course. Anyway, it's not your mother."

"Believe me, that's not the issue."

"One difficulty is, she has no car," Susan continues, ignoring her sister-in-law. "Even if I offer to stay for a few days, I don't have one down here either. So, what if Danielle and the kids go back by train, or by air, and you stay on with me, Dave? Then we could sort out proper care next week, when offices open again. What do you say?"

"Sorry. Can't possibly stay beyond tomorrow. Out of the question."

"I see. I'm prepared to stay here, even though it's a bank holiday weekend, and one of the busiest times in our calendar. It's putting terrible demands on Frank, who's supposed to be the chef, not front of house."

"I know. He's a splendid chap. But there is just no way I can stay here beyond tomorrow. I have important things to sort out before filming starts. With the school, and all my university teaching. You're not the only ones to have other commitments."

"Christ, Dave, how do you imagine *we* cope in an emergency? You're just talking convenience. But *we* have to hire in more staff, and that costs money, and time to teach them our ways. *And* it's risky, because temps are rarely reliable. You never think of other people, do you?"

"I seem to remember, Dave, telling you to organise a professional nurse days ago. Weren't you supposed to phone Susan, and sort that out?"

"Mother said she doesn't want that."

"Oh, for Chrissake. Your mother couldn't even *talk* at the time."

"Well, I can now, Danielle. Has it occurred to any of you to ask *me* what I want?" They all stare at me. The broken doll spoke.

"I'm not sure any more you're the right person to ask, Mother." Susan sounds unexpectedly belligerent, and her eyes shoot painful arrows into my already aching heart. She turns to the others. "She seems to imagine she can just carry on as before. And look at her."

She waves her arm at me in a histrionic gesture that shows David is not alone with his drama gene, which I can only suppose was inherited from their father. Perhaps they're all actors, Danielle included, all playing their assigned parts in a play written by some malignant dramatist. I appear to be simply audience. Clearly I have no part to play, in which case, I should be left alone.

I'm tired of listening to them. What is likely to happen is that Susan will stay on, the others will leave, and we'll take a taxi to the surgery on Tuesday. If I survive that long. It would be good to know exactly how much time I have left, but I doubt if I need worry about finances any more. My main concern now must be to ensure that any professional assigned to care for me by my loving family cannot override my express wish to die here, in my own home.

47

Simon

Simon erupted into the music room. "Ali. Guess what?"

Tani was sitting on the piano stool, gazing at the black and white keys she dared not touch without permission. "Grammar said okay. I know she did."

"Is it all right? Did Grandma say?" Ali asked. "Come on, Simon. We're waiting."

"Never mind that stupid music - we got an emergency!"

"Music's *not* stupid! *You're* stupid."

Alicia put her arm round the shoulders of her outraged small cousin. "Calm down, both of you. Now, Simon, what on earth's the matter?"

"D'you know what our parents are doing? Just cos Granma has got ill and looks a bit funny. D'you know what they're plotting?"

"Plotting? What do you mean?"

"They're like the baddies in a video, that's what I mean. Guess what? They're gonna make Granma go to a old people place, and we'll never see her again."

"How do you know this?"

"Cos I heard them, o'course. And Granma doesn't want to go."

Ali sighed. "Poor Grandma. I can quite believe your parents think they know best. They always do. But I can't see there's anything we can, like, *do* about it, Simon."

"Why not? Granma doesn't want to go anywhere. She told me."

"We can ask Mr Feetwad to help," suggested Tani. "Mr Feetwad is a music teacher, he c'n do magic."

"Yeah. Great idea, Tani. Mr Fleetwood is Granma's friend. He'll save her." Simon rushed to the door. "Come *on*, Ali."

"Just a minute. How on earth can we, you know, ask a stranger to interfere with your parents' plans?"

"He's not a stranger. He's our friend."

"Yeah, he's gotta piano. And yummy red jam." Tani giggled, and Simon joined in.

"Right. I can tell you've been to tea." Ali considered the matter. "Tell you what. Let's go for a walk, and you can, like, let off some steam. And if you can find this chap's house, well, you know, we'll see. I'm not promising anything."

Ali sounds like a grown-up, Simon thought. They always say they're not promising. But she'll have to help us when we get there 'cos we have to rescue Granma.

The parents and Auntie Susan were still plotting at the table on the terrace, as Simon, Alicia and Tanya walked past. Granma was asleep on a garden lounger beside them, huddled under a faded blanket, looking very grey and very old.

"Going for a walk," Simon informed them, and hurried up to the gate.

"Yeah," confirmed Tani, and she giggled.

Their mother frowned, then gazed at Alicia. "No more mud, I trust."

"Of *course* not."

"You got your mobile, Ali?" asked Susan.

"Course I have. Come on, Tani. Let's, you know, get moving." My own mother in on the plot, Alicia muttered to herself as they joined Simon in the lane. Really, you couldn't trust anyone.

Simon was sure he could find the right house, because he remembered exactly how they went there in the car. Easy-peasy. Along to the corner, where Dad helped them climb over the wall, then up the straight bit of lane that led to the field where the badgers used to live. Not something he wanted to think about. Above their heads were huge blackberry bushes, and Ali was so slow, he had time to eat some. Round the corner, and down the steep lane towards the sea, which looked dark and threatening, as though it could just spill over and drown all the houses below. Down they went, between high hedges of stone covered in dusty gorse and pink campion, and the sky was the same grey as pigeon's feathers. Which made him think of the poor pigeon again, and the horrible cat eating it while it was still alive. He wished he didn't have these horrible memories.

A strong wind swooped on them, and they started jogging to get warm. Past the two houses that stood on top of a steep wall above the lane, one with an old fashioned well in the front garden; down to where the road widened and bullocks poked their heads inquisitively through the trees bordering the farmer's land; then round the corner near the well with a cross on top. Ali stopped, holding her chest like Granma did.

"Hang on a minute, Simon. I have to catch my breath."

"Come *on*."

"Crikey." Ali took a deep breath, and then puffed a lot. "Oh, dear. I haven't got your stamina, you know. I shouldn't have, like, skived off games."

"Do come on, Ali. The house is just up there." Simon pointed along the lane that ran past an old house with battlemented walls.

"Maybe we could go that way," Ali said, still breathing heavily. "We could walk back up the valley. But listen, you two. Absolutely no getting wet or muddy. You hear?" Tanya giggled. "I mean it, Tani. Your Mum would never let you go anywhere with me, like, ever again."

"Whatever," Simon said impatiently. "Let's go." He set off again, perfectly sure he knew where to go, past the houses built on the side of the hill, so that their roofs were lower than the road, on to where the trees began and the road ended, and a pathway dipped into the valley.

"Come *on*, Ali. It's here." Simon pointed up beyond the last gateway in the lane, to a large stone building half hidden among trees.

"Good grief, you've found it!" Ali's mobile twittered the signal for a text received. "Just a sec, Simon ... All right, all right, I'll leave the text for a mo. Stop pulling my arm. We have to, like, think. What are we going to, you know, tell this Mr Fleetwood?"

"I'll tell him, don't worry," Simon assured her. "I just need you to come with me. 'Cos you're grown up and so he might listen. They never listen to children, you know that."

"True."

"And my Mum will be really mad when we tell him," Simon added, provoking his cousin with conscious deliberation.

Ali grinned. "Oh, dear. Perhaps we'd better not then."

Tani was halfway up the driveway. "Come on, you slow pokes."

Simon thought Mr Fleetwood looked a bit put out when he opened his front door, so he had to say something pretty quickly. "Mr Fleetwood, please. You gotta help us rescue Granma!" He hoped that was enough. Grown-ups always told children to go away, ages before they ever had any idea what you needed to tell them.

"Goodness me! Simon, isn't it? What are you doing here?"

There. They never listened. Never. "Please. You must help! Granma's gonna be carted off to a old people place, and she doesn't want to go. We need you to help us."

Simon saw that woman Mum wanted to run over appear behind Mr Fleetwood in the hallway. She was dressed in horrible pretend leopard-skin jersey, and she was giggling at something. The big man turned to her. "Do you know anything about this, Belinda?" She shrugged and shook her head. He turned back to Ali: "I'm Norman Fleetwood. Can *you* throw some light on this extraordinary episode?"

"Hi. I'm Alicia Franklin, and I think my grandmother, you know, Irene Harper, is your friend."

"Yes, indeed. So you're another of her granddaughters. Are you musical too?"

Alicia smiled. "I do love music, but I'm not, you know, special. Not like Tani here."

Norman gazed down at the blonde curls and piercing blue eyes of the five-year-old with perfect pitch. "Yes, you're a natural, aren't you, Tanya?"

"You gonna do magic? You gonna make our Grammar stay?"

"I don't think I can do anything like that, Tanya."

"Ohohohwer!" Tanya's wail startled two chaffinches out of the magnolia tree, and Simon cried: "Gollee! You *need* to, Mr Fleetwood, you *need* to!"

"Alicia. You're the oldest. Please tell me what is going on."

Leopard Woman pushed past and draped herself on one of the low walls of the front porch with a stupid smile on her face, like in a telly ad.

"I know we should never have come here, and I am, like, very sorry. I didn't really, you know, think we'd find you."

"You *said*, Ali, you *said!*" Simon couldn't believe what he'd just heard.

"I understand. But you are. So please explain."

"Well, like, our grandmother is rather ill, and our parents are worried about her."

"Very understandable."

"But you see, they want to send her to hospital, or into a care home, you know. And she doesn't want to go."

"Ha, ha, I can see it now," Leopard Woman chuckled. "Know-it-all Danielle organising her mother-in-law to within a hair's breadth of losing her reason, and the lovely Reeny turning to her little kiddie-winks to rescue her."

"Belinda! That will do." The horrible woman blinked. "Perhaps, after all, I had better find out what is going on. You children can come with me in the car. I will take you home and have a quick word with your parents."

Simon and Tanya started leaping up and down in glee, but Alicia frowned. "What have we done?" she whispered to Simon, "What are your parents going to say?" And he whispered back, "Don't care. Mr Fleetwood is gonna rescue Granma, so there."

48

Irene

I open my eyes. The three adults are leaning on elbows on the round wooden table, heads huddled together, like conspirators in a B-movie.

One of the workmen has hoisted a large cardboard box onto his shoulder, is carrying it into the house. How much longer can they possibly be? The same thought apparently occurs to David, for he watches the chap, then stands up, strides into the house. Masterful, that's today's performance.

A car clangs over the drain cover, crunches across the gravel, and parks beside the Volvo. Then Norman strides across the terrace. With the children. All of whom are straggling behind, as though anxious not to be the first to arrive. David emerges from the house, goes over to greet this unexpected visitor. Danielle and Susan look at each other and frown.

"Norman. Come to visit, Mother."

"Irene. How are you, my dear? The children told me you are ill, so I came to find out if there is anything I can do."

"The children?" Danielle asks, puzzled.

Norman looks at Alicia, but Simon says hastily: "Yeah, Mum. It was my idea."

"And mine."

"Yeah, Tani and me, we asked Mr Fleetwood to come and stop you sending Granma away to some horrible place she doesn't want to go. That's why he's here. So there!"

"You *what*?" David is so angry I can see why Simon thought of him as a gorilla. "Come inside this instant. Both of you. How dare you poke your noses into things that don't concern you?"

"Hang on a minute, Uncle. Why don't you listen to what Mr Fleetwood has to say?"

"Norman?"

"David. And Danielle. And all of you. I don't really have anything to say, except that, as an outsider, I can see the children are very upset. And I do know that my dear friend, Irene, has always said she would never move away from this house. That's all. It's not my business. But I did feel I should say a few words."

"Thank you, Norman, my dear friend."

"How do you feel, Irene, my dear?"

"Improving." We smile at one another, glad of our long friendship. "Good of you to drop in like this."

"Can I offer you a cup of tea, Norman? I'm Susan, by the way. Irene's daughter."

"Susan, yes, I remember you as a young girl." He looks around, and I know he sees evidence of workmen and the simmering anger of the parents. "I won't stop, if there is nothing I can do. I can see you have your hands full."

"Do sit with me for a while, Norman dear." Perhaps his gentle presence will calm the others.

He hesitates, and I put out my good hand to him. Susan turns a chair so that he can sit beside me. "I don't want to interfere, Irene. I was a bit concerned though – young Simon seemed to think you might be forced into a care home against your will, and he was so upset, I couldn't just pretend I didn't know."

"I apologise for my son's behaviour," Danielle says. "No doubt his older cousin thought she knew better."

"Your children had good intentions," Norman assures her. "I don't feel you need to apologise to me at all."

Danielle raises her eyebrows.

"They were only doing what they thought best for me, Danielle. Their Grandma. I feel very much loved."

"I rather think everyone is doing what they think best for you, Irene dear," he says to me quietly.

"I expect you're right, Norman. Between you and me, I wish they wouldn't. I do wish they would *ask*."

"Oh, my dear. I know what you mean. When Joseph was dying, we were both tormented by advice - from almost everyone we knew. All well-meant, of course. Poor old JoJo. He wanted to stay in his own home too."

We clasp hands. Sharing memories. And the same desire for ourselves.

"I wish I'd insisted, you know, Irene." Norman's sunken cheeks have taken on a haunted look. "The hospice was very kind to us both, but it wasn't the same. He wanted his own bed, his own things round him. And we could have had a Macmillan nurse. I still feel I let him down."

"Oh, Norman, my dear." I wish I could comfort him.

"Excuse me, Norman," David says. "Workmen to deal with inside. And naughty children to chastise. Thanks for bringing them back. Simon. Come with me."

I try to sit up. "David. Please. Simon meant well. Let him be."

David raises his dark eyes to the glowering heavens and sighs. "Temporary reprieve, Simon." He strides inside.

Norman pats my hand and stands up. "I must go, Irene dear. Phone me if there is anything I can do."

"Thank you for bringing the children back. And for being so understanding."

"My pleasure."

Susan sees Norman to his car, then returns to deal with her daughter. But Danielle has already waded in. "I've told you before, I won't have you involving my young children in your stupid escapades."

"Actually, Aunt Dani, it was Simon who involved me. As we've already explained. Why don't you *listen*?"

"What on earth made you call on Mr Fleetwood like that?" demands Susan. "How *could* you?"

"See, I didn't actually think Simon would find his house. But when we got there, like, we had to explain."

"And you chose to meddle in matters that don't concern you. If you were my daughter, you'd find yourself in deep trouble."

"I think you can leave this to me, thank you, Danielle. Alicia is *my* daughter."

"I trust you will teach her not to interfere in other people's affairs."

"What about you, you old cat? You do nothing *but* interfere."

243

"That will do, Ali. Really. Please go up to your room and calm down. We're all upset, and we don't need to make things worse. Do we?" Susan looks unwaveringly at her daughter, until the girl nods, and goes inside. "Now, Danielle. I would appreciate if you could avoid criticising my daughter again. Is that clear?"

So even my grandchildren are now entangled in the tussle over my disintegrating body. Everyone fighting with everybody else. Such a jolly, joyful family reunion.

49

Irene

"**H**ow are you feeling now, Mother?" Susan smiles at me, as though nothing untoward has happened. "You looked a bit grey earlier, so I thought I'd let you sleep."

"Your children are all very kind-hearted and well-meaning, I hope you both realize that. You should be proud of them." Danielle raises those astonishingly neat eyebrows, and turns away. Susan winks at me.

"I think, Mother, we've got the message."

The sun has gone, and the air smells of the Arctic. I attempt to move my limbs, but my body is trapped in a glacial crevasse, white at the edges, blue in the depths.

"I'm getting cold here. I think I'll go inside."

"Good idea."

Raising this delinquent body turns out to be an even greater struggle than usual. I need a mechanical hoist. Left arm won't work, left hip screeches whenever asked to work, right hip and knee both jerk and jag, and then my lower back starts to scream. Both women come to help, one on either side, lifting me gently, but I can't stop panting with the pain.

"Sorry about that, Mother," Susan says, once I'm at last installed in my reclining chair. "The weather turned much too cold for us to stay out. It was thoughtless of me."

"Not your fault, Susan. I could have moved earlier. I wonder – could you fetch me the duvet from the cupboard under the stairs, darling?" And there's a pain around my heart, a growing darkness in my chest that I'd like to keep to myself. Just in case.

She bundles me up warmly. "I'll get you a pot of tea too. For central heating."

"Lovely idea."

I close my eyes, examine the encroaching pain. Beneath my left breast, around my ribs, up to the left shoulder, down that damned useless arm.

Growing now, into my neck, my ear. Dammit, dammit. I scrabble for the spray. Squirt the chemical into my mouth, one, two, three. This is getting to be a bad habit. Euch, it tastes vile. Come on, work, damn you. We can't have another attack now.

Susan brings in a tray of tea, which she places on the small table beside me. But I have to ask her for an aspirin. I can't pretend this is not happening, not any more.

She hurries back, hands me the glass of water with the fizzing tablet. I drink it down.

"Darling. Please. Don't say ... anything yet. Let the men go first."

She looks at me for a long time, deciding, then stoops and kisses my ugly, damaged cheek. "All right, Monster Mother. We'll wait till the stair-lift is finished. If we can. But I'm staying with you."

I grasp her hand with my right one. It, at least, still functions. "Thanks."

I close my eyes. I feel her move to the settee nearby. On my right, away from the pain which seems determined not to leave me. Damn. It's neither one thing nor the other. Bad angina, yes, but not a full-blown heart attack. Just pain, persistent pain, which should be diminishing now. But isn't.

"Mother?" David appears. "The stair-lift is ready for you to try out."

"Marvellous." Do I have to move again? I suppose so. I think I can. The aspirin seems to have had some effect at last. Stick? Where's my damned stick?

"You sure you want to stand up again?" Susan looks worried. "Dave, you sort it. Mother's really not quite up to it yet."

"It's all right, Susan. Really. I have to try it out before they go." And it will give me a chance to go to the bathroom, glory be! Just the thought makes it imperative that I move. Like Pavlov's dog, my bladder will always respond. "If someone could locate my peripatetic stick, I shall ceremonially open proceedings." I turn to my daughter. "I'm fine now, truly."

David promptly strides across the room, scoops me up in his arms. "No need for a stick, Ma. You have your own personal transport."

I laugh as he carries me out to the bottom of the stairs. "I must have it at the top, though. Don't forget that."

Everyone has gathered to watch. I've never seen my hallway so crowded. And there, waiting beside the bottom step, attached to a long bar that stretches to the top of the stairs, is a cream-coloured chair, with retractable seat and arms and foot-rest.

Discovering how to sit on the chair is an adventure in itself, but once I learn, it's simple, and comfortable enough. The big red-faced chap shows me the controls, and I feel ready to ride. David hands me my stick, I ceremonially press the button, and it works. Very gently, I glide up the stairs until the machine comes to a halt on the half-landing. As instructed, I swivel the chair, dismount and wave to my jubilant family.

"It's wonderful. Thank you, everyone. I shall now take advantage of being up here and go to the bathroom."

A scatter of laughter greets that announcement. I haul myself up the last three stairs. The lift is going to make life a great deal easier, and should surely mean they can leave me now with an easy conscience.

My reflection is a displeasing shock. Really, I can hardly be surprised that my children are concerned. If I were looking at me from outside, I think I'd feel a little uneasy. Even without glasses, my face is crevassed as well as distorted. How unspeakably vile. I was once considered quite a beauty, and now – I look hideous. Like a child's nightmare witch.

I grimace at myself. Yep. Your pride is taking quite a battering, Irene Harper. Should have remembered the fall that pride always goeth before.

Time to go back down. As I shuffle past the long mirror on the landing, I see I'm still bent like a paper-clip. And that ache beneath my left breast, and along my left arm, has not gone, but recedes and then floods in again like the tide.

Simon is riding to the top of the stair-lift, giggling and waving his arms like a Hollywood cowboy. He sees me and jumps off. "Hey, Granma. This is fun. You gonna go back down on it?"

"I certainly am, Simon." Carefully, I descend the short flight, turn the chair to the correct angle, and sit. The downward journey is as smooth as before.

David and the two workmen are waiting at the bottom, one drinking a can of lager, the other a Coke.

"Cheers, Missus. You happy with your new chair lift?"

"Very."

They drain the cans. While one brushes debris into a dustpan and packs away their tools, the other demonstrates the use of remote controls to send away or summon the chair. A remote control is placed on a hook at either end of the run: that way, I should never find myself at a loss, even if a grandchild does play and then leave it at the wrong end. Already, I see that is likely to happen. Tanya is having her turn and might well forget to bring it down when she has finished.

I wave to her, then turn to the workman who calls me Missus. He is completing a complex document, which apparently requires my signature, and my credit card details. Instruction booklet, guarantee and receipt all safely handed over, we exchange warm wishes for the rest of the holiday weekend, and at last David can see them off the premises. A long afternoon, but a useful one.

And, thank heaven, pains around my breast have ebbed. Low tide.

Lord, I'm so tired. As I aim for my comfortable chair, I feel my progress is like the watched pot that never boils. How will I ever get there?

Alicia comes up behind me as I near my destination, takes my right arm to help me along. I see a flicker of distaste cross her pretty face as her mother takes over, helps me lie back and pulls out the leg rest. "Oh, Grandma. You do look done in."

"Feel it a bit, Alicia darling. Don't look at my horrid twisty face, please. I think it'll go away, when I've had a good rest."

"Poor you," she says and her voice is sympathetic. "Uncle Dave's gonna get some champers, you know? To celebrate, like. Good, eh?"

"Lovely idea."

"Do you, you know, like the stair-lift?"

"Oh, Alicia, it's wonderful. Very clever, whoever thought of it in the first place."

Suddenly, everyone is back in the room. Do I keep missing things? Transitions are becoming unexpectedly short, even non-existent. Danielle has brought in a tray of glasses: four empty flutes and three tumblers half full of apple juice. Alicia mutters, "Bitch", leaves the room and returns almost immediately with a further flute, which she adds to the tray with a defiant glare at her aunt. Danielle purses scarlet lips, hands a tumbler of juice to each of her children.

David opens the large, foil-topped bottle with a satisfying bang, and pours sparkling white wine into the flutes. All five. Then he hands one to me, and one each to Danielle, Susan and Alicia, then raises his own.

"To the inauguration of the Hart House stair-lift."

"To the stair-lift!" his audience choruses, and we all drink. It tastes delicious.

I have always loved champagne. And champagne-style wines of quality. Which this one is. I love the fresh, faintly fruity, but tart taste, and the sensation of bubbles in the mouth, and the blissful relaxation that follows.

"Thank you, David, for organising it. And thank you, Alicia, for having the idea in the first place."

I'm really feeling better now, as though the alcohol has widened the capillaries to allow blood to flow more freely. The ache hovers, but in the background, murmuring like the ocean at its lowest ebb.

Alicia's mobile tweets birdsong, and she leaves the room, followed by Simon who has been looking bored and probably wants to find a book.

Danielle stands up. "Time you had your bath, Tani. As a special treat tonight, you can stay up after, and we'll all have dinner together." Tanya gazes at her mother, evidently wondering if defiance is worth while. "*If* you can manage to wash yourself properly, and get your night-things on, without *any* fuss."

The little girl nods. "OK." She trots out of the room, followed by her mother, whose lips I see twitching. Oh, Danielle, let yourself go, woman. You can be quite human.

I look at my watch. Unless my eyesight has gone completely awry, it seems to be nearly seven. Danielle has relaxed her iron grip on the children's routines to an astonishing extent.

"You really, truly feeling better, Mother?" Susan asks.

"Yes. As a matter of fact, I am. Aspirin and champagne, that's the secret."

We both laugh. "If you're absolutely certain, I'll go help Danielle get dinner. She wants it to be a bit special, to make up for all the difficulties that have dogged this holiday."

"What a lovely idea. I'll be fine, darling." And I feel that is the truth.

Yah, boo, sucks to you, Death, as the schoolboy comics of my youth used to say. Go away. Take your scythe elsewhere. You're not wanted here.

.

50

Irene

"**W**ell, David. You must be feeling very pleased, one way and another."

From the depths of the settee, he directs the full wattage of his smile at me, white teeth curved against full, kissable lips, dark eyes that incite dreams. I can believe he will be a startling film success, if simply because of the seductive charm he appears to have inherited from his father. Oh, Martin, how it used to work on me. I laugh inside, as I remember what a fool I was as a young woman.

"Yes, Ma. Apart from your health, which we're none of us happy about, it has all turned out well."

"I'm looking forward to hearing all about your film. So exciting."

"Yep." Those long black lashes flutter, close on his cheeks for a moment, and then he shakes his head. "You know, I don't even want to talk about it. Until I have the script in my hands. Weird, eh?" He grins like a little boy. "You'd think I'd want to tell the world, but right now ... I just want to hug it to myself. Like a wonderful, almost impossible-to-believe secret. Daft, I know."

"My dear boy. You sound almost like a human-being."

He laughs. "Oh, Mother. You do know how to wound a chap."

"By the way, while everyone's busy. What happened with Charles this afternoon?"

"Sorry, I forgot. He brought a revised Living Will for you, and he suggested that it ought to be signed by all of us while we're here, to signify we all understand your last wishes."

"Excellent. And does it state I don't wish to go to hospital?"

"I'm sorry, Mother. I don't know. Didn't think you'd want me to read your private papers without you there." Really? Could he really have not looked, given the circumstances? That suggests a disturbing indifference in someone who is attempting to organise my existence. Or is his automatic response to deny anything that might lead to criticism?

Dismaying to discover I don't trust his word any more. "The papers are on your bedside table, by the way. I thought that the best place."

"And what did he say about equity release?" Though I doubt I will need to worry about money for much longer.

"Hang on. I'd better dig out my notes." He stands up, and for a moment I think he's about to take off again without telling me anything, but I malign the poor chap. He scrabbles in his back pocket, pulls out a crumpled piece of paper. "Right. No difficulty about raising a lump sum, which we assumed you'd want. Up to roughly a third of the value of the house. Or you can do something called 'drawdown' which gives you cash over time. Either way, the mortgage plus interest is repayable by your estate. Which I take it means Susie and me."

"And is he going to arrange a valuation?"

"I didn't ask. But Susie and I can sort you out. When we get back, I'll contact a couple of estate agents, see what the place is worth."

"No, don't bother. But I do want some written information about this equity releasing. You could arrange that for me, if you like. Just so I know what I might be letting myself in for."

"You don't need to worry. None of us would let you get into difficulties."

There we go. Throughout my fairly long life, I've been treated like a child. First, it was because I *was* a child, then because I was female, which seemed to be a defining factor to every male on whom I needed to rely – father, husband, bank manager, doctor (with one blessed exception). And now the same thing is happening with my son, because I'm not only female, but also old. Poor thing, needs a guardian.

Thinking like this is not good. I was happy just now, and want to stay that way.

"So, David, are you likely to be in need of financial help? I'd just like to know."

"Don't worry about me, Ma. I can look after myself."

I laugh at this. "My sentiments exactly."

He gazes at me, indulgent, not bothering to disguise his assumption that his old mother just needs to be pacified, while he and the girls sort out the practical side. Careful, Irene. We don't want an argument now.

"Granma! Look. Look what I've found!" Simon bursts into the room, arms piled with books, eyes sparkling like candles on a birthday cake. "You got lots of nature books, Granma. Can I lend them? Please?"

"You certainly can't *lend* them, Simon," points out his father, and the boy's face closes, like a flower scorched with frost. "You should know better than that."

"*I* can lend them to you, Simon darling, and you can *borrow* them. That's what Daddy means. Different words, see?"

"Yeah." His air is sullen, his joy extinguished. I hope David realizes how much his son needs his approval. Or is he automatically repeating the failings he resented in Jeff?

"Show me what you've found, darling." A couple of large format hardbacks in full-colour, designed by Time-Life to appeal to the curious, one on world wildlife, the other on the extraordinary realities revealed by the electron microscope; a paperback *Dictionary of Biology*; and a leather-bound edition of Darwin's *Voyage of the Beagle*. "A good collection, I see. You may certainly borrow them all, but which one would you want most?"

The boy frowns, then shrugs. His hand caresses the Darwin. A beautiful edition and illustrated with Darwin's drawings. My clever grandson seems to appreciate quality.

I reach for the pen I was using earlier. "If you would hold the book open on my lap, yes, like that." And I write on the flyleaf:

To my darling grandson Simon, with all my love. Grandma.

"There we are. Now this is yours."

His eyes open wide and his face turns the colour of a sun-ripened peach. "Really?"

"Really."

"For goodness' sake, Mother, what *are* you doing?"

"Go away, David. Don't be a pest."

Simon giggles, but before this silly episode can develop, Tanya dances into the room, pink and glowing from her bath.

"Mummy says you gotta come, 'cos dinner's ready."

"Fine. Tell Mummy we're coming, Tani. And Simon. You go put those books back where you found them."

"David, please. Let well alone. I'm lending these to Simon, as I promised. And the Darwin is now his. Surely you can't object?"

For some reason I can't fathom, he looks unhappy. But he sighs, and comes to help me out of my chair, while Simon scurries from the room, carrying the precious disputed books in his arms. Up to his room and into his suitcase, I hope. Why is it, I wonder, that fathers and sons so often get in a tangle?

Raising Irene the Aged is as tedious and as secretly painful as ever. David gives up, lifts me into his arms. "You see, Mother? You need your personal transport, I'm afraid."

I smile up at him. "And when my personal transport is transformed into a film actor?"

"Susie's going to arrange a wheelchair."

David places me in one of the armed chairs at the table, and Susan bolsters me with cushions all round.

"I see."

The meal that follows is a gourmet feast, that I hope the others enjoy, for I'm unable to eat more than a few spoonfuls of the delectable asparagus soup. I toy with a potato enhanced by wine- and garlic-laden sauce from the chicken casserole, but my appetite has deserted me. Fortunately for the *amour propre* of the chef and her chief assistant, everyone else is happy to reward their efforts with praise, scraped-clean plates and empty serving dishes.

Except Alicia, that is. Her appetite seems to have diminished almost as much as mine. Has this unwanted pregnancy brought her the well-known ailments of the first trimester?

"I haven't got a wine glass, Uncle," she points out, in an aggrieved tone. Susan looks across at Danielle, who raises a shapely eye-brow, shrugs and leans back towards the cabinet, from which she takes the missing glass, plonks it on the table in the vicinity of her niece. "*Thank* you, Aunt." David pours the wine, and she raises it to me, and to the table, and drinks. Coughs. Pulls a wry face. "Yeuch."

It's not the wine, which is good. Perhaps she's off alcohol, as I was, I recall, when expecting her mother. Danielle's lips twitch. Alicia glares at her, then pushes back her chair. "Excuse me, everybody. I'm, like … Oh, dunno. Gotta go."

Susan goes to follow her, then changes her mind. "Ali's a bit upset at the moment. It seems that Jilly told Ali's friend, Peter, where she is and why she's disappeared. So now the sisters have fallen out, and Peter is talking of coming down here."

"I hope you stopped him."

"You can't allow that."

Husband and wife speak in chorus, and Susan's voice rises: "Oh, ha, very ha. It's obvious neither of you knows anything about teenagers."

"Yours *certainly* don't know how to behave."

"Oh, for heaven's sake, Danielle! You just wait till that daughter of yours gets a bit older. She'll put a dent in your self-righteousness."

I take a sip of wine, and then another, hoping it might keep up the good work of helping me relax. But I'm feeling breathless and put down the glass. The ache is back.

"What's for pudding, Mummy?"

Susan catches me holding my good hand to my breast, and she does the calming gesture with her hands we always used in our family, like a conductor signalling *piano*, *pianissimo* to the orchestra. David catches on, gestures to his wife with his head, 'watch out for my mother'.

Danielle stands up. "There's ice cream and strawberries for good children who help carry out the dishes without dropping a thing."

"Yeah. Cool." Simon leaps up in the exuberant manner of a healthy young boy, and his chair falls over. His father frowns, emphasises the *pianissimo* beat. Simon picks up a vegetable dish with exaggerated care and tiptoes from the room. Tanya giggles as she tries to imitate her brother, carrying one of my best Chris Prindl plates, knife and fork dangling precariously.

David scoops up a load, makes for the door. "Just hang on there, Ma, we'll be back."

"You're not well, are you, Mother?" Susan's pale face is drawn.

"A bit tired. Is Alicia unhappy or is it the ills of early pregnancy?"

"Both, I'm afraid."

"Anything I can do?" That blackness round my heart is returning, the tide is coming in. Dammit all to hell. My eyes close involuntarily, and when I open them, I find Susan peering into my ravaged face.

"Wouldn't you like to move, Mother? You look pretty done in."

"Good idea, darling." I don't want to focus on the unpleasant drawbacks of trying to persuade this failing body to stand up, and I gaze around my dining room, savouring the elements that have always pleased me: the bookshelves that cover two of the pine-panelled walls; the free-standing Art Deco cabinet, and the Romanian hand-made, stained-glass flutes, so unusual and fragile that hardly anyone ever dares use them, but which I sometimes bring out for myself because I love them. I'd have used them today for the white wine, because it was a special meal. But David always puts them back, as though he's afraid.

"Lean on me, Mother. We can do it."

"Anybody ... can do any .... thing. Right?" My breath is short, but we make progress. Into the hall.

"Grammar's got down. That's not fair."

"Just go sit down, Tanya, and mind your own business."

"Whyee?"

I'm assailed by laughter, and Susan grins at me. "Irrepressible, that's Tani." David's heavy footsteps approach. "It's all right, Dave, we're nearly there."

We reach my chair, manoeuvre this unwieldy chassis into place, and I sink back with relief. That damned pain is definitely spreading. Perhaps I can stop it, before it gets worse.

"Could you fetch an aspirin, please?"

Susan looks alarmed. "Of course." She returns promptly, white tablet fizzing in a glass of water. "Perhaps we should phone a doctor?"

"No. This will help. Just let the others finish their meal and put the children to bed."

"I'm not leaving you anyway." She settles on the settee as before.

"What about Alicia?"

"Oh, she'll be lying on her bed, talking to Peter on her mobile. I take it he's the father?" I say nothing. "Anyway, it looks as though they'll sort something out between them. Would you like some music?"

The opening bars of Mozart's Requiem have been haunting me much of the day, but I feel it's perhaps not the best request to make of my daughter right now.

"Some Mozart would be good. You choose, darling."

She selects Mozart's Clarinet Quintet, my favourite piece of chamber music. As I cannot, at the moment, play my own cherished instrument, this is the happiest choice she could make: the beautiful Allegro, then the long-breathed clarinet melody in the slow movement, and the dancing exchanges with the strings, then the Minuet and Trio, and the wonderful complex Allegretto with variations. I should have liked my playing to have been really good, but it did make me happy. I wonder if Tanya will take up an instrument, perhaps even have my piano.

I recline in the luxury of my own comfortable home, my daughter beside me, bathed in the glorious music of an unhappy genius, and recognize that I have been a fortunate woman. I gaze around the room, salute all the comforts that have served me so well: the long heavy curtains I chose because I loved the colours, the toning carpet and cushions, the comfortable leather-upholstered chairs; the elaborate music centre and the racks of records, LPs, CDs, that have permitted me to hear the greatest composers interpreted by the best performers here, in my own home; the paintings and prints, the bronze sculptures - the entwined lovers, the shy young girl rooted to the ground on enormous feet, and the life-size Arctic tern balanced on one wing tip, hovering by the window, about to fly free. So much have I loved. I have been blest indeed.

51

Irene

Tanya scampers into the room, clambers on top of me, and chisels stab and slash. I hug her close with my right arm, stop her moving and savour her like a banquet, smell the sweet 'n sour tang of little girl's hair mingled with Pears soap, and the strawberries she ate earlier, sense the vitality in her limbs as she snuggles against me. "Night, night, Grammar." She puts her ice-creamy lips to mine, and we exchange a sloppy kiss.

"Goodnight, my precious." I suddenly know that I shall never see this lovely child again, and I hug her to me once more. But she's had enough, and slides down, runs from the room. Oh. That's it. My Tanya has gone.

No, I'm being silly and fanciful. I look around. Death cannot have entered the room yet, I've sent her away. Susan is still on the settee, a book on her knee, not reading but gazing at me.

David marches in: "You gonna help Dani clear up, Suse? She did do all the cooking."

"No, Dave, I'm not. You go and help. Time you did something in the kitchen. I'm watching Mother."

"Does she *need* watching?" He comes over to stare down at me, his brow wrinkling, but Simon bounces in before he can say anything.

"Night, Granma. I gotta go to bed now. Thanks for the book." He grins at me, clearly not in the least put out by my grisly hag-like appearance. "You know what? I think it's just as good as what Mr Fleetwood has got. The drawings are really good, and int'resting."

"You're a chap with excellent taste, Simon darling," I tell him, and then my breath runs out. He gives me a quick kiss on the good cheek, and skips out. I hear him call, "Why's Granma's face all grey and twisty, Mummy?" Oh. Poor darling. What a way to remember your grandmother who wishes you only good things.

"She looks bloody awful, Susie."

"*She* is still here, David .... I'm tired, that's all."

"Let's try to keep upsets to a minimum, shall we, Dave? Our mother is being what she always is – determined to be left alone, and refusing to let anyone know if something's the matter. So I'm watching her."

"Is that enough?"

"We did say we'd respect her wishes, didn't we? So let's try to do just that. Right?"

He raises his eyes in a melodramatic gesture worthy of a television soap. "Just so long as nothing more goes pear-shaped this visit. I'm beginning to feel as jaded as our poor old mother looks."

Did I say seductive charm? I retract. Danielle, you domineering, humourless and, to use Alicia's words, tight-arsed bitch, I wish you joy of your jaded actor husband. The two of you deserve each other.

Oh, Irene, don't. You're doing a David, being offensive and aggressive, because you are afraid. And you, old enough to know better.

I love my son, who has now gone to help his wife. And I love Danielle, who is patient and generous, and tolerant of almost everyone's foibles except Alicia's. It's as well no one can read another's thoughts, for it's so much easier to criticise and blame others when Fate threatens disaster.

Low tide has turned with a vengeance. Pains are increasing, in my chest, beneath and around my left breast, into my back, up my neck to my jaw and down that stupid useless left arm, and I'm beginning to believe I won't be able to fight off this one. How can I tell them? I don't even want them here when Death comes to call.

Have you entered the house, Death? Are you hiding behind my chair? Why didn't you just go away, when I said? You really are *not* wanted, not today.

I scrabble again for the spray, then lie back in my chair, eyes closed, and feel darkness gather in my chest. God, this is really quite uncomfortable. I find I am panting.

Susan takes my hand still holding the spray, strokes it, then places it back against my breast. I feel her hurry from the room, then the presence of all three adults.

"David, your mother is having a heart attack. Call an ambulance. Right now."

259

I take as deep a breath as I can manage. "No ... No ... ambulance."

"Don't be so bloody silly, Mother."

"You know what she said, Dave. We did agree, you and I. She has the right to refuse treatment if she wants to."

"How *can* you two be so blind? You don't call an ambulance right now, she may die."

"We know that, Danielle."

"Don't you *care?*"

"*Danielle!*"

"Lay off, Dani, and don't be stupid. Do you think this is it, Susie? Really?"

"How the hell do I know?" Susan's voice is clogged. "What I do think is that we should try and get her into bed right now."

That part sounds good to me. My own bed, my own pillows, my duvet. Comfort for these raging limbs, burning in the frozen wastes of Dante's Hell. I close my eyes, and all I can see within is a creeping darkness beneath my breasts, but my extremities are alabaster streaked with the purple of slowly surging blood, clogged somewhere in its route and unable to flow through. If I were alone, I should have to remain in this chair. So, children of mine, if you can stick to your promises, I shall rejoice that you are here. For me, if not for you.

David lifts me once again in his arms, looks at my worn face. "Don't you *dare* die on us, Mother. You have a film premiere to attend, and that's months away."

"I ... know." Speaking takes precious energy, and uses scarce breath, so perhaps not. Not too often.

"Am I supposed to stand by and let you let your mother *die?*"

"If necessary, Danielle. Yes."

"Dear God. Irene, I hope this is really what you want."

I nod, and my head swims. "It is ... Danielle," I whisper. "Thank ... you."

The two women follow David up the stairs into my bedroom, and he lays me on the bed. Danielle removes my shoes.

"Why don't you let me undress her, Susan? It's the sort of thing I'm good at. And then I'll leave you with her, if that's what you want."

"You sure?"

"It *is* the one thing I can do for her."

Susan sighs, a sudden gust threatening to release the dammed-up tears in her throat. "Come on, Dave. Let Dani say goodbye in her own way."

The door closes, and Danielle stands beside me as I lie on the bed, gazing down at the twisted ugly carcass my once attractive body has become. "Well, Irene, you really are a bloody-minded old woman, aren't you? How you have managed to seduce me into doing *exactly* what I know is the wrong thing, I can't imagine. You do realize, don't you, that you are running a terrible risk? Right now?"

I smile at her. At least, I hope I smile. The left side of my face appears to have a will of its own, and a darkness within that tugs and twists and pains.

"Please assure me, for the last time, that you know you might die without a doctor, and that is really, *really* what you want?"

I catch her hand with my one good one. "It is .... Danielle ... Please ... Don't ... worry."

She laughs at that, a brief chord on the cello. "Of course I shall worry." She helps me to sit up. "Come on, then. Let's get you undressed and into bed properly."

Once again, I appreciate the skill with which she manoeuvres clothes from this uncooperative body, and the firm gentleness of her hands that seems to calm the demons that have commandeered my nerves and muscles. I refuse to abdicate completely, but without her assistance tonight, getting myself into bed might have been impossible.

"Thank you ... Danielle... You very ... kind."

She stoops, and kisses my good cheek. "Sleep well tonight, Irene, and forget what I said. You're such a tough nut, you'll probably outlive us all."

She leaves the room, and I lie back against the pillows she has plumped behind my head. The duvet conceals the distortions life has bequeathed to my body, only my ravaged face and twisted hands are visible. Sad to leave those I love with such ugly memories.

David appears to have been waiting for his wife to leave. "So how are you now, Mother?" He peers down at me. "Hmm. You don't look very good. Can I get you anything?"

I shake my head. The pains keep surging up into my throat, and then they ebb, and I can believe they are receding. But they come back. I don't want him to watch me.

"I don't want you to die yet, Mother." I have to laugh at that. "I was hoping you'd see my film, and realise that all the aggro I created this holiday will at least have a good outcome. I know I've been a bit of an ass. But I'm not letting anything stop me now, I'm gonna make that film."

I put out my hand to him, and he grabs it with both his own. "Do ... make ... film ... Important."

His anxious face blooms into a smile that fills my bedroom with the scent of magnolias. "You really mean that?" I nod against the pillows, though it makes me dizzy. "Oh, Mother, thank you, thank you." He releases my hand, goes over to the window where daylight is fading, and stares out at a sky tinged the muddy pink of dying roses. "You really helped me, you know. I'm truly sorry I put such deplorable pressure on you with all my hangups, Mother darling. I hope you can forgive me. But I feel I can move on now."

What can I say to make him go away content? Even if my tongue were not impeded by breathlessness, I'd be unlikely to tell him what he needs to know: it's time you walked away from the past; time you took responsibility for your own life; time, too, you recognized your wife's patience and generosity; time you listened to your children's talents and needs.

But all that is advice and I don't like to give advice, not any more. Don't harm others is the only commandment I think that matters; but however much you love someone and try to do your best, you still seem somehow to hurt the other. Perhaps I did harm my son when I divorced his father, even though I tried not to. If you're not a god, how can such unwitting damage be avoided?

"David ... darling ... I'm fine ... Leave me ... go be a star."

He rushes over, envelops me in his bear hug. "I love you, Mother."

"Love you."

262

Slowly and with almost Macready-like pauses for the audience to apprehend the drama, our hero releases his mother, stands at the bedside, gazing solemnly down at the dying woman; then, a broken man, makes his tragic way to the door. Where he stops, looks round at his audience of one, and winks, before leaving the stage.

I clap my hand on my arm. The sound of one hand clapping, as loudly as it can.

52

David

David left the room, a black void heavy in his chest, and when he encountered his son on the landing, he feared he might start to cry.

"Dad," the boy whispered. "Is Granma gonna die?"

His father scooped him up in his arms, carried him downstairs to the sitting room where the boy's mother and aunt Susan were sitting quietly together, not speaking.

"Simon's a bit anxious about Grandma," David said.

"Come here, Simon." Danielle held out her arms. "So are we all, dearest boy."

"I'll go up now," Susan said.

"Bye, Auntie. Mum, I think Granma's dying."

"Gracious me, do you? Why?"

"Is she?"

David and his wife questioned each other silently across the room. What should they say?

"We don't know, Simon," Danielle said at last. "We hope not. But it will happen some time, perhaps quite soon. She is an old lady."

"You need to make it not hurt her, Dad. Please."

"Why do you think your grandmother will be hurt?" Danielle asked, but David realized that his son remembered the reality of nature's cruelty.

"It won't be like the pigeon, Simon. Not like any of the other horrid things you've seen in the garden."

"But what's making Granma die?"

"Your grandma is an old lady, and everyone has to die when they are really old. Like flowers do – you've seen that. But it will be very peaceful. She will just go to sleep, and one day, when the right time comes, she won't wake up."

Simon frowned as he thought about what his father said. "Will you die, when you go to sleep?"

264

"I'm not really old, am I? No one in our family is old like Grandma. So we just go to sleep to renew our energies, and wake up in the morning as we always do. Sleeping's good. Then one day when we are really, really old, like Grandma, and we are tired of being alive, then the time will come for us to die and not wake up. Do you understand?"

"Will Granma mind not waking up?"

David and Danielle looked at each other, tears blurring their vision.

"You know, Simon," David said, "I don't think she'll mind at all."

53

Irene

Susan comes in with a tray, which she deposits on the chest: jug of water, bottle of wine in the silver cooler that I always forget to bring out, glasses. She disappears again, returns moments later with my stick and the china potty that has lived under my claw-foot bath for years.

A snort of laughter escapes my increasingly constricted throat.

"Danielle's idea. Practical, eh?" She hides it under the chair. "Would you like some wine?" She holds up a bottle of Domaine-bottled *Pouilly Fuissé*, dusty around the neck and damp from ice at the base. From my small cellar. Good.

"Please."

She manipulates the professional corkscrew Frank gave me one Christmas, and clearly has become skilled at the important task of opening good wines that have escaped the ubiquitous screwtop. "Time you drank this, Mother, it's a good year." She pours us each a glass of the golden liquid that smells of the Mâconnais countryside. "Danielle seems to think it might be bad for you, but I thought you'd like it. Dying or not." Her smiles caresses me, and the surge of the dark tide stops for a moment. Does not retreat, but remains steady. As her hand is steady, holding out the glass. "Here's to you."

"And you." I raise the *grand vin de Bourgogne* to her and then to my lips, savour the aromas of white flowers and marzipan, the tangy fruity taste with faint hint of almond. I have had a great deal of wine today, and I feel this delicious crowning glory go to my head. Just as well it doesn't matter. There is appeal in the thought of drinking myself into oblivion. I suspect I see Death's shadow at the door, and I'm not ready to welcome her. Not with my children here. Not until I am quite alone.

It won't be long now. Somehow, I'm sure of it. Darkness is surging in on a renewed flood tide, and growing the pain behind my breast, down my arm, across my shoulder, up into my neck. Fluttering bands slowly begin to tighten across my chest. A large black shadow smothers my heart.

I watch my daughter as I sip the golden wine. She is leaning back in the Victorian nursing chair that came from my childhood home, her long brown hair piled on top of her head, wisps falling loose as they always do, her pale face sadly pensive.

"Alicia? Is she ... all right?"

She turns to look across at me and smiles, her face suddenly lit with the after-glow of the setting sun. "She'll be fine, Mother, and we've agreed, somehow she'll go to university. Such a relief. You were a big help to her, you know, made her see she doesn't have to go through it all alone." She shakes her head, and wrinkles the skin between her lightly-drawn eyebrows. "How she came to that conclusion, living with an obstinate old woman like you, I can't fathom. But apparently she did. Despite the best efforts of her aunt. She was quite determined to do the absolute *opposite* of what Danielle said she should do. But fortunately ..." Laughter makes her hiccup. "Oh, dear, I think I've drunk a bit too much today."

The light has gone, and she stands up, switches on the two lamps.

"Let me top you up a bit, and I'll take this down to the others."

But I cover my glass with my hand. If I must face Death tonight, I want to know when she comes, not fool myself by trying to escape into an alcohol-fumed refuge. She's been mocking me long enough.

"I think I'd like to sleep."

"That sounded better. Less breathless." She peers at me. "Do you want me to go?"

I nod. Oh, yes, Susan, I do. "Please."

"Hmm. I don't like leaving you alone. Not at the moment."

"Please do."

"Oh, Mother." Her voice cracks. "I don't mind, you know, if you do die and I'm there. Really I'd prefer it. I *promise* I won't do anything."

I gaze at my loving daughter, and realize that my deepest instinct – to raise my sharp quills and ward off the world so that I can face Death alone – is also the one way I have left to injure my beloved child. I don't want to do that. At the end of my life, I have learned that my best intentions

267

have hurt those I love, and while I can't help being the person I am, I can refuse to inflict the pain of feeling rejected.

But as I seek the words to tell her I'm glad to have her with me, the opportunity is being taken from me.

Death has entered the room and stands at the end of my bed. Tall and cloaked in black, and on her shoulder, not a scythe, but an owl with wide unblinking eyes.

I reach for the wand, fumble for the button to raise the bed-head as far as it will go. Trying to stand on the floor could end in humiliation, but I must be upright. I need to meet her properly.

Susan senses something has changed, moves to the bed beside me, crawls across and takes my hand. I squeeze her fingers a little, to let her know I know and am grateful.

But then I am alone with Death. A dark light radiates from her empty eye sockets, and she grins with those tombstone teeth that have mocked me so long. Tongues of fire undulate like snakes where her mouth should be. I nod to her, for Time has joined us. He carries the scythe. And I know I am to pass into the shadows. To the end of all pain, all striving, and all love. My guttering flame is to be blown out.

Music floods the room, cellos throb, violins dance and sing, a clarinet fills my mind with the sounds of paradise as the bands round my chest tighten intolerably, make me cry aloud.

Death smiles. Susan weeps. Music lives on.

If you enjoyed this book, please let others know. Why not post a review on amazon.com or amazon.co.uk or Goodreads? Reviews help readers find new books and new authors.

Writing is a lonely business, so I love to hear from my readers. My email is: erm@elizabethmapstone.co.uk Thank you for your support.

Just a little extra...
A list of the music mentioned can be found at the end of the book, with web-links to recordings wherever possible; also a list of David's quotations with their sources.

Acknowledgements

Maggie Gee and Jacob Ross both gave me great encouragement during a competitive Arvon novel writing course and I am especially grateful to Jacob for the kind review he has permitted me to quote.

Luigi Bonomi added to my (always wavering) self-confidence by awarding me First Prize for the opening chapter in an Oxford Literary Festival Writing competition.

Katie Isbester, Founder of Claret Press and *éditeur extraordinaire*, helped make this a better book with her meticulous editing and inspiring insights.

Fellow writers Olivier Bosman, Marissa de Luna, Debbie Martin, Tim Arnot, Rob Triggs and Dave Richardson deserve special thanks for their detailed reading of an earlier version. As do my loyal readers Lise Roberts and Akita Fowler, who have lived with *The Porcupine's Dilemma* since its first inception.

I'd like to say a special Thank You to all my friends in the Abingdon Writers Group, the Oxford Writers Circle and Writers in Oxford who have been so kind to me as old age threatened to derail my plans to complete this novel; and especially to Barbara Lorna Hudson and Sylvia Vetta who have been so supportive.

As always, Michael Abbott has given me invaluable technical help, and my husband John Tyerman Williams has continued to be the perfect partner.

Irene's music (in the order mentioned)

Nymphs and Shepherds (Danielle)
A song by the English composer Henry Purcell, from the play *The Libertine* by Thomas Shadwell.
> Nymphs and shepherds, come away,
> In this grove let's sport and play;
> For this is <u>Flora's</u> holiday,
> Sacred to ease and happy love,
> To music, to dancing and to poetry.
> Your flocks may now securely rest
> While you express your jollity!

1929 recording of Manchester Children's Choir (Columbia label)
https://www.youtube.com/watch?v=-vkpqHECZtE

The Parlour Song Book, A Casquet of Vocal Gems,
A collection of Victorian parlour songs introduced by Michael R. Turner, with music edited by Antony Miall. published by Michaael Joseph, 1972.

Helen Reddy, "I Am Woman"
Irene's vinyl LP is from EMI Capitol Records 1972. Grammy award for song I Am Woman which became the anthem of the feminist movement during the radical 1970s.
Helen Reddy - 'I Am Woman' (Live) 1975 - YouTube
https://www.youtube.com/watch?v=MUBnxqEVKlk

The Well-Tempered Clavier, is a collection of two series of Preludes and Fugues in all major and minor keys composed for solo keyboard by Johann Sebastian Bach. Public domain recording by Kimiko Ishizaka, released 19 March 2015.
Bach: Well-Tempered Clavier, Book 1 | Kimiko Ishizaka
http://music.kimiko-piano.com/album/bach-well-tempered-clavier-book-1

Grieg's Triumphal March
Triumphal March from "Sigurd Jorsalfar" by Edvard Grieg.
www.bbc.co.uk/music/records/nz3qbw

Aida, opera by **Giuseppe Verdi**, set in Egypt. Several subscription recordings on YouTube.

Die Meistersinger von Nurnberg by **Wagner The Master (Prize) Song** sung by Peter Anders
https://www.youtube.com/watch?v=gXU93xvie-4

Bach's Brandenburg Concertos
Irene has several different versions, but the one chosen by Alicia is the 1995 EMI Seraphim compilation with Yehudi Menuhin on CD.
Excellent recordings of all six concerti conducted by Claudio Abbado
https://www.youtube.com/watch?v=hbQORqkStpk

Gervase de Peyer playing Mozart's Quintet for Clarinet and Strings
http://www.eavb.co.uk/lp/extrapeyer.html
Clarinet Concerto in A K622: III. Rondo (Allegro)" by Sabine Meyer/ Berliner Philharmoniker/Claudio Abbado conductor
This is from the 1954 recording which Irene has on vinyl LP.

Mozart's Requiem
Irene's recording is the 1991 Philips CD with Sir Neville Marriner conducting the Academy and Chorus of St Martin in the Fields.
Mozart - Requiem in D minor (Complete/Full) [HD] - YouTube
https://www.youtube.com/watch?v=sPlhKP0nZII

Mozart's Clarinet Quintet in A
This being her favourite piece, Irene has several versions. Susan chooses the Decca 1985 recording with Antony Jay, clarinet, and Christopher Hogwood directing The Academy of Ancient Music.

David's Literary Quotations (in order of appearance)

Cry havoc and let slip the dogs of war (W. Shakespeare, *Julius Caesar*,III,i)

Doomsday is near. Die all, die merrily. (*Henry IV, Part I*,IV,i)

wonderful, wonderful and most wonderful wonderful (*As You Like It*,III,ii)

O my prophetic soul. (*Hamlet*,I,v)

tale Told by an idiot, full of sound and fury, Signifying nothing (*Macbeth*,V,v)

As flies to wanton boys are we to the gods;
They kill us for their sport. (*King Lear*,IV,i)

Tomorrow, and tomorrow, and tomorrow ...
to the last syllable of recorded time. (*Macbeth*,V,v)

Dost thou call me fool, boy?
[All thy other titles hast thou given away;] that thou was born with.
(*King Lear,* I,iv)

Blow, winds, and crack your cheeks! Rage! Blow!
You cataracts and hurricanes, spout
Till you have drench'd our steeples, drowned the cocks!
You sulphurous and thought-executing fires,
Vaunt-couriers to oak-cleaving thunderbolts,
Singe my white head! And thou, all-shaking thunder,
Strike flat the thick rotundity o' the world. (*King Lear*, III,ii)

[…] dwindle[d] into a wife. (W. Congreve, *The Way of the World,* IV)

Let's contend no more, Love, Strive nor weep.
All be as before, Love. Only sleep! (R. Browning, A *Woman's Last Word*)

Lightning Source UK Ltd.
Milton Keynes UK
UKOW02f0620200916

283385UK00001B/57/P